The Day the
Swallows Spoke

The Day the Swallows Spoke

DALENE MATTHEE

MICHAEL JOSEPH
LONDON

MICHAEL JOSEPH

Published by the Penguin Group
27 Wrights Lane, London W8 5TZ, England
Penguin Books USA Inc., 375 Hudson Street, New York, New York 10014, USA
Penguin Books Australia Ltd, Ringwood, Victoria, Australia
Penguin Books Canada Ltd, 10 Alcorn Avenue, Toronto, Ontario, Canada M4V 3B2
Penguin Books (NZ) Ltd, 182–190 Wairau Road, Auckland 10, New Zealand

Penguin Books Ltd, Registered Offices: Harmondsworth, Middlesex, England

First published by Tafelberg, Cape Town, 1992
First published in Great Britain 1993

Typeset by Datix International Limited, Bungay, Suffolk
Set in 12/13 pt Monophoto Ehrhardt
Printed in England by Clays Ltd, St Ives plc

A CIP catalogue record for this book is available from the British Library
ISBN 0 7181 3730 2

Thank you, Undine, for allowing me
to use your diamonds

BOOK ONE

One

SHE NO LONGER ASKS, no longer argues, she knows:
Africa does not want white children. If you have a
white skin you can't take shelter anywhere – not even in
the south, at its feet. Not any longer. It's best to pack up
and find yourself somewhere else to live – before the river
bursts its banks.

Two

WHEN SHE GETS BACK to her flat from work that afternoon, she takes the six uncut diamonds from the pocket of her skirt and puts them on the table at the window so that the mountain can see them too. Six little round-edged chips of waxen glass. No, not glass. Glass is not so alive. The man and his wife had both said that they were diamonds.

She tries to find a sense of guilt or wrongdoing within her, but does not. Only a feeling that the diamonds are not happy on the table. She picks them up and holds them against her cheek: cool, tiny stones.

She remains standing there, looking out over the roofs and treetops towards the massive, towering mountain peak to the west of the town. *Her* mountain.

Actually, it's part of a long range of mountains spanning the foot of Africa from west to east, separating the coastal strip from the interior of the country.

Two years ago, when the house agent brought her here to see this bachelor flat on the second floor of the building, the mountain filled the whole window. She told the woman she would take the flat. To the mountain she said: 'I won't be staying here long, but while I do, you will be my only picture, and adornment.'

She turns away from the window and puts the diamonds on the bed to make a soft cushion for them. They're strange little creatures and she likes them. No two of them are alike. Four are translucent, two are clouded. They're neither round nor square, they seem to be made up of tiny triangles with light inside . . . Little shining stones. Little stones holier than stones from the veld.

It was an ordinary, middle-aged couple, Mr and Mrs Shirley, who came to Carr & Holtzman Real Estate that morning inquiring about houses in George. Decent people. Elvin Carr, the senior partner, was out with a client and Bernard Holtzman, the junior partner, was busy organizing the afternoon's golf over the telephone. One of the two typists, Christel, showed the couple into her office.

The Shirleys wanted to get out of Zimbabwe, but they still wanted to hold on to Africa, so they were trying to buy a house as far south as possible.

Coincidence? It did not matter. She was under the impression that everybody who wanted to get out from up north had done so long ago.

The fifth house she showed them invited them in and took them. In the back garden, the woman sat down on a rusty chair, her body saying, 'This is where I want to be, I go no further.'

Mr Shirley wanted to know if the owner would be prepared to lower the price.

'It's most unlikely,' she told him; 'he originally asked R10 000 more.'

'It's difficult to get money out of Zimbabwe, Miss Rossouw. Especially such a large amount. In our case it has been a matter of waiting until an insurance policy was paid out to me here in the Republic of South Africa. Now it seems that it is not going to be enough.'

The woman who rented the house came to the back door and shouted, 'It's a rotten old shack, it will have to be rewired from top to bottom!'

'I've told them that.'

'My contract says I must have three months' written notice.'

'I've told them that too.'

They did not want to see any other houses.

She suggested that they go back to the office for tea. They seemed reluctant to give up the place, but at the same time they wouldn't discuss arrangements for a mortgage. While they were waiting for their tea, she got a feeling that there was something they wanted to tell her. Or ask her. It was only later that she realized they had been weighing her up.

'What did you say your name was?' the woman asked.

'Araminta. Araminta Rossouw.'

'I don't recall ever having heard the name before. Is it a family name?'

'Yes. From a Scottish great-grandmother on my father's side.' She is used to questions about her name. Sometimes, when the situation calls for a bit of a laugh, she adds the story of the old man that was in the church the morning her father baptized her, who went home afterwards and gave his newborn calf the same name.

The Shirleys were ill-at-ease.

'Are you from George, Miss Rossouw?'

'No.' In her heart she said: I'm actually a ghost, still looking for a home.

'We're staying with friends on their farm outside the town,' said the man. 'We've looked at many places that are up for sale around here, but we have found nothing we liked until now. The last place you showed us is what we've been looking for all along – but we're R15 000 short on the purchase price.' The next moment he put the little stones on her desk. 'Perhaps you know someone who would be interested in buying these?'

'What are they?' She honestly didn't know.

'Diamonds.'

Diamonds? Diamonds are set in rings. Diamonds are

huge, brilliant stones set in sceptres and crowns, and kept behind walls of thick glass . . .

'Uncut diamonds,' the woman whispered, nervously. 'A black man gave them to my husband long ago in exchange for some tools.'

Uncut diamonds?

'They should be worth more than R15 000,' the man said anxiously. 'But we will accept fifteen.'

'Well . . .' It was a rather startling situation – but interestingly so. A contract of sale usually read 'subject to obtaining a mortgage'. This one would have to read 'subject to the sale of six uncut diamonds'. 'Well . . .' She didn't quite know what to say.

'My wife and I are the last people to want to get you into trouble, Miss Rossouw. We only thought that, through your work, you must have contacts with many people . . .'

Joop Lourens.

Everyone in the village where she had grown up said that the wealthy Joop Lourens had made his fortune from diamonds. Even after he had taken the deputy mayor of the village to court for defamation of character and won the case, the rumours still persisted. 'I think I know somebody who might buy them, but I'm not sure.' A flicker of movement, like hope, crossed the woman's face. 'Wait!' she cried, 'don't expect anything, because I can't promise anything.'

'Can you trust this person?' the man asked. He made it sound alarming and hush-hush. As it would have to be, but they had not stolen the diamonds and Joop Lourens could always say no.

'It's someone I've known since I was a child. If you're prepared to take the chance and leave them with me, I'll go and see him.'

'Does he live here in George?'

'No. He lives in a village about an hour's drive from here.' In her heart she was starting to wonder if she had not perhaps spoken too hastily. Joop Lourens was the last person in the world she would want to upset.

7

The man said, 'Whatever you can get above R15 000, you can keep for yourself, Miss Rossouw.' Offering an incentive.

'If you buy the house, sir, I will be getting commission. That's all I want. And please remember I only said I know someone who *might* buy them.'

'Of course.'

When Christel brought in the tea, the man quickly put his hand over the diamonds.

She took an option on the house and went and told Elvin that she would not be at the office the next day. As she works for commission only, she can more or less come and go as she pleases. Not that it's a privilege she exploits; each client, every potential transaction offers the possibility of earning money, which is of the utmost importance at this stage of her life. As it is the property market is quiet, and there are several estate agents in town competing for whatever business there is.

It's not a nice occupation. It's an almost daily intrusion into people's lives, like peeping through keyholes, but it was the quickest way out that she could find.

She has made an ark of her flat, to survive in until she reaches safe ground. No close friendships, no unnecessary explanations later on. No cat, no dog to get attached to, no tears.

Only the African violet a client had given her as a present. And the mountain.

And one easy chair, one bed, a second-hand stove and a fridge; one little table with an upright chair at the window, a chest of drawers with a mirror, a bookshelf for her books and her great-grandmother's little porcelain bowl. Four cups and saucers, four plates, four knives and forks. Four. In case her father and mother came to visit. Or her sister Marian.

After the first six months, she made one exception: she bought a second-hand television set. Weekends in an ark can be very lonely.

But she no longer watches the news or reads the newspapers. Right and wrong, truth and untruth are streams that have run together, forming one roaring, swelling river. No matter where you put your bucket in, the water you draw up is never pure.

And a mountain that looks through your window every day becomes more than an adornment – it becomes a presence. You learn to know every cliff and gorge and prominence on it. Its colours: changing shades of blues and greens; grey rock-faces; its huge, bluish-black silhouette on a moonlit night.

You get to know its moods. Its gladness after the rain, when silver cascades rush down the slopes like laughter. Its bitterness when there is no rain, and thousands of pine trees in orderly rows drive their tongues deep into the earth at its feet and suck its springs dry.

She cannot go to the mountain. They rape women that walk alone in the mountains.

Joop Lourens. There's a story that he and his brother both fell in love with the same girl in their youth. Magda was her name. When Magda chose Stefaans, Joop moved away. Presumably heartbroken. After almost thirty years, the long-lost Joop came back a wealthy man, bringing with him a wife, Sally, and an only child, Wilhelm. They bought the house below the rectory. The day they moved in, she and her sister Marian had had to take round a goodwill tray of tea and cake. Their mother had other things to do. Marian had been at high school at the time, and she was still at primary school.

Sally was a soft and tiny woman; if she had had feathers, she would have been a turtle-dove. Joop was tall, with a big stomach, and spoke to you as if you were a real person. Wilhelm was the same age as Marian, a little girlish, but not silly or shy at all. He showed them how he could pull his father's wickedly expensive car in and out of the garage.

Before long, the story began to go round that Joop Lourens had made his fortune out of 'you know what'.

Three

SHE DOES NOT PHONE to say that she's coming. She takes a chance and starts off early the next morning.

Just outside the town, a small brown hawk sits on a telegraph pole and she winks at it as she passes: a hawk or an eagle at the start of journey is always a good omen. They're lucky birds. And she will need luck, for somehow she is no longer sure that it's all right to approach Joop Lourens . . .

Nevertheless, she is feeling excited.

When you've planned and calculated every step you have taken for the past two years, six diamonds falling into your hands is something to awaken your spirit of adventure.

The road is quiet. The sky is clear and blue, her thoughts can go wandering . . . If Joop Lourens buys the diamonds and the Shirleys buy the house, half of the commission is hers to take to the bank, to pay off another slice of the loan on her car. With the commission Carr & Holtzman paid her the previous week she had paid off the last of her student loan – that was over and above the R2 500 she had had to repay to her father, money which she had borrowed from him when she started work at Carr & Holtzman. *And* she has a little nest egg in her savings account.

Would she have been able to do all that in two years on a teacher's salary? Never.

And with each rand that is added, her wings are growing. The moment they're strong enough, she'll start to fly. Far away. Like the birds in the sky, she'll be free to soar between heaven and earth, while behind her South Africa can cry for peace and liberation until Doomsday! When she lands it will be gently, like a phoenix, so that she crushes nothing under her feet, and she will live on the morning dew!

I'm making up fairy-tales now, she says to herself, smiling – perhaps it's nectar a phoenix lives on?

It doesn't matter.

She will not be as stupid as the Shirleys, she'll go far across the sea.

She wouldn't have minded keeping the diamonds for herself and taking them with her, though. There is something magical about them.

Among the books on her shelf, only two had anything to say about diamonds. One was the dictionary: 'Colourless or tinted precious stones of pure carbon crystallized . . . hardest naturally occurring substance . . . a rough diamond, person of intrinsic worth but rough manners . . .' That's like Klaas Muller. His skull is unusually hard too; it took her a long time to get it into his head that there could be nothing between them.

The other book said a diamond is just a piece of charcoal with a finer education. No two are ever alike. The rarest, most expensive ones are the colour of clear water, or the palest blue, and without a speck of dirt or a crack in them. In the very next paragraph it said that in the East a diamond with a speck of black in it is much sought after as a talisman, because it represents a stone with a soul.

What if the biggest one of the six is a clear white and Joop Lourens doesn't know it? What if it's not true that he made his money from diamonds?

She sees another hawk by the road.

It's October. The earth is green. After the harbour town of Mossel Bay, 400 kilometres east of Cape Town, patches of wild flowers colour the veld purple and pink and yellow and white. Above everything, surrounding everything, is an infinity of blue: the sea in the distance to the south; the long range of mountains to the north; the sky from horizon to horizon. Blue. The colour of tranquillity and harmony . . . and peace?

Always, when she drives round here, she weaves herself a dream. She pulls out the telegraph poles and electricity pylons, she sweeps away the farmlands and the houses and the roads; she slips through time's door and finds herself running across the field as a little yellow-brown bushman girl.

She abandons herself to this dream on purpose, to feel what it must have been like to be really free. For the bushmen were the only children of Africa who had ever lived free in the south of the country: they were tough, wild, mystery children who had come from nowhere and lived in harmony with nature and with each other for hundreds of thousands of years. Unencumbered by possessions.

When she dreams her dream and escapes from the present, she is a girl with protruding buttocks in one of the little bands that roamed the coastal strip between the sea and mountains, hunting and gathering, migrating from one hunting area to another. Seldom more than eighty to a group. Blissfully unaware that the earth beneath their feet is called 'Africa' – or of Moses in the far distant north between the bulrushes in the land of Egypt . . .

Time was light and dark. From new moon to full moon. Cold time. Warm time. When all had enough to eat they danced a happy dance; a sad dance for hunger or death.

No one ruled. The great Spirit that lived where the sun comes up sent the rain that made the veld green and the game plentiful. The same Spirit sent the drought that prevented them from staying in one place for ever, getting fat and lazy. Hunger forced the bushmen to get up and move on . . .

She sees the truck with the trailer approaching the cross-roads ahead . . . About two hundred metres before she reaches the junction, she realizes that the truck is not going to stop, it is going to go straight across without looking. In the seconds that follow, her body obeys the orders that her brain shouts and she starts slamming on the brakes: harder! harder! Brake! The distance between the truck and the car gets smaller and smaller . . . Then she begins to turn, missing the trailer by centimetres.

It is not until after she has crossed the Gouritz River bridge that she begins to recover from the shock. She cannot find her way back to the bushmen . . .

About the time that the wise men from the East saw the Star rising over Bethlehem, the first of the tall, thin, browner beings were entering the toe of Africa from the north, invading the valleys of the south with their herds of cattle and flocks of sheep. This was game of a kind no little yellow-brown hunter had ever seen before. Game that did not flee from bows and arrows . . .

The cattle-owners. People with possessions. The Koikoi.

Tribe after tribe, for centuries, they kept on coming south. Some of the groups were hundreds of men and women and children and slaves strong, their cattle and sheep numbering thousands. Plus warriors with bows and arrows and spears, because cattle and women were always prey to looters.

The game fled in their path. The bushmen too. Like baboons, they found shelter in the caves and gorges of the foothills of the mountains. With their twig paint brushes they spilled out their anger on the walls of the caves.

End of the bushmen.

Gradually. A thousand years would pass before the West started out in search of a sea route to the East round the foot of Africa. In every bay along their way, they asked the natives where they could find the land of the rich and mighty Prester John, hidden in Africa's darkness.

She thought it was a legend.

And she had thought that diamonds were pretty little dead stones. But they would not sleep in the drawer next to her bed. Nor in the tissue box. Or on the window-sill in the moonlight. Only after she had got up for the fourth time and put them in the hollows of the African violet's leaves did they settle down.

Maybe it was her imagination. Maybe it meant something.

And always, when she went walking with the bushmen, she would be edgy afterwards. The air smelt dirty, the water in the taps tasted foul, her feet wanted bare earth under them – and she is gripped by anguish because she cannot move any faster!

In ancient times you could pack up your few possessions and start walking; now you must have money first. Enough money.

Four

JOOP LOURENS HAD BEEN good to her.

Six years ago, when she and Frans de Villiers had scandalized the village, it was his hand that lifted up her chin so that she could see some light again.

She was in her second-last year in school. Frans was the new history teacher: tall, fair and sunburnt, as if he had come straight from the sea on a surfboard. When she looked him in the eyes for the first time in class, she knew she had done so enticingly. On purpose. Perhaps she really is the bitch her mother later made her out to be, because at that moment the most wonderful desire had welled up in her to feel his touch on her body.

At first she felt the most glorious happiness taking root in her. After a few weeks, when she was filled with it, it became an all-devouring and restless doubt. If he was feeling the same, why didn't he make an opportunity to speak to her? Was he afraid because it was so very forbidden? Was he unable to act because of the fact that her prison was the rectory and his the house of old Miss Sara Saayman, of which he was renting half?

Or was he waiting for *her* to make the first move . . .

Did she dare to?

What else could she do?

It was April, the days were short, darkness came early. She told her mother she had to go to Helga's with a maths problem after supper. She chose her streets carefully . . . she climbed over old Miss Sara's granadilla hedge at the back and knocked on his door.

It's a brook of cool, clear water. When you take off your shoes and walk into it, you are still just a child-girl; on the other side you have become a young woman. You have discovered the secret of all life: love. You're with the most fabulous man, who tells you to go home, but still holds you tight.

The year was almost out before they were caught – naked in bed, by old Miss Sara herself – and the whole village went up in flames.

Her mother hit her again and again; she fell against the kitchen sink, she called out to her father, but he just stood there in the doorway, his face filled with rage and loathing. He didn't lift a finger to stop her mother in her mad rage. She will never forgive herself for angering them and humiliating them like that.

She did not go back to school for a week. Every morning she was called to the study to kneel in prayer; first her father prayed and confessed her sin, beseeching God's forgiveness for her. Then her mother. Then she herself. She will never forgive them, that they made her kneel before God to pray a lie.

The rest of the day she lay on her bed, waiting for Frans. Every car that came past in the street, every knock on the door, every ring of the telephone was him sweeping everything out of his way to get to her . . . Waiting. Waiting. Waiting. Until everyone around her became ghosts and she growled at them if they dared to come a step too close.

Only towards the end of the week did her mother have the courage to come and ask if she could possibly be pregnant. No. Was she sure of that? Yes. Her mother did not ask how she could be sure. She probably needed to convince herself that they had not really slept together.

*

16

No one told her that he had left the village on the Friday, that a temporary post had been found for him in Cape Town. She had found it out herself on the Monday morning when she went back to school. It was like standing stock-still while a rock slowly comes down on you, crushing you into the ground. She did not cry, she did not open her mouth to say a word. She simply stood there dying.

When the scandal in the village had burned itself out, when all the mothers with daughters thanked God in the silence of their grateful hearts that it had been the minister's daughter that had been shamed, and not one of theirs, *she* became the ghost. A ghost clinging to the hope that he would send her a Christmas card explaining that he could not say goodbye because they would not let him. That he still loved her.

The Christmas cards came and hung like gaping beaks over the string in the dining-room – but there was none from him. On the day after Christmas Day, she had to take back Aunt Sally's dish and she found Uncle Joop alone in the kitchen when she got there.

'Is it no better yet, child?' he asked, without reproof.

'No, it isn't.' She could admit it openly to someone.

'I cannot tell you how sorry I am for you, Araminta.'

'If only I knew why I haven't heard from him!'

'Perhaps you'll understand if you let me tell you how life works.'

'Understand what?'

'When we are born, each of us are given a certain number of rivers to cross during our lifetime, trials and tribulations to teach us about living. At this moment, you are crossing your first difficult river and with it you are gaining years of experience. I can see it in you.'

'Don't say that, uncle. All I want to know is, did he love me or didn't he love me!'

'If you even have to ask the question, Araminta, the answer is no.'

'I can't accept that.'

17

'I know. It's one of the hardest things in life to have to find out that someone does not really want you. It remains an open sore for a very long time.'

'It was the circumstances!'

'Go on, shout. Aunt Sally's gone round to Aunt Martha's.'

'He couldn't cope with the circumstances.'

'You are a very beautiful girl, Araminta. You're a rare kind of girl. I remember the time when you and Wilhelm were holding hands; he came home from school one day and asked his mother if she had noticed that all the girls in the village with fair hair have blue eyes. Except Araminta. Her eyes, he said – and he really did say it – are deep and dark and full of light. When Frans de Villiers saw that light, it made the man in him so reckless that, although it was forbidden, he could not keep his hands from the most wonderful thing that will ever tempt him in his life.'

'He *did* love me!'

'In the flesh he did. One day, a man will love you with his body and his mind and his soul, and then you'll know the difference. Not yet. Today you're longing for Frans de Villiers and you don't even realize that you're crying for the moon.'

'I'll never love another man in my life.'

'You will. We receive enough strength to help us cross our rivers – it's up to us whether we waste it floundering about in midstream for too long.'

'It's not fair.'

'All's fair in the end. You'll see. And after every river we've crossed, we get a little reward, and time to rest before we have to take on the next. You'll see. The first river on our way is almost always the river of love: while we are young and still strong swimmers. It prepares us for the better love to come.'

'It hurts, Uncle Joop.'

'It will go on hurting for a long time yet. It's not like a pain in your toe – you know when it's gone. This is a pain that goes away without you knowing it – only long after-wards do you realize that it was your hurt pride that took the longest to heal.'

Three years later, when she ran into Frans de Villiers at Stellenbosch, she understood how true Uncle Joop's words had been. She felt nothing. Except for that something that remains between two people who have once loved each other. Even if it had been in the flesh only. Even if they've grown to hate each other.

Five

ALMOST NOTHING HAS CHANGED in the centre of the village. The only new building is the bank, standing there like a self-confident, untouchable place full of secrets.

Uncle Joop and Aunt Sally are glad to see her. They want to know how her parents are getting along in the new congregation at Bloemfontein. Has she been to visit them there? Not yet. Is Marian still teaching in Paarl? Yes. Is it true that she has got engaged? Yes. To a man who also teaches in Paarl.

She is invited to look at some of Wilhelm's latest paintings. She has to stay for tea.

At last she speaks out: 'Aunt Sally, if you don't mind, I would like to talk to Uncle Joop alone.'

'Of course I don't mind. Shall I ever forget how you came to him when you were in trouble that time?'

'At least I'm not in trouble this time, Aunt Sally.' But old woman looks as if she does not quite believe her.

And apparently Joop Lourens does not either. The minute he closes the door of his study, he asks, 'Do you have problems, Araminta?'

'Not as such, uncle.'

'When are you going back to university to finish your studies so that this property-selling nonsense can stop?'

'You've asked me that before, and the answer is still the same: I have no intention of going back.'

'I wish I knew what has happened to the Revd Rossouw's once cheerful daughter. A girl, that in spite of everything, left this village with her head held high.'

'Come now, Uncle Joop! Do I look unhappy or something?'

'I get the impression that you've come to a standstill. And at the same time you're as restless as a trapped animal. I ask myself, what's bothering her?'

She laughs. 'Perhaps it's having to stand still while my feet want to start running!'

'Where do you want to run to?'

She must be careful, the old man is sharp. 'To where the man of my dreams is waiting – hopefully the right one this time.'

'Your tongue and your eyes aren't speaking the same language, Araminta. Why did you want to see me alone?'

'I've come to ask if . . .' She takes the diamonds from her pocket and places them on the desk in front of him. 'If you would buy these.' She sees how his body stiffens in the chair as if from shock. It's not the way she had planned to do it, she had wanted to explain about the Shirleys first . . .

'Where did you get these?' He makes it sound as if it's a bomb she has put down in front of him.

'A client of mine needs R15 000 urgently,' she says. 'They want to get out of Zimbabwe and buy a house in George but they haven't got enough money. They are good, honest people – please don't look at me like that, Uncle Joop!'

'Go and give these back to them immediately!'

'I just thought . . .'

'You thought *nothing*!'

Oh no, she had not meant to upset him like this. 'I'm sorry, I think I've made a terrible blunder. Please forget about it.' Should she take the diamonds and go? 'Honestly, I didn't mean to upset you.' He is still staring at her – he does not make a move to help her over her mistake. Perhaps he wants her to leave . . .

21

'Sit down.'

She sits down again. 'I wish there was some way I could undo all this.'

'Why did you come to me?'

'Because. Because I thought you might be able to help these people.'

'Answer my question.'

No, she's not going to.

'Why did you come to me, Araminta?'

He means to know. She says the words as fast as she can: 'Because the people always said you made your fortune from diamonds.' She sees how it hurts him. How disillusionment leaps into his eyes and his body starts to sink back into the chair. She didn't mean to hurt him like this . . .

'Are you telling me that they still said that, even after I won the case against Jan Trap?'

'I'm sorry.'

'Answer me!'

'Yes.' He sits there as if his whole body is slowly absorbing blow after blow of defeat and dismay. 'Please, Uncle Joop, say you'll forgive me!'

He just looks at her. He takes off his glasses and wipes his eyes; when he puts them back on there is something like hatred in his eyes. 'You see, Araminta,' he says, 'man shows very little forgiveness. I left this village by the back door. When I returned, I entered at the front and for that they have never forgiven me.' His bitterness is welling up and spilling over.

'That's not true.'

'You won't understand. They would have accepted it, if I had stayed here and moved up slowly, street by street, for that is how most of *them* proceeded. Had I come back without one of my legs, it would have been all right too – but I came back with money, and that was unforgivable. Every beggar and collector comes knocking at my door, because I'm good enough for

22

giving. But never a knock at my door from someone from this neighbourhood coming to invite me or Aunt Sally over for a cup of tea. Not for a birthday, not for Christmas, not for anything. It's like a never-ending punishment.'

'I never realized you felt like that . . .'

'For myself I don't mind, but I didn't want it for my Sally.'

'To me, you were always the nicest people in the whole neighbourhood. I swear it.'

'You give and you give. But you're human, so you also want to be liked. Even though it does sound a silly thing for an old man to be saying.'

'*I* like you.'

He looks away and stares at the wall behind her . . . slowly he begins to tap on his desk with his fingers . . . 'You say these people want to get out of Zimbabwe?'

'Yes. But they don't have enough money.'

'Did you tell them you were bringing these to me?'

'No.'

He stops tapping. Starts again. Stops. He seems calmer. When he turns back to her, he seems to have made up his mind. 'Diamonds, Araminta, are not play-things,' he says, taking a writing-pad from the drawer next to him. From the holder on the desk he chooses a pen; there is a sense of purpose in every movement he makes. When he starts to write, he doesn't hesitate. . . . When he signs his name, it's a kind of seal he puts on it. It's like a moment of reckoning, of getting even. He takes an envelope and writes an address on it. 'Your good fortune is your ignorance and innocence, and the fact that you came to me. Your clients' good fortune is that I once had to get out of Zimbabwe too. This letter is addressed to a man whose name you never – *never* – reveal to anyone. If they ask you ten years from now whom I sent you to, you say you've forgotten the name – even if they put a gun to your head.'

23

'I give you my word.' Then it was true what they had been saying all these years?

'The man will trust you and buy the diamonds because it's me that's sending you to him. Take the people their money and wipe this day from your memory together with the name of the man. Tell yourself it was a dream in which you dreamt of an old man in his moment of deepest bitterness.'

'I promise I will. Thank you. Thank you very much.'

He folds the letter and puts it into the envelope. 'Do you have this clear? *This has never happened!*'

'I promise.'

'Good. Now take this, and if you really want to thank me, do so by going back to university while you still can.'

'I don't want to go back. I want to live and become a happy person.' Careful, she thinks, you're sounding childish. 'That does not mean I'm not happy now – it's only that I don't want to discover when I'm old one day, that I've been stoned to death because I was afraid to run.'

'What are you saying?'

'I didn't put that quite right, let's forget it. But, uncle, there's something else I've been wanting to ask you for a long time, but never had the courage to.'

'What?'

'Did my father ask you for the money that allowed me to go overseas with the student choir?' Perhaps she never asked because in her heart she still hoped that it was her father that had given her the money. The old man does not answer. 'I want to know, Uncle Joop. I have the right to know.'

'Why don't you ask your father?'

'I'm asking you.'

'Yes, I did give him the money. If I could have chosen a daughter for myself, I would have wanted her to be like you. That's why I gave him the money.'

'My father should not have done that.'

24

'Would you rather have stayed at home?'

'It's too late to ask that now. All I know, is that my life would have been different if I had not gone.'

'Why?'

'Perhaps we are not really able to choose.'

Six

WOULD SHE HAVE STAYED at home, if she had known about the money, she asks herself as she drives away. Did she have a choice or was it predestined? Was it one of the rivers that she had to cross? Was it something as simple as a guardian angel with a warped sense of humour that had pushed her towards her destiny?

She never intended to join the Village Choir when she went to university. Marian was in her final year and had been a member of the choir since her first year.

She, Araminta, went to university because it had offered hope. Escape from school and home and village where the shame kept following her no matter how hard she tried to put it behind her. University was putting on new clothes, leaving the old ones behind. It was the place where Future began so that you could get to Now.

Disillusionment is a narrow bed in a small room on the third floor of a hall of residence, surrounded by rows upon rows of other rooms filled with strangers and corridors smelling of menstruation. Every morning, thousands of multicoloured ants came out the rooms in all the blocks, making for a multitude of classes. A multicoloured ant, she followed the thickest line to the BA classes in sloping lecture-rooms as big as concert-halls, where the lecturers and professors stood far below. It was a huge open prison, you could escape if you wanted to, but you were too

26

frightened. You didn't know which door to escape through.

Nothing was right. Not the clothes old Miss Lily had made you, not the shoes they had bought you. God only knew how you were to make do on your weekly pocket money. You didn't. And your father would not have five cents' mercy on you, for sure!

Twice she changed her subjects before it was too late to change them again and she was trapped: Afrikaans-Dutch; English; geography; psychology; history. The only consolation was the fact that she would only have to take three of those subjects in her second year. And two in the third.

If she got that far. She would stand in front of the mirror in her room asking herself: Why am I here? Who am I? What's life? How am I ever going to get all the experience that I need? She was afraid to look too deep into her eyes, afraid of what she might see . . .

A man came hammering on the rectory door one day. It was early on a Monday morning. When her father opened the door, the man shouted, 'Reverend, why don't you get the hell out of here and go and live in black Africa, where you can preach to the fucking communists?'

Marian got such a fright, she started to cry. No one ever spoke like that at the rectory. Their mother took them to the bedroom and told them not to be upset, it was only a nasty man who had not liked their father's sermon the day before. She, Araminta, didn't know what the sermon was about because she always daydreamed in church.

When the man had gone, her father came and stood in the door, tight-lipped. 'Children,' he said, 'I think you're old enough to understand the tragic incident that happened here just now.' She was twelve, Marian fifteen. 'I want this to be an example to you of the blindness of most of the Afrikaners. And an indication of why we Afrikaners have become the most hated people on earth.'

It was as if a little hole had been bored into her skull and the words from her father's lips had poured through it. When the words got inside her head, she said to them: You're not true!

So the words went away.

Later that day, she did, however, take down the atlas and turned to the page with the large orange land in the centre: Africa. Until then, South Africa had been an ordinary land made of earth and rocks and mountains and plants and people and animals – not really part of Africa. Africa was a far-off place. Somewhere else. But then she saw that South Africa was Africa's feet and that they were living on its toes. Suddenly she *knew* where she was living. A fear came over her – not as for snakes and spiders, but as for lightning that could strike you when it wanted to.

Until that day, she had not even understood what it meant to be white. A white skin was something that you were born with, like arms and legs. Then one day you start *becoming* white: gradually. Later you stand in front of a mirror in a hall of residence and you ask yourself: Who am I, what am I doing here, where am I going?

Finally she went to Marian and told her that she had decided to give up studying. Marian laughed and said everyone goes through that, especially students from the country. Come do a voice test and join the choir; it's fun and you make a lot of friends.

The choir was the Village Choir. A smaller choir than the university choir, but just as popular and praised by the critics after every performance. Often even more highly than the university choir.

She passed the audition, and from the very first day enjoyed every moment of it. In the beginning she was just Marian's younger sister. Later, after Marian had finished her studies and left, she became the leading soprano. Jakob Hart, the self-appointed clown of the choir, was the leading tenor and everyone thought there was something between them.

There was. But not what they thought.

At the end of her second year, there was talk about the choir going on a short overseas tour in the June of the following year. It felt like a dream that could not come true.

A dream costing money. For although the choir had good sponsors, every member still had to contribute R800 plus pocket money, another R400. R1 200 in all. By a certain date everyone had to bring the necessary consent and guarantee from parents or guardians.

R1 200. Her father would have a heart attack.

It was early autumn. The streets and pavements were strewn with leaves that crackled under her feet as she wandered around, trying to find the courage to phone home. Every little gust of wind sent more leaves fluttering down to the ground like large, brown moths – no, like small bank-notes . . .

Having to ask Ignatius Rossouw for money was no fun.

She had been in standard three before she had found out that the church was paying her father to preach and her mother to play the organ. She had always thought that her father took some money from the collection plates on Sundays to pay for the week's bread and newspapers, and for the rest they lived on the meat and vegetables and stuff the farmers and other members of the congregation used to bring to the rectory.

Occasionally, she and Marian got pocket money from visiting grandparents, and sometimes lucky enough to find a lost coin in a pew when they played in the church – which was against the sexton's rules.

The day she discovered that her father was getting a monthly salary, she thought up a clever plan to get a bicycle.

'Father, you said in church this morning that everything comes from the Lord.' She had chosen Sunday lunch as the time for her attack.

29

'Yes, Araminta, so I did.'

'Does money come from the Lord as well?'

'Everything comes from the Lord.'

'Why does He give some people lots of money and others only a little?' She honestly wondered about it sometimes . . .

'The ways of the Lord are not always clear to us, Araminta.'

'Do you think God will give me a bicycle if I ask Him nicely?'

'No, because you don't really need a bicycle.'

'Will you give me a bicycle then?'

'Eat up your food.'

The week after, the sexton's brother brought her a bicycle his children were no longer using. She had to write the man a letter of thanks, and Marian had said that when the time came Father would undoubtedly go begging for his coffin as well.

She needed R1 200.

In the end she didn't have the courage to phone home and ask for the money. She got a lift home for the weekend and went to ask in person.

'Let's get this straight, Araminta,' her father had said. 'You are the leading soprano. Correct?'

'Yes, Father.'

'Well in that case I see no reason why the sponsors shouldn't pay for all your expenses.'

'They can't do that, Father! And I don't want them sending a hat round for me; I'd rather tell them I can't go!'

'Don't be impertinent! Your academic record, has not been good. You do not deserve to go abroad at all.'

'You don't understand, Father.' Her academic record had already been discussed ad nauseam, and was a subject best avoided.

30

'You're quite right, I don't understand. For it makes no sense that a student, with As all the way through school – except for a temporary decline – can be struggling with a simple BA degree at university.'

'I'm not struggling as such, Father. I've already tried to explain to you many times that I have to understand things for myself. I have to find my own way. It's no use understanding only what the professor wants you to understand from piles of photocopied notes. Especially in history.' That was the last subject she wanted to touch.

'You know what I think about that. You know how much time we've wasted already on discussing it. As long as the Afrikaner keeps hanging on to a single view of history, we'll remain pillars of salt like Lot's wife. Anyway, we must learn to look ahead, not backwards!'

'That's right, Father.' Careful, she said to herself, we must not get into another senseless argument.

'In this country only one thing matters, and that is to find solutions to our complex situation as quickly as possible in order to bring about justice for everyone.'

'As you say, Father.'

'Your indifference worries me.'

'General Smuts said that the most brilliant men in the world came here to solve South Africa's problems and every one of them went back defeated.'

'Because the solutions to our problems lie within ourselves!'

'Yes, Father. At this moment the solution to my immediate problem is R1 200, and I have no way of finding that within myself.'

'Where do you think I can get it from? Everything is getting more expensive by the day. I must make provision for us to have a roof over our heads when your mother and I eventually retire.'

'I realize that, Father.'

'Perhaps you should stop singing in the choir and apply yourself wholly to your studies! Have you thought about the consequences if you don't get your degree at the end of the year? You have a teacher's bursary.'

'You know something, Father? There's a girl in the choir – her name is Heidi – she invited the whole choir to her home in Durbanville one Saturday. Three bathrooms, a swimming-pool, three garages. She and her brother both have new cars, she has the most beautiful clothes. And neither her father or her mother have been to university – they have a real-estate business. Both you and Mother have years of university training and what have you earned for it? We never have money for anything.'

'Granted. But earthly goods aren't everything. We must look for real values.'

'I would so much like to go abroad with the choir, Father. Please.'

That was the Friday afternoon. On Saturday morning, she had seen her father going round to Uncle Joop's. Later he gave her a cheque for R1 200. The next morning, during the church service, she had gone into his study and found a savings-bank book with R17 840 in it, and she said to herself maybe he had gone to Uncle Joop on a social visit.

She would always remember what it had felt like when the aircraft began to move faster and faster down the runway and finally left the ground. At that moment the dream came true. Gone was all the hard work, the hours spent in rounding off every piece on the choir's programme, the fear that something like flu might force her to stay behind.

The choir consisted of twenty-one members: twelve women and nine men. A final meeting was held shortly before their departure. For the first part, the men and the women were taken separately. Helen Pearce, wife of Dr Groenewald, the tour leader and conductor, spoke to the women; Dr Groenewald himself spoke to the men. What Helen Pearce said, with great embarrassment, was that no sleeping together during the tour would be tolerated. It was assumed that Dr Groenewald had said the same to the men.

The joint meeting afterwards was a disappointment. They were once again informed that in England they would only perform before invited audiences. Their participation at the choir festivals in Scotland and Wales would be unofficial, because they were South African students. There would be no publicity. They were to avoid confrontation at all times and in no way advertise the fact that they were from South Africa.

'The anti-apartheid campaign in Britain is particularly strong and well-organized at the moment,' Dr Groenewald assured them.

In other words, they had to go and perform like sneaks.

Early on the Sunday morning, after a flight of fourteen hours, they landed at Heathrow Airport. Jakob Hart made a final 'announcement' from his seat next to her while the plane taxied to a halt.

'Ladies and gentlemen, we have just landed outside Londinium, ancient city of Romans. Today known as London and the heart of the myth of myths: democracy.'

'Cut out the politics!' one of the others joked.

Jakob carried on with exaggerated portentousness. 'Bear it in mind, ladies and gentlemen, that sixty years before Christ, this enormous city, where there are more inhabitants today than all the white people in the whole of South Africa, was just a hamlet consisting of wooden shacks and a single wooden bridge crossing the River Thames.

'Think of that time, think of how the people of the land rioted against the rule of the Romans, looted and burned, so that extra warriors had to be called in to force them to submit for three more centuries. When at last the Romans went away, new looters came from across the sea to rule for another six hundred years!'

'You must be joking.'

'No I'm not. At last, William the Conquerer came across the Channel with his mighty Norman army and took the land from the Saxons–Celts–Angles–Norsemen and said: "Now it's mine." His descendants continued the wars, and blood, my friends, flowed across this land as it does over the floor of an abattoir. Blood mixed with blood: at last the Norman–Saxon–Celt–Angle–Norsemen were of one blood – a new people had risen and they were called "the English". Today, dear friends, everyone in this land is equal before God and the Law: the princes and the punks, the lords and the ladies; whore, bore, duchess and dame; earl, bricklayer and marquess.'

You could never be sure whether Jakob was being serious or playing the fool. A tall, lanky, reddish-blond law student in his fourth year; brilliant according to his classmates.

Of all the girls in the choir, Jakob had chosen her to walk with or sit next to. Perhaps it was because he knew she was 'safe', that she would not expect more. For Jakob was one of those people that gave the impression that he knew exactly where he was going, and that nothing and nobody would stop him.

It suited her. Her body didn't react yet when someone touched her; it was still drained after Frans.

On the very first morning they had to get up early and go for a work-out session in the park opposite the hotel where they were staying. Matthys Okennedy did a cheeky thing that first morning: he pinned a small South African flag on to his track-suit. Dr Groenewald asked him to take it off.

On the Monday, a special bus took them to South Africa House for rehearsals. Afterwards, when they went to Trafalgar Square luring armfuls of pigeons and taking photos, a rowdy demonstration against Nelson Mandela's detainment and against apartheid was taking place in front of the building. Dr Groenewald asked them to stay away from it. Two of the men, however, slipped away to go and talk to the demonstrators. When they got back, they said the demonstrators were planning a round-the-clock demonstration against South Africa until apartheid was ended and all the political prisoners had been released. Nobody seemed particularly interested.

That same evening they gave their first performance before a small but most appreciative audience. On the Wednesday, the choir left by bus for Scotland, and performed in Edinburgh the following night. Everybody said afterwards that had they been allowed to compete officially, they would undoubtedly have taken the first place.

And everywhere they went, the people were friendly. A wary kind of friendliness. They looked at you and spoke to you as if from a distance, as if you were not quite to be trusted or something.

A different kind of people. More refined. Higher people. Hollow people. Not hollow as in empty, hollow as if all superfluous passion had been pared away over the ages . . .

In Wrexham, in Wales, the choir received a standing ovation. Afterwards, a small confrontation developed when a man from the audience wanted to know why there were no blacks in the choir. Somebody pointed out to him that there were two coloureds, but the man was not satisfied. Lucius and Tyrone were apparently not black enough for him.

For the last four days of the tour, the choir was back in London. On the first night they performed with two other choirs in a small theatre in Islington. Only one more performance remained, the one scheduled for the second last day, at the residence of the South African ambassador.

During the morning of that particular day, most of the group went to see the Tower of London.

Afterwards, she always wondered why it had had to happen. She didn't plan to go to the Tower; she and two of the other girls were going to go to Madame Tussaud's.

Then she changed her mind. Or perhaps it was her angel that pushed her on to the coach.

The guide that took them through the Tower was a neatly dressed, middle-aged man with thick glasses.

In the middle of the enormous fortress stands a big castle; he told them that it was the castle William the Conquerer had started to build as a defence against his riotous subjects, nine hundred years ago, and as a strong-hold from which to exert his will. One of the later kings had the tower whitewashed and so it got its name, the White Tower. The walls of the castle measure fifteen feet thick at the bottom and thirteen at the top. Or something like that. She could not quite hear what was being said, because Matthys Okennedy kept on passing remarks at the back, reminding them that the first for-tress at the Cape, built some 340 years ago, had walls measuring twenty feet thick at the bottom and sixteen feet at the top. And that it had been built in order to guard the English from taking control of the sea route to the East round the Cape.

The guide got cross with Matthys, but carried on.

The White Tower, he said, also served as a state prison later on. Captives of high birth were housed on the top floors; prisoners from the lower classes were chained to the stone walls in the cellars. Prisoners might be detained in any of the thirteen towers on the inside wall till it was time for their heads to be chopped off.

'I remember it well,' Jakob suddenly pipped in. 'My own head was cut off here some four hundred years ago.'

'Don't talk bloody shit!' somebody said, amongst the laughter.

'Pity it grew back on askew!' someone else chipped in.

'Ladies and gentlemen, may I please have your attention!'
'Sorry!'

The guide went on to say that Macaulay, the historian, had said that the Tower was the most godforsaken place on earth. Before he could continue, Matthys butted in again.

'According to the old sea-captains, the Cape of Good Hope was the most godforsaken place on earth,' he cried.

'I wouldn't know,' the guide answered with a sneer. 'I've never been there.'

Later, attention was shifted to the large black ravens, hopping around and trying in vain to fly. Someone mentioned that it had been prophesied that the throne of Britain would fall on the day that the last raven left the fortress. That's why their wings are clipped.

'Well, I'll be damned!' Matthys called out once again. 'That means we'll have to start clipping our wagtails' wings!'

'What do you mean?'

'The wagtail is the white man's emblem. The day the last ones fly away, it will be the end of the white man down in the south of Africa.'

'Are you making this up?'

'Of course not.'

'But in that case, the blacks can simply start wringing the wagtails' necks!' That was Jakob.

'Don't be silly!' one of the others cried.

'Ladies and gentlemen . . .'

The guide asked those who wanted to see the Crown Jewels to follow him.

Are there angels that take you by the hand and lead you where you are destined to go?

First you shuffle along in the queue through a hall full of glass cases in which all sorts of royal objects are displayed: golden dishes, sceptres, candlesticks, rows upon rows of trumpets, medallions, royal robes woven with golden thread. Your eyes could only jump from the one to the other, in an impossible effort to take it all in.

'Where's the king's crown?' someone wanted to know.

'I suppose we're going to come to it.'

Shuffle, shuffle. Down, down, down steps and through the most incredibly thick door: CHUBB. You're in a large, dusky vault with black walls. Light comes from a group of glass cases in the middle, filled with the treasure. Golden altar dishes . . . swords in jewelled scabbards . . . a salt-cellar as big as a small castle . . .

'Keep moving,' a guard says from the semi-darkness.

You are not allowed to stop and look.

Velvet-capped crowns with arches and circlets encrusted with precious stones. Hundreds of stones, emitting tiny rays of light. Large stones. Small stones. Bright stones, blue stones, green stones, red stones. Large white pearls.

'Move on!'

'Araminta, the man's talking to you!'

'I can't look at it all so fast!'

'You've got to keep moving!'

It's like being allowed to see something forbidden, something wonderful, untouchable, unbelievable – but only for the wink of an eye.

'Look, there's the Star of Africa!' Lucius Muller, walking in front of her, pointed out the diamond. 'There, in that sceptre with the cross. It's part of a colossal diamond that was found in a mine outside Pretoria.'

It was the most incredible stone. Like pale blue ice. As big as the palm of a child's hand and cut in the shape of a pear. 'Star of Africa', it said on the plaque.

'Move on!'

She could not move on. She wanted to reach out and tap on the glass wall and say to the diamond, 'Look, we've come to visit you! We're from the same land.'

'Please keep moving, ladies and gentlemen!'

The diamond was longing for home. She knew it, she felt it. She saw it through the glass. It was too tightly clamped in the sceptre, it was too crowded in the case and the lights shone too brightly. Her feet began to move forward, but in her heart she begged them to take the diamond out so that she could hold and comfort it. When she couldn't see it any longer, a feeling of helplessness welled up in her against the power that guarded it. Something akin to hatred.

38

When they got outside, she deliberately wandered away from the others to be alone for a while. She could not understand why the diamond had upset her so. She would gladly have spent the last of her money on going back and seeing it again, but it was half-past twelve. They had to be back at the coach at one o'clock.

She was thirsty. She stooped down for a drink of water at a drinking fountain but she did something wrong, because the water came out with a gush, splashing all over her face . . .

Perhaps shadows from the future fall on you as a warning – perhaps you only turn them into shadows of foreboding afterwards.

A little way beyond the tap was a small square fenced off with chains. Written on a plaque were the names of five women, a lord and an earl whose heads had been cut off on that spot.

When she turned round, Jakob was staring at her intently – not Jakob the clown, but the Jakob whose head had been cut off long ago.

On their way back to the hotel, there was great merriment on the coach. Some of the students had bought some finger puppets from street vendors and were putting on an impromptu entertainment for the others.

From the back of the bus came other strange noises and shouts, which remained a mystery until a very disgusted Heidi explained: 'They've bought a book with naked girls in it. I saw Paul buying it.'

'That's nothing,' said Yolanda, 'I bought a *Playgirl* full of naked men yesterday! I'm going to smuggle it home in the bottom of my suitcase.'

'*Naked* men?'

'Naked as the day they were born. Only bigger.'

'It's illegal to take pornography into our country and you know it!' Heidi retorted, indignantly. 'Anyway, it's downright immoral!'

'How can paper pricks be immoral?' Yolanda teased.

When the coach stopped at the hotel, there was a scramble for bags and packages and cameras and a last laugh, and no one apparently noticed what was happening on the pavement. More than half of them were out of the coach before they realized that a group of demonstrators was blocking the entrance to the hotel.

It was a demonstration against *them*!

The coach pulled away and left them right in front of the demonstrators' posters: 'RACIST PIGS!' 'FREE MANDELA!' 'VILLAGE CHOIR GO HOME!' Some were holding up their clenched fists in the air shouting, 'Amandla! Amandla!'

Because she had been one of the first to get off the coach she was standing right in front of the demonstrators and uncomfortably close to them. Dr Groenewald appeared from somewhere and told them not to react, but to start moving away, one by one.

It was not that simple. In front of them were the demonstrators, behind them the street and the traffic, on both sides of the pavement, crowds of pedestrians, so that they were kept there in a huddle.

There were about fifty demonstrators. Mostly young hippies; only two were black – a handsome young man with a thick beard, wearing a tartan cap, and a middle-aged woman with a shock of hair, wearing a red dress.

'Amandla! Amandla!'

'What does it mean?' one of the girls asked in distress.

'If you really don't know, it's time you woke up!' somebody snapped.

'It means "Power to the People",' someone whispered.

The worst thing was the eyes of the people around them. Eyes looking at you with unconcealed contempt, and somewhere in your head there's a little hole . . .

Dr Groenewald urged them to start moving away. She stepped to the left and managed to get past two of the girls next to her. She was still in the front, however, and she felt sure that the woman in the red dress was watching her. She wasn't sure, as the woman was wearing glasses.

With difficulty, she managed to reach Matthys Okennedy, who was standing right at the end. Had she stayed where she was, it would not have happened. 'Amandla! Amandla!' a demonstrator shouted. Without warning, Matthys raised his fist in the air and shouted back, 'To hell with Amandla! I'm a Boer and where I rule, I rule!'

Her first thought was 'Thank God he said it in Afrikaans, they won't have understood!' But red-dress came rushing at Matthys like a vixen, shouting, 'Hold your bloody tongue, you white-arsed Boer!' In Afrikaans.

Then it happened. She, Araminta raised her hand to give Matthys a push and tell him to keep quiet. The Red-dress must have seen the movement differently, because the next moment the woman spat at her, right in the face.

She fled through the demonstrators to get to her room. But neither soap, nor water, not the hardest scrubbing, nor shampoo, nor a facecloth or towel, *nothing* takes away spit from one's face. Or hatred from a woman's eyes.

One after the other, the others started coming to her room to ask how she was. As if she were sick. They came and sat on the bed and on the floor, they leant against the walls till the room was filled with voices: 'I would have spit back at her' . . . 'I would've slapped her' . . . 'Why didn't she spit at Matthys?' . . . 'Don't look so upset, Araminta' . . . 'How come the demonstrators knew we were staying at this hotel?'

She stood in the door leading to the bathroom and covered her ears with her hands, but the voices wouldn't go away: 'They get paid to demonstrate' . . . 'Did any of the spit get into your mouth?' . . . 'Where is there an ashtray?' . . . 'Did she give you a fright?' . . . 'Where's Jakob?'

Suddenly Retief Human cried out, 'Calm down, everyone! Don't you realize that we have earned every drop of that woman's contempt? Every drop!'

For a moment it was dead quiet. Her hands dropped to her sides. Matthys Okennedy came up from the floor like a lion that had detected a movement too close to its lair.

'What did you say?'

'You heard.'

'You fuckin' traitor.'

'Leave it, guys!' Someone was trying desperately to calm them down.

But Retief and Matthys were on their feet. 'That woman,' Retief said calmly, 'spat on behalf of the millions of oppressed people in our country. People who are deprived of all political rights.'

'Bullshit! They have more rights than many whites in South Africa! The bloody workers' unions rule the country and when they don't get their way, they strike and loot and destroy, and the government just keeps on giving in. And you say they have no rights?'

'Hear, hear!'

She did not want to listen. She wanted to flee from the room, but she could not get to the door and her shoes were missing. One after the other they joined in, words collided with words like stones hurled across the room. It was no longer a choir that sang together in harmony, it was a collection of gaping mouths emitting distorted sounds.

'People, please!' someone urged. 'We have the most complex society in the whole world and no fighting is going to solve any of our problems. Only reform and negotiation.'

'Like hell! Only birth-control can do that – one black baby is born every thirty-seven seconds. It's the fastest-growing population in the world, and the whites are paying for all the fun.'

'If you've taken all political power for yourself, you have to pay whatever the cost.'

'*Nkosi sikelel' i-Africa!* God is on the side of the oppressed!'

'Napoleon said that God is on the side of those who have the strongest army.'

'Yes? And look what happened to Napoleon.'

'You're all talking bull and you don't even know it!'

'My aunt's emigrating to Australia.'

'My uncle and his family are there already.'

'No solution will be found for South Africa's problems unless a redistribution of wealth takes place.'

'Don't worry, the blacks are stealing the lot anyway.'

'So is the fucking government!'

She went down on her knees and started looking for her shoes.

'Have the police ever dragged your mother from your home in the middle of the night? Have the police ever shot at people in white streets?'

'You speak with the tongue of an agitator, you take exceptions and make them the norm.'

'The world expects us, the five million whites, to provide hospitals and houses and schools and whatever to twenty million blacks.'

'You speak with the tongue of the capitalist.'

'That's right. Why else would the blacks be streaming south towards the wealth of the capitalists, not north to the breeding grounds of the communists?'

There was a little hole in her head . . . 'Will you please get out of the way so that I can find my shoes!' No one took any notice.

'They're going back to the land that we stole from them, that's why.'

'We didn't steal land from anyone!'

'Are you saying that it's fair that only thirteen per cent of our territory has been granted to all the millions of black people?'

'Yes. For what the clever dicks never add, is that something like seventy per cent of our land is inhospitable!'

'And that gives you racists one more loophole to jump through, but one day there won't be any loopholes left.'

'I see in the papers that the blacks in London are also frustrated by the way things are going; they claim it's mostly the fault of the police. It's the same as back home.'

'Will you stop it!' One of the girls started to cry.

'Back home the main problem is the police with their Caspirs and guns.'

'Shooting at children running away.'

'I've told you not to turn every goddamn exception into the norm! Every time there's trouble, the bloody agitators send the children up front to start fires and throw stones; that's what they do!'

'Have you ever seen a child carrying a dead child?'

She pushed her way to the door and fled. Without her shoes.

Even the desolation of a desert could not be more frightening than walking barefoot in a city, thousands of kilometres from home. The worry of not knowing where you are, or where you're going. The fear of the demonstrators, of running into the woman with the red dress . . .

Neverending streams of cars, buses, taxis, people. No one knows you're fleeing.

Only you do. Somehow you've been sentenced without your knowing what your punishment will be. Foolishly you had thought you could simply go on living, and reach happiness eventually. Now suddenly you know it's a dream.

You're white. You were born in the wrong place. Somebody once said, 'Life is seven storeys high. At the top dwell the godly and the good; it's far off and very high up. Down at the lowest level live the perverts and everything that's evil. One step higher is the abode of politics and lies.' That afternoon in London she added: If you live in South Africa, you can try as hard as you can to climb up, but you don't get any higher; they grab you and pull you back to the place of the lies, no matter where you are. No matter that you've seen the most beautiful diamond

44

deep inside a dark place and felt a speck of light within yourself for a moment.

When it got dark, she asked a stranger the way back to the hotel.

And nothing Helmut Groenewald did that night could bring out the old sparkle in the choir. Something was gone.

The following day she crept into the cocoon of the orange-tailed SAA Boeing to be taken home: not across Africa, but round the continent. Africa did not want its airspace polluted by you.

When they arrived at Jan Smuts Airport the next morning, it was Jakob who took over again while they taxied on the tarmac.

'Ladies and gentlemen, we have just landed outside the city of gold, Johannesburg. Bear it in mind that a hundred years ago there was not a single street or building or stockmarket here, and no Soweto either. It was open veld with a few head of cattle here and there. Think of the words of one of our earlier statesmen, Reitz. Remember he said it would be better if we rid ourselves of this place before it destroyed the noble character of the Afrikaner, the Boer. Reitz, ladies and gentlemen, was not a man of vision, he did not foresee that it would be this murky cloud of smoke that would cause the damage in the end. Smoke from the millions of shacks where poor people dwell; poisoned smoke from the chimneys of the thousands of factories and power stations and all sorts of places where poor people work. Think of all the thousands that have to riot and plunder and murder in this terrible state of pollution and allow me to say: Welcome home!'

No one laughed.

Most of the students changed flights to go down to Cape Town. She flew to George where her parents were waiting for her. From there it was a little more than an hour's drive before it was 'welcome home' for her.

45

She ate, she slept, she talked. Everyone said she was looking well. No one noticed the spit on her face. Not even Uncle Joop.

The night before she had to be back at university, she took her father a cup of tea in his study. On purpose.

'There was a demonstration against us in London, Father.' She made it sound as if it was nothing in particular.

'Was there?'

'Yes. A black woman with eyes full of hatred spat at one of the girls, in her face.'

'That was a bit drastic, wasn't it?'

'I thought so too.'

'Was it a well-organized demonstration?'

'It seemed so.'

'What was the purpose of the demonstration?'

'It was about telling racist pigs to go home and free Mandela.'

'Why is it always Mandela only? What about Sisulu and all the other political prisoners?'

'The girl said afterwards she was sorry she didn't spit back.'

'That would have been typical of what we do in this country. We do not ask people why they're spitting, we spit back or put them in prison.'

'But that girl didn't do anything, Father! At least she would have felt better if she had retaliated.'

'Was it you the woman spat at, Araminta?'

Her father wasn't stupid. 'What makes you think that?'

'It just crossed my mind . . .'

'I suppose in a way she spat at us all.' But the words sounded false.

Seven

THE ADDRESS ON THE envelope is that of a Mr Samuel Sundoo in Woodstock, Cape Town. It sounds like a back-street place. Had it not come from Joop Lourens's hand, she doubted whether she would have had the courage to go through with it.

All day long, on the Sunday, she has to stop herself from getting into her car and driving to Cape Town. If she did, she would have to stay the night somewhere, and hotels cost money!

Samuel Sundoo. It has a strange ring to it. Indian, perhaps. If he is Indian, he should at least know *something* about diamonds. For centuries, the West went seeking all its diamonds in India: overland on foot, on camels. After the discovery of the sea route round Africa, they were taken to the West in little canvas bags on the sailing ships. Diamonds for the adornment of the rich and the royal.

When Jan van Riebeeck was sent to the Cape in 1652 to establish a way-station on the sea route between West and East, he was given a handful of Indian diamonds to take with him. He had to show them to the indigenous Koikoi and ask them if they knew what they were. No, they didn't. When he showed them pieces of copper and gold, however, the answer was always yes, yes . . .

*

The mountain is a hazy blue, almost as if someone had painted it too light and featureless against the sky.

She takes the diamonds from the violet's leaves, rinses them under the tap and gently dries them on a towel.

A rather worried Mrs Shirley phoned on Friday afternoon to say that she and her husband had only realized afterwards that they might have made a mistake in involving her with the diamonds. If she were to get into trouble, they would be responsible. What trouble? All sorts of trouble. Can she really trust the person? Of course.

She didn't tell them about Samuel Sundoo. Joop Lourens would not allow her to get into trouble.

She keeps the diamonds in the towel and puts them on the table by the window. When they catch the sun, the light in them is lots of tiny sparks of colour . . .

One carat is the weight of one seed of a carob tree. It says so in the book. When the old traders didn't have any carob seeds, they used grains of barley as weight. Samuel Sundoo will not be using grains of barley, though.

Really big diamonds are very scarce and are always found in the shelter of a rock. It makes sense: without shelter you can be trampled into the ground no matter how tough you are. And only 10 per cent of all the diamonds that are being taken from the earth can truly be called precious stones. The rest are full of faults and are set in cheaper rings, or used in tools such as grinding-wheels and lathes.

What if Samuel Sundoo says all six diamonds are good for industrial use only? Say he offers her something like R5 000 for them? Then she takes them back to the Shirleys and that is the end of it.

'Don't worry,' she tells them aloud. 'I will not let them make tools of you.' The Bible says stones can hear.

She has found out more about the Star of Africa too. They say it's the biggest cut diamond in the world and of the purest, palest blue. The mother-stone weighed more than 3,000 carats, and was found in the shelter of a rock outside Pretoria in 1905. Three thousand grains of barley. She went to the Greek on the corner, bought a packet of barley and counted out three thousand grains. It took her nearly the whole of Saturday afternoon. When she was finished, it was only half a cupful, which did not seem quite right. Perhaps barley had bigger grains in the olden days.

The old Transvaal government bought the diamond for something like R300 000 and presented it to King Edward VII of Great Britain for his sixty-sixth birthday. One lot of Boers hated the British; the others said, 'We must forgive and forget, and give them our most beautiful diamond. What's the use of standing up against an empire as strong as that? We've tried it to our doom and sorrow.'

The king had had the diamond cut and polished into more than a hundred pieces. The largest, 530 carats, was set into the Sceptre of Kingly Power and Justice; the second largest, the 'Lesser Star of Africa' of 317 grains, was set in the king's crown.

R300 000 for 3,106 carats in 1907. Seventy years later, a stone of 354 carats was found in the same mine and sold for R10 million. It didn't make sense.

And it's not right: a stone lives for millions of years, man only seventy, more or less . . .

She irons a dress to put on and goes to church, taking the diamonds with her.

Bernard Holtzman and his wife sit two pews in front of her. Elvin Carr will not be in church, he's Methodist. Christel and her husband are Apostolics. Lizzie, Carr & Holtzman's second typist-cum-secretary, will not be here either, she's coloured and Catholic . . . Why does Lizzie sometimes stay behind at the office when Elvin has to work late? Don't jump to conclusions, Elvin is old enough to be Lizzie's father . . .

Klaas Muller is in the deacon's pew. Klaas used to be a schoolteacher, but left the profession to start his own paint shop in town. When she moved to George, he was one of the first people to knock on her door, asking if she was new in town. Yes. Does she belong to the Dutch Reformed Church? Yes. May he come in for a moment? He's the deacon of the ward, and will be making the monthly collections. Sure. He wanted to know where she worked. Where she came from. What her father did for a living. If she was engaged to be married or anything? No. Neither was he.

The following evening, he didn't come collecting, he came visiting. The next evening, he came a little earlier. And he kept on coming. She told herself it didn't mean a thing, he was just coming to chat. Mostly nonsense. But at least he could kill a spider or replace a washer in a tap for her.

Then suddenly, he didn't only want to chat any more, he *insisted* that she come and sit on the bed with him, and after that she never opened the door to him again.

Ralph Linde is also in church. With his new wife. His second. An irritating, nagging insurance agent, to whom she has already explained a dozen times that she's not interested in taking out any insurance and that her reasons are personal.

Joris Oosthuizen is officiating and stands in the pulpit reading from the Epistle of James. Joris's father and her father were at university together. She suspects that her father contacted Joris when she came to George and told him about her. Perhaps asked him to keep an eye on her. Because Joris came to call on her even before Klaas Muller did. Prying, cautious.

'Don't you think you should have persevered with your studies?'

'No.'

'Don't you think teaching would have been a much safer career than selling property?'

'Not for me.' She knew he meant well.

'Don't you think you might have acted a little too hastily? We all go through periods of doubt, it's part of life. After a time one sees clearly again.'

50

'I do see clearly.'
'Are you sure?'
'Yes.'

They say that if you put a diamond in the hottest of fires, a very bright light shoots up and then it vanishes without leaving a trace of ash behind . . . How long do one's traces remain behind you after you have gone? Your hair, your nails . . .

'". . . ye that say, Today or tomorrow we will go into such a city . . . and buy and sell, and get gain . . ."' She suddenly sits up and pays attention to what Joris is reading. '"Whereas ye know not what shall be on the morrow. For what is your life? It is even a vapour, that appeareth for a little time, and then vanisheth away. For that ye ought to say, If the Lord will, we shall live, and do this, or that . . ."'

Why is he reading that?

'Whereas ye know not what shall be on the morrow.'

Joop Lourens will not send her into trouble! Not knowingly.

Eight

It *is* kind of a slum area. And Samuel Sundoo *is* an Indian. She wants to leave as soon as she can and never come back.

The wooden stairs she had to climb to get to the first floor are old and worn and as steep as a ladder. The carpet underneath her feet is so dirty, weeds could grow on it. Up in the corners of the room, spiders' webs are sagging down like little hammocks under years of gathering dust.

The only thing that does not fit is Samuel Sundoo, sitting across from her at a most untidy table. There is no dust on *him*. The suit he's wearing is certainly of the best, and so is his shirt and tie. His head gives the impression of being square; perhaps it's the way he combs back his smooth, black hair from his wide forehead. Thin lips, stern mouth, very white teeth. His eyes say: I belong to East and West – I know many secrets. I am who I am, I need nothing of you.

From the moment she walked in, he was openly hostile, as if to make sure that she will not feel welcome.

She arrived shortly after twelve. The address on the envelope was that of a simple little fruit and vegetable shop. When she asked to see Mr Samuel Sundoo, a plump woman wearing a yellow saree appeared from the back like a watchdog, and stared at her coldly. She asked again to see Mr Sundoo. The woman said she was at the wrong address. It left her no choice; she told the woman she had a letter for Mr Sundoo from Joop Lourens. The woman took the letter and disappeared out the back again.

When she returned, she took her to a door next to the shop, right on the street, and motioned to her without a word to climb the stairs.

Samuel Sundoo was sitting behind the table with the letter open in his hand. From his gesture, she gathered that she was to take the chair on the other side of the table.

'Identity document?'

'I beg your pardon?' It's about the first word he has spoken.

'I want to see your identity document.'

'Sure.' She takes it from her bag and hands it across the table to him. Will he ask for the diamonds, or should she hand them over as well?

'Did you come alone?'

'Yes.'

'Next time you phone and make an appointment.'

'There won't be a next time. I'm sorry for being a bother – it's a rather long story.'

'Why are you so nervous?'

'I've never been in a situation like this before. I'm not sure what to expect.'

'Where are the articles?'

She takes them from her pocket, unwraps them from the tissue and hands them over. It feels like giving away a cat or a dog you should have kept . . .

He switches on the lamp on the table and takes a small magnifying glass in a black frame from the inside pocket of his jacket. With a pair of long tweezers he picks the diamonds up one after the other, holds them to the light and looks at them through the magnifying glass. When he is finished, he places them in a little brown envelope, gets up and leaves through the door behind him without a word.

53

She remains where she is. She waits.

She hardly moves. It's worse than waiting your turn at the dentist. The incessant noise of the traffic down below makes it impossible to hear if he's in the room on the other side of the door or what he's doing. She thinks to herself, what if he does not come back? They say Indians can be very sly.

It must be more than ten minutes since he went.

What if he does not come back? What is she to tell the Shirleys? Why didn't she ask him if they were worth anything while he was examining them under the magnifying glass? How long should she wait before accepting that she has been tricked?

Someone is coming up the stairs from the street. Her heart starts beating faster – the door at the bottom was not locked, nobody knows where she is, they can murder her right here . . .

It's Samuel Sundoo. Carrying a yellow plastic shopping bag. 'The stones are of reasonable quality.' It's all he says before he gives her the bag.

In the bag is another bag, a smaller one.

When she gets to her car, she is shaking so much she can't get the key into the lock of the door. It's not the door key, it's the key of the petrol tank. Relax, she tells herself, it's over. But her body will not listen.

She does not dare open the bag when she is in the car; all kinds of loafers are loitering around. She must get away and find a safer place.

She has difficulty getting into the traffic, she has difficulty staying in the right lane. There are too many cars and trucks simply stopping where they want to!

What if it's only paper he has put in the bag? Or a loaf of bread? She puts out her hand to feel . . . it's not bread. It feels like banknotes.

Never again must anyone come and put six diamonds on her desk. Never. Not even a single diamond.

There's nowhere she can get out of the line of traffic to find a safe place to stop. The first chance comes at the turn-off to the Strand, half an hour later, and in Beach Road she finds a place at last.

The tide is out, the beach is a wide stretch of sand. For a moment she just sits back and becomes a student again, for this is where they always came swimming and holding beach parties. Everything is the same: the sun, the sea, the sand. Old people with bandy legs, walking along the water's edge and leaving long trails of footprints . . . See what's in the bag. Not yet . . . Some walk fast and upright as if denying old age with a show of gusto. Small children play around their mothers who are lying in the sun, tanning their winter-white bodies . . .

Suppose it's pieces of paper cut to the size of banknotes he's put in the bag?

The old Portuguese seafarers, trying to find the tip of Africa, had trouble getting any crew for their ships, because it was firmly believed that the earth came to an end here in a boiling sea. If you got too close, the sun would burn you black, for that is why all the people of Africa were black . . .

Look what's in the bag!

It is packs of R20 notes: R200 to a pack – R20 000 altogether.

Just before sunset, she's back home. And exhausted. Since the morning she has been on the road for almost ten hours.

She dials the Shirleys' number as she promised she would. Mrs Shirley answers.

'Yes, for R20 000.'

'How are we ever going to thank you, Miss Rossouw?'

'If you're still interested in buying the house, you can come and see me at the office tomorrow morning.'

'We'll be there. Thank you very much.'

'Not at all.' In her heart she adds: Just don't ever ask me to do this again.

55

Before she opens the curtains, she lifts the frill round the legs of the arm chair and puts the money under the chair so that the mountain will not see it.

When she opens the curtains, every grey rock-face stands out in the last light of the sun. The mountain is as massive and noble as ever.

I did not steal it, she says. I swear I did not.

She goes and lies down on the bed, watching the darkness setting in and the first flickering star come out high above the mountain. Something is gone. It's the diamonds. The bag with the money has a different kind of presence, but she is aware of that too. The whole time. If the Shirleys buy the house, it will add another feather to her wings . . .

More and more stars are coming out, shining like little diamonds in the sky. There must be diamonds in the sky, they have found some in meteorites . . .

How much longer would it take? How much farther must she go?

Is it the money under the chair that's making her so restless? For two long years she has been telling herself to be patient: it's a river she's crossing step by step; if she keeps on going steadily she will eventually get to the other side.

University was a different kind of stream. One that pulled you in relentlessly and carried you along graffiti-covered banks you had to learn by heart, stuff into your mouth, smear over your eyes, while you slowly realized you were living in two different worlds.

The first was eating and sleeping and attending classes; going to the beach, having fun. The second was called South Africa. Daily sneers with razor-sharp teeth from posters tied to lampposts in the main streets. Or framed outside the cafés: 'MORE SANCTIONS DEMANDED AGAINST SOUTH AFRICA.' Cars drove past without a care. 'MORE ARRESTS.' Streets full of people: white, brown and black walked past the posters, unconcerned. 'ARSENAL FOUND

56

IN SOUTH CAPE.' Shop-windows displaying the most beautiful things; you promise yourself you'll have lots of money one day. 'RIOTS.' Victoria Street was a lush green tunnel of old plane trees – you could have sworn they were oaks at first.

'NATIONAL FLAGS BURNT IN STUDENT VIOLENCE.' Cafés full of students and people eating and drinking. 'MORE SAA LANDING RIGHTS SUSPENDED.' Tourist with thick-soled shoes took pictures with long-nosed cameras. 'SCHOOL BOYCOTT SPREADING IN BLACK TOWNSHIPS.'

It felt as if lightning was waiting to strike . . .

'BEAT UP A BLOODY BOER TODAY!' It was written in big black spray-paint letters on a wall near one of the men's halls one Sunday morning. That same day, one of the Sunday papers carried the headline: 'Another 140 held near Crossroads – babies parted from mothers.'

The tunnel of trees started to turn into skeletons of bare brown branches. The winter grew colder and wetter. Spring arrived and brought back the green, and in the summer, her first year mercifully came to an end.

The day after she arrived home for the Christmas holidays, her year's results were in the post and her father called her to his study.

'How is it that you have such a bad report, for the second time this year?'

'I'm sorry, Father.'

'Sorry about what?'

'Because I'm not the way you want me to be.' She said the first thing that came into her head. He would not understand.

'How do I want you to be?'

'Like Mother and Marian. Mother agrees to everything you say, Marian agrees to everything Mother says. She never does anything wrong, it's always me that causes the trouble.'

'Surely, you can't still be having trouble adjusting to university?'

'I'm having trouble adjusting to life, Father.'

'We all go through times of incertitude. The secret is not to get stuck in the process of adjusting and sorting things out, but to think about the future and work at it.'

'What future, Father? According to you and most others, there is no future for us. Not in this country. Not if you're white. Not if you're an Afrikaner.' She wanted to pull him from the pulpit and see him without his surplice just for once!

'I've never said there is no future for us. There will be a future for us if we are prepared to make sacrifices and adjustments. If we're prepared to reform and stand together in the struggle to achieve justice for everyone in this country.'

'How do you think five fishes and two loaves of bread are going to be shared between twenty-six million hungry mouths, Father?'

'A fatalistic attitude, Araminta; it suggests an inherent laziness to get up and fight for what is just.'

'Maybe we should simply pack up and leave, Father. For how is justice to be done? We are less than three million white Afrikaners, about as many coloured Afrikaners. Two million English people, something like one million Indians, six million Zulus, three million Xhosas, three million Northern Sothos, two million Southern Sothos, one and a half million Tswanas – at least I got full marks on this – one million Swazis plus a horde of smaller nations and immigrants – and everyone's fighting for a piece of the fish. Or a whole fish. Or all the fishes! And you say we must stand up and fight for justice? Whose justice?'

'I'm worried about you.'

'When does the struggle come to an end? When can one start living without having to feel guilty because you want to be happy? When does one get to *life*, Father?'

'Why are you so defiant, child?'

'Because I'm sick of being confused! You know what I

did? I went to Cape Town with a friend one night to attend an illegal meeting where we were incited to all sorts of actions and methods of civil disobedience, so that we could help to make this country ungovernable. They said the rulers are living like fat cats while the poor are getting poorer. On a big white board the words "KILL GOD AND SET MAN FREE" were written in big red letters. They spread out the national flag on the floor and everyone had to walk over the flag while singing a freedom song. I didn't know the words of the song, and I felt as little for the flag I had to trample on as for the whole commotion. It was nothing but more walls made of words which I couldn't see behind!'

'Why did you attend the meeting then?'

'To prove myself – to struggle. Everybody's struggling for some cause or other. Every day we're being told on campus that the time has come for every student to make a stand. I don't know what stand to make. It feels to me that if I'm to make a stand, I'll end up like a stake fixed in one place – I'll never be able to walk any farther again.'

'Whether you like it or not, one has to make a stand sooner or later, otherwise the wind comes and blows you all over the place.'

'Lucius Muller, that sings with me in the choir, also attended the meeting. I always thought we were friends, but suddenly he was speaking English and snubbing me. When it was said that the Afrikaner and his language must be phased out as quickly as possible, he cheered the loudest. He could just as well have slapped me on the face.'

'Over-sensitivity, daughter, often arises from fear or unwillingness to adapt to changing circumstances. Changing people's ideas is what is needed in this country to create a better South Africa for us all. I was delighted to hear that your rector has proposed open universities. At least we can now begin to address that black mark against us. We must pray unceasingly, however, that the government will come to its senses before it's too late.'

'Perhaps one should get as much out of life as possible, before "too late" comes, Father.'

'Perhaps you should go to the beach less often, next year, attend fewer dances on Saturday nights and pay more attention to your studies!'

'Marian is a tell-tale.'

'Marian is as worried about you as your mother and I are. She's worried because she won't be there next year to keep an eye on you.'

'You know something?'

'What?'

'I went to another meeting as well.' She made another attempt to shock him. 'On a farm outside Stellenbosch. This time the national flag was draped on the wall. The meeting was opened by a reading from the Bible – about how God made a place for David on the earth, or something. Another student rolled out a large map of Africa – the whole map was coloured in black except for a little white spot in the south. The main speaker of the evening said our forefathers had toiled and died for this, our only place on the earth. That the time has come when we must fight for it again. After that we had to sing the national anthem. All four verses. I only knew the first one. When they finished singing, someone shouted: "We will not lie down and be slaughtered!" Now I keep on seeing us lying with our throats cut!'

'I'm going to make an appointment for you with Uncle Ernest.'

'I don't want to go to him.'

'He's a good psychologist; he's my brother, he'll understand.'

'I'm not going to him! I want to drop my studies; I don't want to go back to university! Please, Father, let me go and work!'

'I don't think you're capable of making decisions of that kind at this time. One does not simply give up at the end of one's first year. The answer is no.'

*

She had to go back.

They called her down to meet a visitor one afternoon. When she got to the lobby, she found Wilhelm waiting for her. A brand-new Wilhelm, back from Europe after two years. His hair was done in a long pony-tail, his coat was of the softest yellow leather; a long, red, tasselled scarf hung round his neck, almost to his knees. She reached out to him as if to fresh hope.

'Were they ever nasty to you over there because you are a South African?' she asked him over dinner that evening.

'Not once.'

'And because of the fact that you're an Afrikaner?'

'Afrikaner? You're talking about something from the archives, my dear Araminta. Get up to date! The oxen have been put out to grass, the wagons are rotting in museums!'

'I'm serious.'

'My having been an Afrikaner – God knows what it really means – is something I've renounced long ago.' There was contempt in his voice when he said it.

'How can you forswear what you are?'

'You are reborn. You open your eyes to a new world, you join the struggle and start living!'

'What struggle?'

'Any one, as long as it's against P. W. Botha and the fascist apartheid government of this country, *ma chérie*! We, the new generation, will make up for what has been done to the black people of this country.'

'What wrong did you and I do to the black people?'

'We are the children of the culprits. Children of Malan and Verwoerd. But we have the will and the power to make it right again. Langenhoven said, each generation must bury a mistake. Or something to that effect. We will stand by the might of the majority, we'll wipe apartheid

61

out under the noses of the assholes and let the will of the people triumph!'

'Don't talk so loud, people are staring at you.'

'I love it.'

'It bothers me that I'm a member of the most hated nation on earth, Wilhelm. One moment it makes me ashamed to be alive, the next moment I want to stand up for my right to live. I know apartheid is wrong. But every day my eyes see wealthy and well-educated black people, wealthy and educated brown people, very wealthy Indians. I ask myself: How come they've not been plunged into misery by apartheid?'

'If that's the way you talk your way round the issue, my dear, it's better and safer for you to go and teach somewhere deep in the Karroo and leave the struggle for those that know. For those that can feel. For those that can see pain.'

'I want to know what I, myself, am guilty of. I want to know why I have to pay for the wrongs others have committed!'

'You're very pretty and very naïve. I think you're rebelling against your father for some reason or other. Frans de Villiers, perhaps?'

'I don't know.'

'Don't make life miserable for yourself, darling girl. If the world has decided you are guilty, you're guilty – don't dispute it, accept it.'

'I can't.'

'Then I feel sorry for you.'

That very same night she took the Bible, laid her hand on it and said aloud, 'I'm no longer an Afrikaner, I'm Araminta Rossouw.'

But it made no difference.

Still, she got through her second year with less difficulty. She took less notice of campus politics. Less notice of prospective members of the students' council making political speeches during the lunch hour – she simply chewed louder and looked up at the ceiling. She read no newspapers. She walked down Plein Street looking at her feet, not at the headlines grinning from the lampposts.

Choir practice was an island to escape to. It was fun afterwards in Jakob's flat or somewhere else. Sundays: going to the beach or sleeping out in the open at Kogel Bay.

'Father, I'm working two nights a week in a restaurant now, I found it impossible to manage on my weekly allowance.'

Afrikaans-Dutch, English. And history, in which she was trying to find herself. When she got lost, she retraced her steps and started all over again, for somehow, somewhere, she had to find meaning.

Time after time, she fell behind, knowing her father was going to have another fit because of her marks, but she had to find her own way. Once she had found it, she would throw away what she didn't need, but at least she wouldn't be throwing away something she should have kept.

And then, one day, she began to see the pattern that spread like a crack through everything, getting wider and wider . . .

Nine

THERE WAS A GIRL by the name of Paula in the same hall
of residence. Paula was a drama student, and she used to
read palms for R2. Sometimes, especially at weekends, the
girls had to put their names on a waiting-list outside her
door.

Before long, the hall committee decided fortune-telling
was not allowed and spoke to Paula about it. She took no
notice. Next, the members of the hall prayer group spoke
to her. She took no notice of them either. So then it was
the duty of the house-mother to call her in, and this time
she was threatened with some law or other against
fortune-telling.

Just in case this was not bluff, Paula went and picked
up acorns, which she then sold at R2 each, reading the
palms for nothing. There were even rumours that she paid
all her class fees from the money she made by selling
acorns.

Shortly after the choir came back from abroad, and
about a week after the start of the last semester of her
third year, she went to see Paula for the first and only
time.

It was an ordinary room, nothing witchy or anything.
Most outstanding perhaps was Paula's very wide and
colourful dress and her strikingly happy eyes.

She bought an acorn and laid her hands on the table as

Paula showed her. Paula looked at her hands, she frowned, she looked, she frowned . . .

'What are you seeing?' She was getting a bit worried.

'I'm afraid I don't quite know what I'm seeing,' Paula admitted.

'What do you mean?'

'I don't think you've come here to find out what most of the girls usually come for: does he like me or not; am I going to get married and have children, will I have lots of money one day . . .'

'Am I not going to get married and have children?'

'Yes. Eventually.'

'But?' She was now very worried.

'There are good, strong lines in your hands, Araminta, but there are also lines that I have never seen in a hand before.'

'Bad lines?'

'Not necessarily.'

'You're not lying to me, are you?'

'I don't know. I honestly don't know. Maybe you should tell me why you've come here; perhaps I can try and puzzle it out.'

'I came here hoping to feel better. Everything is so complicated, and I'm so terribly confused!'

'Confused about what?'

'When I came to university, I thought I would at least learn where I was going and why. Now I'm almost at the end of my third year and I'm still going nowhere in particular. Apparently no one in this country is, except that we're all heading for chaos. Especially the white people. We, the white Afrikaners, even more so, because Africa does not want us, the world does not want us . . .' She didn't care if she sounded melodramatic. 'Personally it feels to me that I have no right to belong anywhere!'

'You certainly are confused,' Paula said. 'Have you got a pack of playing cards?'

'I don't want to play cards!' she snapped. 'Don't you

understand? I only want to be an ordinary human being, I don't want to feel guilty because I'm alive! There are times when I think I'm going out of my mind; perhaps there's a line on your hand that says if you are?'

'There is. But it not in yours, I promise you. As you've just said, many people are confused today. Have you got a pack of playing cards?'

'No. But the girl in the room next to me has. Why?'

'Go borrow the eight of hearts from her. Put it between your pillow and the pillowcase and sleep on it for eight consecutive nights. Before you fall asleep, wish for a clear and tranquil mind and you will find it. Don't skip a night.'

She would have put a rock in her pillow. Silly or not.

After the first night, she would have sworn that she was feeling better. Stronger, less angry at her 'fate'.

The second day.

'TEAR-GAS FIRED AT CROWD'

On the third night she had the most terrible dream about floods. Everything was threatened by brown, muddy water.

'STONE THROWING: MOTORIST IN SERIOUS CONDITION'

The fourth night.

'DOWNPOUR: 200 LEFT HOMELESS'

The fifth night. She had to work out a history question: '*A critical evaluation of American involvement in Vietnam since 1954.*' She got halfway with it and then tore it up.

'CONGRESS: DOES THE AFRIKANER HAVE HIS BACK AGAINST A WALL?'

She slept little on the sixth night.

And the seventh night.

'USA CALLS BACK LEGATE'

She had another question to work out: '*The Israeli–Arabic conflict from 1948 to 1973 and the factors enabling Israel to defeat the Arabic states in four consecutive wars.* Or something like that. She couldn't care less.

'Two heavily armed ANC terrorists arrested during police raid,' she heard over the radio. 'Bomb exploded this afternoon at two o'clock ... Black South Africans plead for stronger economic sanctions against South Africa ... Minister in fraud scandal ... Large-scale corruption in Black Management Committees is being investigated ...

The eighth night. The card had made no difference. It was a childish thing to do anyway.

She got up and went to the bathroom to wash her hair. While she stood over the bath, her hair foaming with shampoo, the strangest feeling of outrage started to gather in her. One moment it was like hitting a wall of anger, the next moment the wall was gone. She started crying, and it was awful to cry with your head down because everything runs back up your nose. She rinsed her hair, put a towel round and sat down on the edge of the bath. She had the most curious feeling that it was growing lighter around her.

I am Araminta Rossouw, she suddenly cried out inside herself. I am me. I'm sitting on the edge of a bath in a woman's residence somewhere on the foot of Africa while the earth is silently spinning through the air with me and everything else that's on it. If I want to live, I will have to emerge from the ashes of the sins of people long dead, and go and find a place for myself somewhere else.

She had said it. It was the most wonderful, unbelievable moment of liberation; the moment when at last she knew exactly what she had to do.

She went back to her room and started drying her hair. Warily. She was afraid the light would go away. She was suddenly no longer afraid of her eyes in the mirror ... she was not in the mirror now; she was inside her body, safe as in a house while a storm was blowing up outside. She had crossed the river of university – and somehow she would deal with her father and mother and Marian. She would have to work in order to earn money. She was not afraid: if it meant a new river, she would take it on boldly, for on the other side she would be born anew.

She would find herself another fatherland.

She turned away from the mirror and started making her bed. When she took the card from the pillow, she saw that it was the eight of diamonds, not the eight of hearts as Paula had said. In her haste and anxiety she must have taken the wrong card that night.

It was of no importance.

She didn't go to her class. She never went back to classes again. She started packing her things.

Late that afternoon, Paula came to see her, saying rather sheepishly that she had suddenly remembered that it had to be the eight of diamonds and not the eight of hearts that must be put in the pillowslip.

Ten

A MONTH AFTER SHE sold the house to the Shirleys, Bernard Holtzman came into her office one Monday morning and closed the door behind him. He doesn't normally do that. And he's not at ease, which is also unusual.

'I warn you, Bernard, if Elvin has sent you to tell me that Carr & Holtzman don't want me any longer, I'll go and work for the opposition.' She says it outright, but with some apprehension. Three estate agents in the town had had to find other employment in the previous month. She had sold one back-street plot, Bernard one house, Elvin not a single brick.

And Bernard's smile is not real either. 'You know, Araminta,' he says, 'you've been with us for something like two years now and I still don't quite get you.'

'Why should you be concerned about that?'

'It's normal for people to form opinions about each other, isn't it? Especially people working together. But the moment I think I've got you worked out, you go and surprise me again.'

Why is he speaking in a whisper? 'How have I surprised you this time?'

'Is it true that you have sold six uncut diamonds for the Shirleys?'

It's a stone hitting her on the back. The Shirleys have betrayed her! Is it possible? For a moment she can't say a word. 'Where on earth did you hear such a thing?'

'Relax; don't look so alarmed, you can trust me. The Shirleys have become very good friends of Elvin's and they told him. Confidentially, of course. They wanted him to know how much they owed you. Personally I think you've done them an enormous favour. From the little I know about you, I suspect that you would not have taken the chance if you had not been sure of your own safety.'

'I have nothing to say to you, or to Elvin, or to the Shirleys!'

'Easy now! Trust me. There's a reason why Elvin told me.'

'I don't want to hear it.' She wants to reach out and cover his mouth with her hands.

'Araminta,' he says, imploringly, 'my only brother, Dirk – you've met him – he's co-owner of the garage where you bought your car. Jan du Toit is his partner. It took everything they had between them to buy that garage a couple of years ago; today they're ruined. People are not paying what they owe and the country's in a poor economic state because of the political troubles. So last year, Dirk went and did a stupid thing: he bought R20 000 worth of uncut diamonds in the hope of making some money to bail them out and . . .'

'I don't want to hear this.'

'Please listen. They're in a deep financial mess. He had no trouble getting hold of the diamonds, but he can't find a buyer for them. He's been to Johannesburg and Durban and even Graaff-Reinet, to see a couple of so-called buyers, but not one of them would bite. They think he's a police trap.'

'So you heard a rumour that I had sold diamonds for the Shirleys and now you see me as your brother's deliverer. Forget it.' The Shirleys had no right to talk about it.

'He'll pay you commission.'

'I will not hear a word of what you're saying.'

'He'll be happy if he just gets his money back.'

'The answer is no. And please, you'll have to excuse

70

me; I have an appointment for ten o'clock with a client that wants to have a look at Mr Blom's block of flats.'

'I know.' He gets up. 'Perhaps we can have another talk later on – when you're not in such a hurry. And by the way, Wynand Blom is himself in bad financial shape. He bought too much property on the strength of rumours of an oil find in the sea in this area. I'm sure, if he sees a cheque-book, he'll bring his price down quite a bit.'

'I'll keep that in mind.'

'We'll talk later, then?'

She does not answer him. When he's gone out, she remains at her desk, with a sick feeling in her stomach. Every step I take, she says to herself, I go as inconspicuously and carefully as I can, and then land myself in trouble because of a favour to others!

'Somebody's looking pretty despondent this morning!'

When she looks up, Ralph Linde, the pressing insurance agent, is standing in the door. 'I was just wondering if this Monday could get any bluer. Then it did.' Ralph Linde always gives the impression that he's come to save you from any possible disaster.

'Is your car insured, Araminta?' he asks as he pulls out a chair.

'No.' She had not expected it of the Shirleys.

'How are you going to do your work if it gets stolen?'

'It won't get stolen; there's an angel sitting on its roof.'

'They'd steal it, angel and all. Rex Meyer's car was stolen from his yard on Saturday night and that's only a block away from where you are living, Miss Smart!'

'My car won't be stolen.' But in her heart she's suddenly not so sure. 'If you're trying to sell me insurance, you're wasting your time. And mine. I'm just about to go out with a client.'

'I can't understand how you can take the risk of not having insurance these days. Do you realize that a car gets stolen every ten minutes in this country?'

71

'How much will it cost to insure my car for a short period of time? Per month.'

'I can work something out for you from about R200.'

'Forget it. I don't want to insure my car.'

'A hundred and fifty.'

'The angel's cheaper.'

The man she takes to see the flats, a Mr Lotter, has apparently also heard about Wynand Blom being in trouble and wants the place for about half the asking price. She tells him it's less than what Mr Blom paid. He says he knows that. She tells him she does not have the heart to go to Mr Blom with his offer. 'What kind of an estate agent are you?' he asks. 'You're supposed to act in my interest, not Blom's! If you're worried because your commission is going to be less, I'll see that you get something extra under the counter.'

She waits until late in the afternoon before she phones Wynand Blom with the offer. He says he'd burn the place down rather than give it away to a jackal for nothing.

Every rand counts. She carefully calculates every commission in advance; the commission she would have got for the flats would have been the biggest she has ever made on any transaction: R10 000. Ten extra feathers for her wings. And yet, she is relieved when Wynand Blom turns down the offer. Every rand counts, but she does not want money with the fingerprints of a money-shark like Lotter on it.

When she gets home shortly after five, a tall, attractive man with a big moustache is waiting at her door. Dirk Holtzman.

'Mr Holtzman,' she says, coldly, 'I wish I knew of a civilized way of asking you to leave.'

'If you did, I wouldn't blame you, Miss Rossouw.' He admits it frankly.

'Do me a favour then, and go away. Please.'

'I've got to talk to you. All I'm asking is five minutes of your time. I'll go down on my knees for it.'

'Five minutes, and the answer is already no.'

She unlocks the safety gate, then the door, and walks in ahead of him. 'Sit down.' He hesitates, then chooses the armchair. 'Mr Holtzman,' she says, taking the chair at the table, 'you are confronting me with rumours for which you have no grounds, and I don't like it. Everything I have to say, I've said to Bernard this morning.'

'I have great sympathy for the way you feel,' he says, quietly. 'You did something dangerous for those people as a favour and they went and let it out. As a result, I have now come knocking at your door in my own hour of need; tomorrow everybody comes running and the day after you land in trouble. All I have to offer you is my word of honour to protect you, and the fact that I can make it worth your while. Apart from paying you commission, I can introduce you to Piet Sinksa.'

'I don't know what you're talking about.' He puts his hand in his pocket and takes out a little drawstring bag. The faint sound of crystal against crystal, of little holy stones . . . Don't lead me into temptation! He opens the bag and holds it out to her: two, four, six, nine they fall into the palm of her hand. More beautiful, bigger, more brilliant than the first six. 'I wish you had not come, Mr Holtzman,' she says.

'If I can just get back the money that I paid for them, it would help relieve my situation.'

'I wish you weren't doing this to me!' One moment she wanted nothing to do with them, the next moment she wants to close her hand round them and hold them tight.

'I'll introduce you to Piet Sinksa as soon as he comes again. He's a black; he comes from Kimberley and is the safest contact you could wish for.'

'I'm not interested in meeting him.'

'I just thought I could do you a favour in return.'

'*If* I decide to sell the diamonds for you, the commission will be sufficient. If I do.'

'Miss Rossouw, I'm not here to try and win you over with a sad story. Those few diamonds can't save my business from the trouble it's in. They can buy time for me and my partner, and for our families, that's all. It's almost Christmas.'

Two of the diamonds are quite big; one is as clear as a large drop of dew. 'I will have to think about it first.' In her heart she adds: I just want to keep them with me for a little while.

'As I've said: I'm not here to talk you round, I'm here because I'm desperate.' A hint of anxiety is breaking through his composure. 'Every year you say to yourself that next year things will be better, next year there will be an upswing in the economy, and before you know it, the year has gone by without its having happened. Things have just got a bit worse: the country, politics, everything. If the government reforms too fast, too many people shift to the right; too slow and they begin to support the left, while the world pushes harder and harder with sanctions and boycotts, forgetting it's the blacks that are hit the hardest. If I close my business tomorrow, there will be four black families eating porridge for Christmas. And the ordinary labourers as well, of course.'

'I'm nobody's Mother Christmas, Mr Holtzman, I've told you I will have to think about this first.'

'If you do decide to help me, how long will it take to sell them?'

'At least a week. And you'll have to trust me and leave them with me.'

'I trust you.'

She gets an appointment with Samuel Sundoo for the Friday afternoon at two o'clock. She searches her conscience for a sense of guilt and does not find it. Only a feeling, that wherever she puts the diamonds, the light there becomes brighter.

And as with the other six, these want to sleep with the

African violet as well, and in the mornings they lie on the towel in the window talking to the mountain.

For three whole days they're hers. Ancient little stones to play with and make riddles of. Where do they come from? Where will they be going? For fun, she tries to sort them into four categories: one in the category of the most beautiful, two in the next category, the two yellower stones in the third category and the four least brilliant ones in the last . . . No, it doesn't seem quite right.

She searches until she finds something about Indians and diamonds. They say the oldest link between man and diamonds is in India. That only the members of the two most primitive castes in the land, the Tora and the Jhara, used to be allowed to scrape the diamond-bearing gravel from the river-beds after the rainy season. All of them – men, women and children – could help with the washing of the gravel and spreading it open on planks in the sun, but only the women were allowed to sort out the diamonds. She likes that. The women sorted them into the four customary groupings: without a magnifying glass, by the light of the sun and by rolling them between forefinger and thumb.

One grouping for each of the four kinds of people on earth, they said. The scarcest, purest and most beautiful for the holy men that guarded all knowledge and religion. The next most beautiful, for the kings, the noblemen and the warriors. The yellower or browner stones for the merchants and tillers of the soil. And the greatest numbers of stones, those that were not suitable for gems, went to those in servitude.

Would it be possible to put a diamond back into the earth so that it could grow purer before you took it out again? Surely not. Can a human being grow purer while living, even if he wasn't born a gem?

After the women had sorted the diamonds, the best ones were taken to the jewellers. But a jeweller would never cut a diamond, for they believed that diamonds were made of holy substance and that it was never to be wasted. They would just rub one diamond with another to make it shine a bit more, because diamonds are already 'radiant beings' in themselves.

For three whole days the nine diamonds are hers.

Eleven

AT HALF-PAST ONE on the Friday afternoon, she parks her car on open ground near Samuel Sundoo's. It's raining incessantly. It's not really a parking lot, it's a muddy site where a building has been demolished, but it's the nearest place she can find.

Because it's still early, she wants to stay in the car till it's time for her appointment, but the windows keep on misting up and she can't see who's walking past. It's not a safe area. Perhaps it's better to turn up a little early.

'Miss Rossouw,' Samuel Sundoo says as she sits down opposite him, 'when you have an appointment with me for two o'clock, it's two o'clock. Not ten minutes to or ten minutes after. Two o'clock. It's an absolute rule of this game.' He speaks particularly good Afrikaans.

'I'm sorry.' Game? Last time she promised herself she would never come here again; now she says it in capital letters.

She gives him the diamonds and he does exactly what he did with the others – except that he examines the largest of the stones for a second time under the magnifying glass and puts it in a separate envelope. Like the last time, he gets up and leaves through the door behind him. At least she now knows what to expect and is less nervous.

She had hoped Sundoo would be friendlier. More willing to talk to her. There is great knowledge and respect in

77

his hands when he holds the diamonds. She wanted to ask him what he sees inside them.

She waits longer than the last time.

And he does not come back by way of the front stairs, but by way of the door through which he left. He carries a smallish box on which 'Sunrise Toffees' is written. He places the box on the table in front of her and waits. She gets a feeling that there is something she should do . . .

'Miss Rossouw,' he says, reprovingly, 'at a certain stage of a transaction, you are supposed to ask what I'm prepared to pay for the articles. After that you are supposed to count the money in my presence.' He says it like a lecture to a simpleton.

'Joop Lourens said I could trust you.' On the spur of the moment, in an attempt to make conversation, she says the first stupid thing that comes to her mind and asks, 'Mr Sundoo, is it true that the tigers in the forests of India are stronger than the lions of Africa?'

'Yes.' Not a word more, as if every fool would know it.

'But Africa's diamonds are more beautiful than India's?'

'Yes.'

It's no use, he does not want to talk to her. He's waiting for her to open the box. When she lifts the lid, she draws back her hands with a jerk, for in the box is the most money that she has ever seen together in her life! 'How much is it?' she asks in alarm.

'Eighty thousand rand. One of the stones is a particularly good one – a brilliant white.'

Twelve

THERE IS A GOD of heaven and a god of the world. She has worked it out for herself. The God of heaven is like light that permeates everything, but because the people can't see this God, they've made themselves another god – a mighty god that rules over everything. And next to her on the seat of the car is R80 000 worth of god in a Sunrise Toffee box.

'Don't think!' she says aloud. Keep on going, concentrate on the traffic and stay in the right lane.

R80 000! It's like a power that has got into the car with her. A force that seeps from the box and grows stronger and stronger. Everything it touches is freed. It's deliverance from evil: it's merciful. Promethean. It's everywhere within the car, within her, like a joy that grows until it becomes fearlessness.

Eighty thousand rand.

She wants to put her hand in the box and take out bundles of the notes and throw them out the window so that others can pick them up and share her gladness . . .

Somewhere ahead, there's a road turning off to the airport. Her passport is in her bag. She could buy a ticket to London and exchange as much of the money as possible for sterling. There's a man in George that does it every year when he goes overseas. She could buy a ticket to Switzerland or Austria – not America or Australia – find herself a place to live in the greenest valley, surrounded by mountains with snow on their peaks and become a new person. Liberated. A residential permit to live on this earth. A burden to no one, she has enough money to see her through till she has learned the new language. She applies for permanent residence ... she finds work ... somewhere, the man she's going to marry and have children with is waiting for her. And her children will not be burdened with iniquities they have not committed, and no one will ever spit in their faces!

It's not stealing. It's a short cut put in a Sunrise Toffee box for her. She will count out Dirk Holtzman's R20 000 and send it to him. He said he would be happy if he could just get his money back. It's not stealing! It's a stroke of luck that she has contrived and which she has the right to profit from too.

Cars are hooting. At her: the traffic lights have turned green.

Sixty thousand rand if she sends Dirk Holtzman his money.

Twenty minutes later, she passes the turn-off to the airport.

She promises herself she will be coming back sooner than she had ever planned. She says it aloud. She drives past because she does not want to leave with only the clothes she has on. That would be deserting. Because she does not want to leave without saying goodbye to the mountain. That would be rude. Because she does not want the violet to die without water. That would be cruel. The day she leaves, she will do it in an orderly way.

Bernard said Dirk would be glad just to get his money back. She has a little over R7 000 in the bank. Plus outstanding commission amounting to another R4 000. Plus the money she'll get on the sale of her car and furniture, plus R60 000 – that's more than R71 000. And she had been aiming for R60 000.

She must find somewhere to stop and count out Dirk's R20 000. No, of course she can't stop with so much money in the car. She must drive carefully. Not too fast. She must not get home before dark and run the risk of being seen . . .

The freeway takes her through the southern outskirts of the city. On one side of the road lies the last of the middle-class residential areas, closed in, with ugly grey concrete walls. Then through cold, industrial areas. Past the first tin shacks standing out above the sand dunes and Port Jackson bushes: the overflow from an unstoppable flood of a black squatters' camp.

Don't look.

In the distance, she can see the road crossing the formidable blue mountains like an upward-slanting scar on the side of the mountain . . . R60 000 . . . The very same mountains that had helped to keep the first white settlers trapped on this peninsula for more than thirty years. On the seat next to her, in a Sunrise Toffee box, is the power that brought them here, the subjects of the largest, wealthiest trading company in the world: the Dutch East India Company. White slaves that had to see to it that there was fresh produce and whores for the passing ships that carried the riches from the East.

The sixty directors in Amsterdam freaked out at the cost to the company of the station at the Cape. Each guilder it cost meant a hole in the final profits to be shared out. For more than fifty years, their ships had sailed round the Cape, managing without a staging post along the way; throwing dead seamen overboard had been much cheaper. However, when Cromwell cut off the King of England's head, threatening to grab the whole world for England, and the oceans as well, the Dutch quickly sent Jan van Riebeeck to the Cape to put up a fort and a hospital.

Year after year the ships brought the same complaint from the directors of the company: 'Why isn't the Cape self-supporting and a profit to the company yet?'

Because of the drought, my lords. Or because the winter storms have washed away our gardens. Because lions broke into the company's enclosures and killed the cattle; tigers took the sheep, wild cats devoured every duck and chicken . . .

Dirk Holtzman said it would help him if he just got his money back . . .

Because Harry, the Koikoi interpreter, had disappeared with the company's cattle while the Commander was reading the sermon on Sunday, as the company had decreed he should; for in order to save money, they had decided not to send a minister to the Cape.

Eighty thousand rand.

Where does coincidence begin, where does it end? What is in your blood, what do you pick up along the way? After ten years, when Jan van Riebeeck left, only three of the original settlers that had come with him stayed behind: Hans Ras, Pieter van der Westhuizen and Willem van der Merwe. The others had either died or deserted. Her mother's maiden name was Van der Merwe.

In a Sunrise Toffee box lies the power to buy herself free from every consequence of the staging post between West and East.

In her second year at university, a lecturer in history had once suggested that she should try to use less imagination and more intellectual rigour if she wanted to obtain better marks.

They had to do a paper on the first white settlers at the Cape. In a moment of wilfulness she had written that she had come to the conclusion that God had fenced in the first white settlers on the peninsula because there were so few of them; there were something like 90 000 Europeans in America when there were still only 300 at the Cape, including women and children. Perhaps God had weighed them too and found them wanting in strength to cope with the wilderness which awaited them. So He mixed in a little

82

German blood, but it was not right yet: they were too pale for the blazing sun in the south. A touch of Koikoi blood. Still too white. A little slave blood from the East. Too fair still. Eventually the darker blood of the French Protestants fleeing from Europe was added as well. Blood mixed with blood, and a new people rose between the East and the West; when enough umbilical cords had turned to dust in Africa's soil, God let them go.

One thing is for sure: the Lord above might have foreseen this new nation, but the lords of the company certainly did not. All that mattered to them was the profits – and to have enough hands at the Cape to work with the spade, or hold the guns if trouble should come. For if they were to remain the wealthiest trading company in the world, their enemies had to know that their defences were strong. But defence costs money. Lots of money. If your coffers are empty, your teeth are pulled. Whoever controlled the best spice routes and commercial strongholds in the East, controlled the coffers in the West. There was no time to worry about a new people growing on the toe of Africa.

There were no ears to listen to their pleas for help either. They started moving deeper and deeper into the valleys between the mountains, building themselves dwellings along the streams. Sowing wheat. Planting vineyards. Putting up schools and churches.

Some began trekking over the mountains, saying they were tired of being white slaves of the company. The company was in any case going bankrupt from waging wars and from officials stealing from it to fill their own pockets. No help was forthcoming from the mother country. They no longer had a mother country. Governor Willem van der Stel said they must stop looking towards the sea where their parents had come from; they were born *here*. So were their children. This was now their country.

With their wagons and oxen, their wives and children,

their Bibles and hymn books, their guns and household goods, their servants, their slaves, their horses and cattle and seed, they crossed the towering mountains. Some trekked north. Most trekked eastwards in the direction of the place where the hunters and cattle traders reported the earth to be fertile, with grazing and water, where the sour grass grew that fattened the livestock quickly . . .

To get across the mountains, they took the wheels off the wagons and dragged them. The sick and the old, the babies and the lambs, they carried . . . And now she, Araminta Rossouw, is crossing the same mountains by way of a beautifully tarred road.

Africa showed little mercy to these new children at its feet. Scorching them with the summer sun, freezing them in winter. The beasts of prey got their livestock: lions, tigers, jackals. Bushman arrows and Koikoi spears picked them off; they trod on adders and scorpions, their wagons rolled down the cliffs.

Africa tormented them with its worst droughts and its worst floods. It grew the piss-grass that made their cattle drown in their own piss water; the livestock that survived were decimated by every kind of pestilence.

It made them cling to the God of their Bibles. It made them see His greatness, His vastness, his mercy. It gave them shelter on the hillsides. It gave them rest in the valleys and time to sow and reap for bread. It let them drink at its springs.

It made them strong.

The weak and the old were buried along the way.

Some it made too hard.

Those that wanted to go no further unyoked their oxen and marked out their own boundaries. They spoke a new language, a new spirit had sprung up in their bodies. They were free.

Three hundred years later, they are the most hated

people on earth, and in her is a bitterness that does not want to go away! It makes her fight against a sentence she cannot accept.

Eighty thousand rand.

She must drive slower, get the money home safely. She will have to stop at a café in the next town; she has had nothing to eat since that morning. What about the box? What if someone breaks into the car?

She stops at Riviersonderend and takes the box with her into the café. She orders a sandwich and coffee. She wants to go to the cloakroom, but what about the box? She takes the box with her. When she comes back, her order is ready, but she's no longer hungry.

As she passes Riversdale, a huge, silvery-white full moon rises in the east as the sun goes down in the west behind her. In her mind she runs across the veld in the direction of the moon, over the bushes, dams, farms, over the mountains. For a little while she becomes calmer but she cannot dream too long, the traffic is too heavy.

An hour and a half later, she's home.

She puts the box on the table and opens the curtains. The mountain is a giant spectre in the moonlight. 'It's eighty thousand rand,' she says, challenging it to disapprove. 'Dirk Holtzman said he would be more than pleased to get his money back. That's why I'm going to take the rest for myself, and I'm telling you now, it's not stealing!'

The mountain is a mountain, it cannot hear.

She opens the box and shakes the money out on the bed. It's in bundles of R20 notes secured with rubber bands. The money is unhappy, the elastic is too tight. One by one she starts to pull the bands off, letting the smaller bundles of notes fall on the bed. In each of the forty packets there are ten bundles of ten notes held together by paper clips . . . she starts taking off the clips and as they come free, she throws them up in the air . . . they begin to breathe, they float down on to the bed and to the floor like clumsy oblong wings . . .

There's a force in her room stronger than anything she knows. It scares her. It gladdens her. It flies out of the window and down to the street. It fills the sleeping shops, it rides in the cars passing by. It's in the houses, the people's clothes, their food, their carpets, chairs, tables. It's in everything . . .

Here it stays in abundance, there it passes by uncaring. It is Fate's mate, holding you back when you want to advance; pushing you until you stumble.

It is the power that determines whether you eat or starve; sleep warm or cold; the power that makes people cry, laugh, toil, steal, beg, murder, fornicate, gamble . . .

'Jakob, what is money?' she asked one day when she was tired of trying to make ends meet on her pocket-money.

'Money is a woman, Araminta,' he said. 'Full of secrets. The rib from which man has to make a soul for himself, his power for good – or his downfall. She has within her the strength to make him a god or a devil. If he takes her as his whore, she dies. When she's dead, he pursues her; desires her night and day, because her ghost will lift up her skirts to him and tease him to madness.'

'I don't know what you're trying to say.'

'Don't worry, just see to it that you never become a whore.'

She's tired, she must get some sleep, but the money will not let her. She plays with it, arranges it in rows round the edge of the bed. She stacks it up and builds a tower with it. The magic that was in the diamonds is in the money too. She swears it is. Only it is much clearer in the diamonds, more sparkling. The money is a reflection of diamonds seen in a mirror. And the notes will not let her put the rubber bands round them again, or put them back in the box. She can leave the bands off, but she has nothing else to put the money in.

She draws the curtains and starts counting out Dirk Holtzman's share.

It's not stealing, she says to herself.

At a quarter to nine the next morning, she puts the box on his desk and sees the hope come into his eyes.

'Never ask me to do this for you again,' she says. 'Never.'

'I give you my word. How much did you get?'

'Count it yourself. As payment I want two things: commission and Piet Sinksa. I would like to have the commission today; I want to see Piet Sinksa as soon as possible.'

'I'll phone and leave a message with his sister. How much did you get?'

'How long will it take him to come?'

'It depends if he's got diamonds already, or if he still has to get them. He usually supplies a man at Mossel Bay; I've only been in luck that one time.'

'Don't try your luck again. How long will it be before he comes back?'

'I had to wait about a month.'

'Phone him. Tell him I want good ones. And send my commission round to my office.'

Just once.

Just once more will she go back to Samuel Sundoo. For herself this time.

When she woke up that morning, she knew she had to put all the money back in the box. She must walk out of the country, not flee from it on Dirk Holtzman's money. She will make her own short cut.

Just once.

The mountain was in one of his green-grey moods when she opened the curtains that morning. Every rock and wooded gorge smiled at her. Don't be cross with me, she said in her heart; you live for ever, I don't. I cannot plod on and on in the hope of getting out of this land eventually.

Two messages are waiting for her at the office. The one says that Wynand Blom wants to see her urgently, the other is from a man by the name of De Villiers who was in the office the day before looking for a house to buy.

'As I was taking him through to Elvin,' Lizzie said, 'he noticed the name on your door and stopped as if he had seen a ghost. He asked where you were. I said you had gone to Cape Town and you would be back today. He said he'd wait. He asked you to phone him as soon as you came in this morning; he's staying in a friend's holiday cottage at Herolds Bay. I've got the number. He wants you to meet him there.'

De Villiers? 'What does he look like?'

'Very nice man. Tall and blondish, but married, unfortunately; a broad ring on his finger.'

'I see.'

Frans de Villiers. It must be. Deep inside her something stirs – that something that remains between two people . . . No. It's the old hurt of knowing that someone did not really want you.

She rings up Wynand Blom. He wants her to contact Mr Lotter and ask him if he's still interested in the flats and if they could come to an agreement. It's most urgent.

When the god of the world gets his hands around your throat, he does not easily let go again. Perhaps it's a she, though, as Jakob had said.

'Good morning. May I speak to Mr Lotter, please?'

'Speaking.'

An hour later, Lizzie starts preparing the deeds of sale for the flats and Elvin comes to her office to congratulate her.

'It's no wonder our opposition's looking for a lady agent; they think it's a matter of appointing a pretty girl. Congratulations, your commission should make up for the quiet months we've had.'

'It's thieving.'

'What?'

'Blom is the loser in this transaction. Lotter, Carr & Holtzman and I are the winners. It's not fair.'

'It's business, my dear! And Blom isn't paying your commission, Lotter is.'

'I know. I may ask you for an advance before the deal goes through.' When Piet Sinksa comes, she must be ready for him.

'I can write out a cheque for you now, if you want me to.'

'No. I'll ask you when I need it. Thank you.'

'A pleasure. And I want you to know that I thought about you a lot yesterday – from the way Bernard rushed out after Dirk phoned him earlier on, I gather that you managed to help him.'

'Yes. I've sold his problems for him.' She throws it in his face. 'I never want to hear about it again, or have it discussed in any way!'

'You need not worry.'

Lizzie comes in and says, 'Araminta, you mustn't forget about Mr de Villiers.'

'Do me a favour, phone and tell him I can't leave the office right now, I've got clients coming in to sign contracts. Ask him if he could come here.'

Lizzie and Elvin burst out laughing. 'You're still afraid of going out alone with a man, aren't you?' Elvin teases.

'At least this one will be in broad daylight, not after sunset,' Lizzie says, teasing her. She had landed in a tricky situation once . . .

'It's easy for you to laugh, it was me that had to get out of it. Will you please phone him for me, Lizzie?'

'It will cost you four crossword puzzle answers.' Lizzie firmly believes that she will make her fortune by winning a crossword puzzle competition.

'It's a deal.'

*

He's older and even more attractive as he stands at the door and a touch of the old fire runs through her body . . .

'Hallo, Araminta.'

'Good day, sir.' As soon as she has said it, she realizes it's a mistake. Suddenly she's the schoolgirl and he the teacher again, and it is quite clear what is going through his mind.

'I couldn't believe it when I saw your name on this door yesterday.'

'I was surprised too. Come in, sit down.'

'Did you know it was me?' He closes the door before he sits down.

'Yes.'

'It wasn't necessary to have the other young lady phone me – I'm here alone, my wife didn't come with me.'

You fool, she says to herself, going cold. 'I had to get some important contracts signed.'

'It's really good to see you again – not just for a few minutes in a busy street, like the last time.'

Bed-hopper. 'Is it true that you're looking for a house in George?'

'Yes. I'm taking up a post here next term. I'm on long leave at the moment, using part of it to find a suitable house – you're still just as beautiful, Araminta.'

'I will show you a few houses, if you would like me to.'

'Of course I would like you to. I don't believe it's coincidence that made me come in here yesterday.'

'We are the best estate agents in town, even if I say so myself.' Play dumb and smile. 'Perhaps it's my luck, the fact that you came into Carr & Holtzman.' Tease him. 'I take it that you've come in advance to see what's available? You're still living in Cape Town, aren't you?'

'Yes.'

'I suppose you'll have to sell the house you've got there first, before you can buy one here?' It's what usually happens.

'No. I've already sold my house.'

90

Great. 'I've got a few excellent properties to show you.'

'I've never come across a girl as striking as you. A girl that can turn a man's heart to wax by one look from those dark eyes that seem to harbour a thousand secrets . . .'

Stop it. 'A very nice house came on to the market only last week . . .'

'Your hair is still just as it was when you were at school. Streaks of gold and brown and honey.'

'Your hair has grown darker.'

'So has my life.'

I'm not surprised. 'Shall we go and have a look at a few of the houses?'

'Are you in a hurry?'

It's you that was always in a hurry. 'One can lose a bargain by as little as an hour,' she points out.

He looks at his watch. 'It's just after eleven now. What if you show me a couple of places, and then we drive down to the sea for a while. Perhaps there's something for sale at Herolds Bay?'

I see through your plan. 'Only holiday cottages. Maybe I'll show you one or two later on.' Keep him dangling until he signs the contract. Every rand counts. If Dirk Holtzman gives her R15 000 in commission for the diamonds – even R10 000 – if Piet Sinksa comes and goes, she can pack up and go.

She shows him six houses before she takes him to the one she has purposely kept until last. The day she started work at Carr & Holtzman, Elvin told her never to try and sell a house to anyone. All she had to do was to sum up her clients, take them to the right door and allow the house to sell itself.

She had a good idea which house would catch Frans de Villiers.

'I noticed a few cracks under the windows at the side,' he says when they're back outside. Finding fault, pretending not to be interested.

91

'They're cracks in the plaster, nothing to worry about.'

'I suppose you agents must cover up as far as you can.'

'I don't.'

'The garden's a mess, it will cost quite a bit to get it right.' That's digging for a drop in the price.

'I agree. But it's a bargain as it is, they're old people, waiting to buy a retirement home.'

'Maybe you should get me an option for a week or two.'

'Unfortunately, the owner does not like the word "option". Perhaps you should get your wife here as soon as you can, to have a look at the place.'

'*I'm* buying the house, not my wife.' As if he's shying away. Why?

'But she's the one that has to live in it and make it a home.'

'She trusts my choice.'

'Do you have any children?'

'Two. The roof will have to be painted.'

'Not for a year or so, but I'll try and get the price down by a thousand or two.'

'Good. Are you coming to visit me tonight?'

'This town and the resorts near by are full of people that went to school with me.'

'Does it matter?'

'Of course it does. You know it does.'

'Can I come and visit you then?'

The transaction is safe, he will buy the house. 'No.'

The envelope lies on her desk when she gets back to the office. There are eight R20 banknotes in it, R160. Plus a little scrap of notepaper with the words, *With the most sincere gratitude. Dirk Holtzman.*'

It's like having reached out to a plank of wood while you were floundering and suddenly the plank turns out to be just a reflection in the water.

R160!

Thirteen

THE WHOLE WEEKEND she is restless and confused. The mountain is covered in cloud and it rains without stopping, a light summer drizzle. She tidies her cupboards. She cleans the inside of the windows. She cleans the bathroom tiles. She bakes some wholewheat bread. She cries a little, but she feels no better.

Halfway through the Sunday, she puts on her raincoat. She has to go out. She will walk and walk until she is too tired to feel angry any more!

One thing is clear: it won't help her if she takes the money back to him and throws it in his face. Or phones him and asks how he could have the heart to give her so little. She has to keep him on her side, he is her introduction to Piet Sinksa.

The streets are quiet.

Most of the shop windows are already decorated for Christmas; strings of glittering Merry Xmases and Happy New Years are strung over lavish displays.

'GIRL BURNS TO DEATH IN BOLAND UNREST.' She catches sight of it by accident, on a soaked billboard in front of a closed café. She crosses the street immediately.

More windows, more beautiful displays.

There is no one else in the streets, except now and then a car – and the pigeons and the starlings and the sparrows pecking in the gutters in the rain. Pigeons and sparrows and starlings are lucky, she says in her heart; if they don't like a place, they can simply fly away. They need not work to get money to pay for an aeroplane's wings! They need not sell diamonds to Samuel Sundoo to get a measly R160 for it.

Marian once stole a packet of sweets in old Mrs Silbert's shop when they were small. She didn't notice her doing it. It was only when Mrs Silbert called them to the store-room and the sweets came out from under Marian's jersey that she realized what was going on. She couldn't believe it. Always, at Christmas, Mrs Silbert used to send a turkey and a Christmas card to the rectory, even though she was Jewish. And Father always used to say: 'What a kind gesture,' and after the New Year he would go and say thankyou himself. And Marian had the nerve to steal a packet of sweets from this good woman?

Mrs Silbert made them sit on the packets of potatoes and said, 'Your father is a good man; what will he say if he hears about this?' She said, 'Aunty, I didn't do it, it was Marian. When we get home, I'll see to it that my father kills her.' 'No,' said Mrs Silbert, 'I want to spare your father the embarrassment.'

So Mrs Silbert gave them a sermon: 'We Jewish people,' she said, 'have an old legend we always tell our children. Every person born on this earth gets two angels to go with him or her: a good angel and a bad angel. The good angel says, "Do good," the bad angel says, "Do evil." For every good deed one does, one gets another good angel; for every bad deed, another bad angel. When Abraham had to sacrifice his son Isaac, he had many good angels that went to plead for him with the Almighty to spare Isaac's life. We must always see to it that we gather good angels to plead for us when we need it. What did Marian do? She listened to a bad angel.'

When they left, Mrs Silbert gave Marian the sweets in any case. On their way home Marian asked her not to tell their father. She told him the minute they got home and from then on they got pocket money every week.

When she asked her father what a legend was, he said, 'It's like a story. It's not really true.' She was very relieved, for where would all the angels have found a place in her room?

Her good angel said, 'Give Dirk Holtzman all the money you got for the diamonds so that you need not flee from this chaotic country, but go with a clean conscience.' Dirk's good angel said, 'You will have to give her at least R10 000 for this miracle, R15 000 really.' But his bad angel said, 'Don't be silly! Give her R160. It's more than enough.'

She walks until she reaches the large residential area to the north of the town. It is Sunday; everything is quiet and peaceful. The gardens are lush and dripping with rain. Big houses. Beautiful houses. White people's houses. Safe houses. Burglar-proofed houses. Beware-of-the-dog houses. Lights that switch on automatically at night when there's any movement. Warning signs that say: 'This property is being protected by the best alarm system . . .'

The first house she ever sold was in this area. Coincidence? When all the contracts were signed, the seller brought her a box of chocolates because the other agents in town had been trying for almost two years to sell the house.

'You see, young lady,' the man suddenly confided in her, 'in ten years there will be no apartheid in this country. These things are worked out long ahead of time. All this talk about reform that will bring peace and prosperity to everyone in the country is a well-planned strategy. To soften up the white man, to manipulate and confuse him so that he will walk straight to the grave they're digging for him. I've bought myself a place just outside of town, my dogs are on their way, and God willing, we'll start putting up the security fencing next week. Mark my words, things are going to get bad in this country.'

She opened the box and offered him a chocolate. 'Why don't you leave if you feel like that?' she asked him.

'You don't transplant an old tree. But I always told my two boys: choose careers you can do anywhere in the world. They did. One is practising medicine in Canada, the other one is a dentist in Australia.'

'Are they happy?'

'They're safe.'

She wants to live in a house that's safe. She wants a man to marry. She's known it since she has met Frans again. Her body's asking for it. A strong man, a good man, a clever man. To love her with his body and his mind and his soul. A man to look pretty for, to be good to. To love. She wants a child and they will live in a house with windows that can safely be left open in a country where hatred has not been planted amongst the people to grow until its runners slowly strangle the hearts of men! Where right and wrong and truth and untruth don't flow together in one stream, flooding everything in its way; where her children will not be the most hated . . .

But between her and a man and a child and a house with open windows lies half the globe, and to get there she needs money. Enough money.

She must turn back home.

There is a short cut through the park, but it is not safe to take it when you're alone because there are vagrants in the bushes. Perhaps she can take a chance?

No.

She will go and live in a land where one can walk through the park in the rain. Where you need not be afraid of the dark; where there are no bolts of lightning waiting to strike.

Joop Lourens is sitting in his car in front of the flat,

waiting for her. She is immediately worried. Did Samuel Sundoo let him know that she had gone there a second time?

'Hallo, Uncle Joop! This is a surprise.' Act cheerful.

'I saw that your car was here, so I thought you wouldn't be far away.'

'You're the last person I was expecting. Is everything all right?' If her way to Sundoo is blocked . . .

'Not much to complain about. I dropped Sally at her nephew's, and said I would come to see how you were.'

'Come inside. I'll make you some coffee.' When they climb the stairs, she realizes that he has grown old, he's climbing with difficulty. 'How is Aunt Sally?' she asks as she unlocks the safety gate.

'Fine. I took her to the doctor's yesterday, and he's happy with her blood pressure and everything. How are you, child?'

'I'm well, thank you. Sit down and have a rest.' She puts the kettle on and sets out the cups, watching him. Why does she get a feeling that he hasn't come just to see how she is doing? 'Will you take milk in your coffee, Uncle Joop?'

'Yes, thank you. How are things in the property market?'

'It's quiet at the moment. But my boss says that it's normal for this time of year.'

'Yes. Fortunately the people from up north are on their way to the sea for the holidays. Many will come to buy a refuge in the south, just in case. It seems to be becoming the fashion. A few have even bought property near us.'

'We don't mind, so long as they come and buy. I'm working on a commission basis, you know.'

'No man in your life yet? You said last time, you were waiting for the right one.'

'I haven't found him yet. But I'm sure he's waiting somewhere; I've just got to keep going until I find him.'

'It often happens that he's right under your nose without you knowing it.'

97

'I'd know if he was there.'

'We had a letter from your father to say that they'll be coming to Herolds Bay for the Christmas holidays, as usual.'

'And I suppose to ask whether Aunt Sally will bake the usual biscuits?'

'She does it with pleasure.'

Something's worrying the old man, it's not her imagination. If he's here because she's been back again to Samuel Sundoo, if he's here to forbid her going there again, she'll put up a fight ... 'How is Wilhelm, uncle? Is he still in Holland?'

'I was hoping you'd ask. He phoned to say that he won't be coming home for Christmas.' The old man stirs his coffee slowly, taking his time before he speaks again. 'As a matter of fact, I'm afraid my Wilhelm has lost his way. We no longer know where he really is, Araminta.'

'Help yourself to biscuits,' she says, relieved. It's not because of Samuel Sundoo that he's here, it's because of Wilhelm. 'You shouldn't judge too harshly, uncle. People are confused because of all the politics going on in this country, everyone's afraid and everyone's reacting in his own way.'

'I know. And I also know that Wilhelm, the real Wilhelm of my flesh and blood, is still there somewhere – it's just that he needs someone to take him by the hand and bring him back to where he belongs.'

'We're no longer sure where we belong, these days, uncle. Perhaps we don't belong anywhere.' What is she supposed to say?

'God has a place for us all. It's the devil that's upsetting everything and misusing man's cleverness for his own ends. If you want to destroy a man, teach him to hate himself; if you want to destroy a people, get the children to hate themselves. Wilhelm no longer listens to what I say, he has learnt to hate his own people, he's mixed up with the wrong crowd, Araminta!'

'Maybe you're right.' What can she say?

'Wilhelm needs someone to bring him back on the right track. That's all.'

'What is the right track? Where is it, uncle?' Surely he's not implying that *she* is the one to do it . . .

'A man that runs this way and that never walks a straight line. Wilhelm must settle down, Araminta. I've been thinking, couldn't you go and talk to him? There was a time when the two of you were close . . .'

'We're still close in a way, uncle.' Please, don't dream the impossible dream, there's nothing I can do to help!

'He will listen to you, my child.' The old man's hands are unsteady, he keeps on spilling coffee in his saucer.

'What makes you think he'll listen to me, uncle?' She gets up to fetch him a clean saucer. She has to mark time and get out of this without hurting Joop Lourens . . .

'It's something I've been thinking about for some time. I don't know any of Wilhelm's friends, he never brings them home. I thought if you . . .'

'Please, uncle, I owe you much, but don't ask the impossible of me.' Doesn't he know Wilhelm prefers men?

'I'm not asking the impossible. I just want you to go and visit him. I'll pay all your expenses; the two of you can travel as much as you want to. I want him to walk with his own for a time.'

'Do you want to send me abroad to see Wilhelm?'

'I know it's a big thing to ask.'

'What if I don't come back?' It's happening too fast . . .

'The reason I want you to visit him is exactly that – I gather from his letters that he's thinking of staying over there for good. I think he's sort of preparing us.' There's undisguised fear in the old man's voice.

'Please, Uncle Joop . . .'

'I know I'm asking a lot of you, Araminta, but he's all we have, and if there's one person that might be able to bring him home, it's you. You need not come back immediately. I remember how you used to fuss when you were a child because no snow fell here in winter – go and see how snow falls. Go see all the beautiful places over there. Take Wilhelm by the hand and bring him home.'

How is she going to get out of this without hurting the old man? 'If circumstances were different, uncle, if I had not already started out in my own direction, I might have considered it.' That was the wrong thing to say, the old man might see hope in it. 'I went in search of my own way – my own knowledge – and found it. Wilhelm went in search of *his* way, and he found it too. But his way and my way are not the same.' What more can she say?

'You can stay away as long as you want to. No matter what it costs.'

'I'm sorry, I can't. I'm so busy already, getting across the most important river of my own life, uncle!' Please, let me off!

'We are supposed to help one another across our rivers.' He's begging for her help.

'I know. But there are rivers we have to cross alone.'

When he leaves, she is left with a feeling of guilt and sympathy for the old man.

But at least he didn't say anything about Samuel Sundoo.

She's safe.

Fourteen

EVERY MORNING, WHEN SHE wakes up, she says to herself: Today's the day Piet Sinksa is going to come with the diamonds, and all day long she carries this hope inside her.

Every time she phones Dirk Holtzman, he tells her she's in too much of a hurry, Piet will come.

'When?'

'Perhaps he's waiting till after Christmas.'

'Did you talk to him?'

'No, to his sister. She gave him the message.'

'Why can't I phone and speak to her myself?'

'Because she won't trust you. She'll think you're out to trap them and then you won't get anything out of them. Piet will come. You just have to be patient.'

She tries to be.

Early in December, the schools close for the Christmas holidays and the holiday-makers start flocking to the resorts in the area. Most of them come from the north. During the day, they come into town in a never-ending stream of cars, causing traffic jams in the centre. The pavements become streams of people milling about, cash registers overflow with the harvest the shopkeepers have been looking forward to for most of the year.

In the afternoons, the streets are dirty, the shops tired,

and here and there a 'Happy Xmas and a Happy New Year' starts coming loose or hanging awry.

Ten days before Christmas, her parents arrive at Herolds Bay for their annual holiday. Marian and Charl-Pierre, her fiancé, are with them.

She now lives in three worlds at the same time: work, Herolds Bay, waiting for Piet Sinksa.

Work. For every prospective buyer that comes into the office, ten viewers – 'just wanted to have a look at what's on the market' – follow. She cannot distinguish between buyers and viewers; she goes to the same trouble for everyone because they all represent the possibility of a transaction, the possibility of a commission. In her own car, with petrol she has paid for herself, she drives them from one 'For Sale' sign to another, until she feels she should add 'Free Tours' to the Carr & Holtzman sign outside.

They complain about how expensive everything is down here in the south; about the way they are treated; about the poor service in the restaurants. How bad the weather is. How overpriced houses are.

She agrees and apologizes.

When she gets home late in the afternoons, the mountain is waiting in her window: quiet and aloof above the din. But she cannot stay too long, she has to change roles; her father and her family expect her for supper every night.

The table at which you are born is the table to which your umbilical cord is for ever tied, no matter how hard you pull to free yourself! The food at this table is different from all others, no matter where it's laid. It's a place of old familiar things: a certain aroma, a taste, the way a serviette is folded, the way grace is said. It's a cloud to which you return with old resentments, guilt, secrets.

'You're too thin, Araminta.'

'There's not much time to eat at the moment, Mother. We're very busy.'

'I don't want to be personal,' Marian says with sisterly bitchiness, 'but judging by the lack of furniture and stuff in your flat, you can't be doing too well. Even your clothes are mostly what you had when you were at university. Seems as if you haven't bought yourself a decent thing in two years!'

'I'm saving up.'

'How much have you saved?' Marian challenges her.

Will she tell? Why not? 'Together with outstanding commission, just over R20 000.'

'*What?*'

She does not look up from her plate to enjoy the surprise on their faces. She knows it's there.

'Well . . .' says Charl-Pierre, the outsider at the table, 'you're tempting me to become an estate agent too.'

'I still owe R3 000 on my car, though.' She adds it as a little damper.

Marian would not give up however. 'Are you telling me you're sitting on R20 000 and you're not buying anything for yourself?'

'Because I'm saving my money for a specific reason.' When she and Marian were small, they used to walk on the wall round the rectory garden and see who would fall off first . . .

'What reason?'

'For something.'

'What?'

'A man.'

They all laugh, except her father. He looks at her with eyes that say: We'll talk later.

The time comes on the Sunday morning, after the two of them had gone for a swim and were sitting on the rocks. It's early still. The tide is in, the sea looks deep and green and the sky is clear. She knows she's going to get some kind of sermon and he's still preparing his opening.

'The morning you were born, Araminta,' he says at last,

103

'I had spent – like most fathers – a night in anguish in the waiting-room of the hospital.'

'I cannot imagine you being in anguish.'

'When the sister came and told me it was another girl, I got up and walked outside, just at the very moment the sun was coming up. It was a strange experience: behind me a new life had just arrived, before me was the sun of a new day.'

'At least you can be sure I'm not moonstruck.'

'Don't be flippant. As a result of that experience, I have always felt there was something special about your birth. Perhaps that is why I always felt confident about you in my mind – even when I was uneasy about you. But ever since we've arrived here, I've been trying to find that confidence and I can't.'

For a while they sit in silence. Then he looks at her searchingly and says, 'Araminta, you're becoming a stranger to us. I don't understand you.'

A cormorant sits on the rocks in the water, his wings spread out in the sun.

She and her mother never really quarrelled. Perhaps about a dress she refused to wear, or a wardrobe that was too untidy, but never because of her being defiant. Rebellion was always against her father's rules. And yet, she fears the day when the door between them will close for ever.

'Father, I want you to know that I love you, even though I'm angry with you sometimes. And I know that you love me too, even when you're angry with me.'

'I think there's something you want to tell me.'

'There is. I'm going to leave the country.' She hadn't wanted to tell him just yet, she had wanted to write him a letter. She waits for his reaction and feels herself go tense. But he does not answer her. Perhaps he didn't hear her above the noise of the sea. 'I'm going to leave the country, Father!'

He smiles. 'I heard you.'

'Aren't you shocked?' she asks.

'No. I was suspecting something far worse.'

'Like what?' She suddenly realizes that he's not indifferent, but relieved! 'Like what, Father?'

'Frans de Villiers's wife has left him. I believe he's taking up a post in George.'

Shit! 'You don't blink an eye because I'm going to leave the country, Father – you're just relieved because you think I haven't got involved with Frans de Villiers again!'

'Have you?' Like fear flaring up.

'No, I haven't.'

'There's no need to shout. I'm not unconcerned about your decision to leave the country. Hardly a week goes by without a student or a member of the congregation coming to me to talk over the merits of staying on or emigrating. I'm sure there are very few people who are not considering it in these troubled times, though many can only dream about it because of the cost involved.'

'You mean there are very few *white* people who are not considering it or dreaming about it.'

'Don't always turn everything into a question of colour, daughter. Times are uncertain for all of us. And if it helps in any way, I can assure you that if I were younger I would have considered going myself. As a protest. But I know now that it would have been a mistake. Protest must happen here. Every day.'

'Father ...' She turns round and faces him squarely. 'Why do you hate your own people so?' She's been wanting to ask him that for a long time.

'How can you accuse me of hating my own people, Araminta?' he asks, appalled. 'How can you?'

It's as if clouds were suddenly gathering above them; she wants to turn back and run for the sunshine, but she can't. 'Sunday after Sunday,' she says, bitingly, 'you get up in the pulpit and spread the gospel, but when you get down again, you help to fan the flames against us! And then, when evening comes, you go on your knees, praying for peace in the land!'

105

'Araminta!'

He is getting angry. Very angry. It's strange, Ignatius Rossouw seldom drops his poise. 'I'm sorry, Father. But this is something that has been disturbing me for years. I can try and understand why others hate us, but why you, Father?' He does not answer her; his mouth is set in an angry slit and his eyes have grown hard. Often, when she was a child, he used to punish her for disobedience by not talking to her for hours. He was like a rock that couldn't hear, no matter how loud you shouted. 'Father, speak to me! Show me your understanding today, not your impatience. I don't want to go away knowing there's hostility between you and me.'

He is gazing far out to sea. 'Your impression, Araminta, that I hate my own people, is one that you have created in your own mind. What you see as hatred is the impatience you have just spoken of. The Afrikaner is in the process of coming out of a long, dark tunnel – many are in the light already, and many are in the twilight just before the light. Too many are still far back in the tunnel, though, and there isn't much time left for getting them out.' He is calm when he turns to her. 'Do you blame me for my impatience? My concern? You call that hatred?' It's as if he wants to put the words in her mind with his eyes.

'Perhaps I've misunderstood you, because you've never put it like that before,' she admits. She knows they're nearing a crossroads where they will either find or lose one another for ever. She senses it and she's afraid. 'Suppose I'm one of those still at the back of the tunnel, will you, bear with me for a moment then, Father?'

'If you'll allow me, I'll take you by the hand and bring you to the light – as I've tried to do so many times, but you always let go of my hand.'

'Because I had to find my own way, I had to find out the truth for myself. Can't you understand that? I don't want to be led, I don't want to be carried, I want to learn to walk by myself!'

106

'Why are you so difficult?'

'You see, Father, I came across a pattern, a little crack that got bigger and bigger the closer I looked.' She knows he is not going to like it, but she has to do it. 'The little crack started when a small group of Europeans came to the foot of Africa, and became a new nation.'

'Surely, you're not still *that* far back in the tunnel!' he says with annoyance.

'I'll be as brief as I can. Otherwise I can't show you the crack.'

'I'll try to be patient.' As if allowing a troublesome child to have her way.

'The Dutch East India Company went bankrupt. Britain came and occupied the Cape in order to control the sea route to the East.' It's like having to find the shortest route through a maze: every word is a step and she must be as quick and as accurate as she can. 'In the end Britain took the Cape and was ordered to give the Dutch £6 million in compensation. For the £6 million they got an enormous piece of land on the toe of Africa. Plus about twenty thousand bushmen and Koikoi tribesmen and thousands of Xhosas fleeing southwards across the eastern boundary as a result of the power struggle between the Xhosa leaders to the north. They also got the company's thirty thousand slaves and a couple of thousand half-castes, who had mostly been born of the slave women.'

'How long are you going to keep me on this rock giving me a history lesson?'

'It's not history I'm telling you about, Father. It's about an open secret but everyone ignores it. And the English got the Boers: about twenty-five thousand men, women and children that said they were Afrikaners. By that time they had already been living along the toes of Africa for decades. An independent people who said they were their own masters.'

'They were always an obstinate lot.'

'It was decided that these Boers must be Anglicized.

Their mutton sheep had to be exchanged for wool-bearing sheep, and the men had to be turned into good workers if they were to get back their £6 million investment.'

'Now you're splitting hairs.'

'They wanted more than their £6 million, Father! The main purpose they had for the Cape was to provide raw materials for the factories in Britain. Especially wool. Tons of it. The area round the eastern boundary was a factory owner's and a Merino sheep's dream.' She goes and sits on another rock so that she can see his face better. His hair has grown grey, but he is still the tall, handsome man with the strong face that always stirs a touch of pride in her because she is his child . . .

'May I say something?' he asks.

The dissent in his voice makes her wary. 'Of course.'

'I'm afraid it's much too late to object to the British occupation of the Cape. For if you do, you are also objecting to the enormous part they have played in civilizing this country.'

'I agree. But that's not what I'm objecting to.'

'Are you objecting to the course of history then? You can't change it.'

'No. But I warned you that I was not talking about history.' She knows if she stops, he will not give her the chance to finish. 'The first thing the English needed at the Cape was cheap labour. In England, the reformers had caused the factory owners – the money-men – untold trouble for using women and orphans as cheap labour. They would put up with no injustices towards the "noble savages" at the Cape.

'So missionaries were brought in by the boatload to make the Koikoi and half-castes, the brown people, industrious and eager for salvation. A plan which failed miserably. Everything that went wrong was laid at the door of the Boers, who were – thank God – not noble savages. Truth and lies were dished up together, as the English were to discover in their own courts of law, but they seldom cared to remember it.'

'Don't try to dip the Boers too deep in honey, Araminta.'

'There's always a little dirt in good honey,' she says, pressing on. 'The English didn't have money to place soldiers on the eastern border to restrain the looting Xhosas, the Boers were a convenient buffer, because they had to protect themselves. All the while the factories in England were pressing for the promised wool, and your face tells me you're dying for coffee, Father! You force me to jump a thousand steps!'

'Try not to fall,' he scolds.

She ignores it. 'I'll skip another thousand stones. When Britain was at her wits' end, she decided to send the sternest governor she could find to the Cape: Lord Charles Somerset. In 1820 he had thousands of people shipped from England and settled them on land between the Boers and the Xhosas on the eastern border – an area where they were already fighting over land and grazing. He gave them Merino sheep and told them to farm the land. And guns to help protect the border.'

'Your great-grandmother, Araminta MacDonald, came out with one of the smaller groups two years later.'

'I know she did. Slowly the Boers became despondent. Britain had freed their slaves but didn't have the money to give them compensation or pay for military protection on the border. The tax collectors never failed to turn up, though. And nobody listened to the Boers, Father. Lord Charles himself went to the border and admitted that they were not the people he had been made to believe. They were good and decent. The lawless individuals among them they themselves banished to Stellenbosch and Swellendam. But according to the records of the English they were all troublemakers, and the record was never changed.'

'Don't get so worked up, child.'

'So the Boers went on the Great Trek. In their thousands, and mostly from the region around the eastern border. They said they would go on until they found somewhere where there were no black people and where they could rule over themselves. The British settlers bought one of the leaders a Bible, and inscribed it: "As a farewell token of our esteem and a heartfelt regret at your departure." In spite of everything, the Boers had got on well with the settlers. They had learned a great deal from them.'

'I'm glad you admit that.'

'The trekkers travelled round the territory of the Xhosas. Northwards and westwards. Right up in the north various groups turned eastwards again, crossing the fearsome Drakensberg Mountains in order to get to the sea, for the republic they planned for themselves had to have a harbour. At last, after hundreds of them had been killed by the Zulus and tens of thousands of their cattle looted, they founded the Republic of Natal.'

'I think you must go a little faster.'

She sees the frown between his eyebrows, but hangs on. 'When the English at the Cape received word that the Boers had a harbour, they were furious. They annexed Natal and the land of the Zulus, and they declared it a British colony.

'So the Boers went back over the mountains. After meeting up with the other groups, they founded the Orange Free State beyond the Orange River, deep inland. A little further north, beyond the Vaal River, they founded the Republic of Transvaal.'

'I take it that they didn't find anywhere where there were no blacks,' he said, smiling.

'No. Trollope said that Africa is a land of black people; it was so, it is so, it will always be so. The trekker Boers did, however, find many deserted battlegrounds where the black tribes had massacred each other. Paul Kruger said we stole no land from anyone.'

'What worries me, Araminta, is that you're not getting an inch closer to the light. You keep on mulling over things at the back of the tunnel.'

110

'I'm asking you to give me a chance to get to the crack that runs through all this.'

'The problem with our history, Araminta, is that we too easily forget that there are other perspectives as well.'

'You're wrong, Father. History has only one perspective – except when it's being dished up as propaganda for people who will believe anything as long as it's twisted to what they want to hear.' As soon as she says it, he jumps up, offended.

'It's no wonder your marks for history were never better than average!' he says, sharply. 'It's no wonder I can't reach you.'

'Please, Father, don't go.'

'I don't think I can listen to any more of this hysterical history lesson!'

'Please wait. If you go now, you'll never understand.'

'No, Araminta, it's *you* that will never understand. It's *you* that prefers the darkness to the light.'

Fifteen

WHEN HE GOES OFF in the direction of the houses, without her, it does feel as if she has been left alone in the dark. She knows he won't turn back.

There had been times, when his unyielding attitude had made him so unpopular with most of the people in the village that she wanted to cry for him. Always, while her mother and Marian were supporting him and spurring him on, she used go to her room and pray: Dear God, please let the people like my father. Or: Please God, let him receive a calling to another village; perhaps he's been in this one for too long.

And he would get a call but he wouldn't accept it. Or he would deliver one of his beautiful sermons on a Sunday morning, and suddenly things improved again.

In the end, his final break with the local church council came after his dispute with them about her mother's salary as organist.

Because of money.

The very next call he received, the one in Bloemfontein, he took.

After a while, she gets up from the rocks and walks across the sand and back into the water. Something feels incomplete, unfinished. Like having to go away, or die, before you

112

have had a chance to say what you so badly wanted to say.

It no longer matters to her whether others understands or not, it is his understanding she wants. So that he won't be sorry because she is his child, that she is not like Marian, that she can't believe blindly . . .

She sees the wave coming and starting to break with a curling, foaming crest, and she knows that if it hits her, it will be very hard, so she deftly dives through it. When she comes up, the next one is upon her and she has to dive to safety again. And again and again. Then she finds herself in deeper water among the bigger waves and turns on her back . . . weightless, suddenly detached . . . It's an infinite cradle of water holding her. It's solitude and peace. The sea is her grandmother, and she's back in her womb.

Gradually she begins to play: she floats, she swims, she dives. She's a fish. A seal. A dolphin. It's a water-dance. It's like flying through a different kind of air . . .

As she comes up again, she realizes that she has drifted out too far between the hills that form the bay. For a moment she panics, then forces herself to be calm and starts swimming to the shore with the waves.

He is waiting for her on the sand. She didn't expect him to do that.

'Do you realize how far out you've been!' he scolds as he wraps the towel round her shoulders.

'I'm sorry, I had a bit of trouble getting back.' She dries her face on a corner of the towel, catching her breath.

'You know how treacherous this bay can be!'

'It's done me good, Father.'

'It most definitely didn't do me good when I came to look for you, and saw you right out there! Don't ever go in that deep again!'

He had come looking for her . . . 'Why did you come back?' she asks.

'Because you didn't come home.'

But she can see from the way he is looking at her that it is not the whole truth. That he too is afraid of them walking away from each other, without having a chance to turn back.

'I so badly wanted you to understand, Father,' she says as they walk across the sand in the direction of the retaining wall above the high-water mark.

He makes no comment. He takes the towel and spreads it flat on the wall for her to sit on. He would never let her and Marian sit on the bare cement in their wet swimsuits. 'Let's talk about other things, Araminta. It's Christmas time, family time. I don't want you to drift away from us any further. Leave politics alone – it does not suit you.'

'But it's not politics, Father! I swear.'

'Well, let's stop digging about in history then. What good can it do?' He's more relaxed. More composed.

'Where else could I have gone digging to find myself? I wanted to know who I was, so that I could be someone. I'm supposed to be ashamed of what I am; if you dare to be cheerful you're accused of insensitivity. People are frustrated and angry and afraid – do you know what fear and anger together feel like, Father?'

'Isn't it just two sides of the same coin?'

'Do you know what it's like to be trapped in a tiny college room with the knowledge you have been searching for, and have found? You want to wipe it from your mind but you can't. It's inside you, it's around you, you can't run away from it, you only grow bitter and more afraid.'

'Of what?'

'Of the fury and fear you can see coming from left and right in this country and that will surely crash into one another somewhere along the line. You see only one side of the coin, Father. It seems as if everyone only sees one side. The black side. You're blind as to what's brewing up on the white side . . .'

'What can be brewing up on the white side except guilt?'

114

'Old anger. New anger.'

'We can't hang on to old anger for ever, child!'

'How do you stop being angry at the axe that has cut off your best hand, Father?'

'What axe?'

'If I tell you, you'll only get angry again and walk off.'

'I won't.'

'The Boers, Father, had their two republics . . .' It's like testing the water first to see whether it's safe to go in or not . . . 'The English said that if they wanted that piece of barren earth without a harbour they could have it.'

'Keep the towel under you.'

'Many English people, and some learned Afrikaners, even moved away from the Cape to settle in the republics of the Boers, for the two British colonies weren't much better off than the two republics.'

'I should have brought your hat.'

She combs her hair through her fingers to help it dry. 'Everything went relatively well until one fateful day in 1866 – or was it '67, I can't remember now – when a Boer child in the Orange Free State picked up a diamond. A beautiful diamond. More diamonds. The English were extremely alarmed. It was out of the question that the Boers could be allowed to own diamond fields! What if they were to get richer than the English colonies? Don't forget, the Suez Canal was being dug; ships would no longer have to come all the way round the Cape.'

He nods his head, a little withdrawn.

'So the English got a Griqua native to swear in court that it was Griqua land on which the diamonds had been found. Then Britain simply annexed one hundred and forty Boer farms and incorporated them in the Cape Colony.'

'Pull up a bit of the towel round your shoulders, you're getting too much sun.'

'Prospectors from all over the world streamed into the country. Money streamed in. A new city began to grow – Kimberley. Five years later the Land Court found that

Britain had done a wicked thing: the land on which the diamonds had been found had been Boer territory. As punishment Britain had to pay the Orange Free State £90 000. They did it with a smile, for within ten years, the diamond fields yielded more than £30 million for Britain.'

'Is that a fact?' he asks, with a flicker of interest.

'Yes. And Trollope said that it was neither the church nor the missioners with their schools, that gave the black man in South Africa his first taste of Western civilization – it was the ten shillings a week they earned in their thousands on the diamond fields that did it. Money. Pay attention now, Father, the crack is getting wider ... Twenty years later, the richest gold-field in the world was discovered three hundred miles from Kimberley: right in the middle of the Republic of the Transvaal where no Griqua could swear the land was his. With the money made on the diamond fields, the English money-men now invaded the gold-fields. Britain urgently needed this gold, for the gold reserves at the Bank of England were dangerously low. Germany and America were fast becoming a threat to Britain's position at the centre of world trade ...'

'Get to the crack, Araminta.'

'Money is the crack, Father! Don't you see? History is just money blazing its trail across the earth, even if there are a thousand different variations of it. Our own history is nothing but a trail of greed. To get hold of the Boers' gold, Britain provoked them with lie upon lie until war broke out over – of all the stupid things – voting rights for the foreigners on the mines! The bankers in London announced shamelessly that the biggest money power in the world was now at war with the country producing the most gold in the world! They described it as truly exceptional.

'Thirty thousand men, women and children died on the Boer side on the battlefields and in concentration camps, Father. All because of gold. Their farms burnt to the ground, their cattle killed ...'

116

'How is it possible that a young girl, on a beautiful day like this, can carry on with such bitterness about the things of the past?' he asks, downcast.

'We are living with the results, Father.'

'We must forget the past and look to the future, Araminta!'

'Don't play dumb, Father!' She cries. 'Where could the Afrikaner go this time? All the territory around their republics had been annexed by foreign powers. All they could do was slowly get up from the ruins and go inside themselves – building a wall to retreat behind where they would be left alone to govern themselves. Don't forget, most of the black people had sided with the English. The wall the Afrikaner built round himself is called apartheid. It is the curse that is about to fall on them while others are getting fat from our diamonds and gold!'

A feeling of helplessness wells up in her. A sadness. Behind her father lies the bay and the houses and the lush green hills. She knows they have reached the crossroads, she wants to put out her arms and hold on to him, but she cannot reach him, his eyes are suddenly cold and angry again.

'Don't you realize that the wall is going to fall on you as well if you don't bury the past, Araminta?'

'No, Father, the wall is not going to fall on me. I'm going away to make my life somewhere else.'

'You're serious then?'

'Yes. The moment I have enough money, I shall go.'

'And if I say to you that the wall will not fall in on us if we open our eyes to the suffering on the other side of it? The present signs of capitulation from the government's side are just panic. The international sanctions are taking effect. With Japan turning her back on us now too, the government knows its time is running out.'

'You're right. In the end it's money that will make the wall fall in. That is neat. But where will the money come from to clear up the rubble.'

'Economic growth will have to be restored.'

117

'If you think it's that simple, you're dreaming, Father. Most of the present propaganda against us is aimed at covering up the crater which the crack has become, and into which we have fallen.'

'In other words, you don't see the hand of God in the history of the world.' It is not a question.

'No, Father. I see only greed.'

'You don't see God's mercy in history, in spite of everything?'

'No.'

'That His only Son was offered on the Cross for the sins of the world?'

'If Jesus had lived in this country, it would not have been necessary for him to have died on the cross for our sins; apartheid is the only sin in this land, apparently!' His face grows pale and he clenches his teeth . . . 'I'm sorry, I should not have said that.'

'I hang my head in shame before God this day because I have failed as a father; because I could not lead the child He trusted to my care to the light.'

'It's not your fault, Father. I only wanted you to know why I can no longer stay in this country that does not want me. Why I want to go and find a place where I can belong to myself. Where I'm not penalized for being an Afrikaner every day, where I'm not supposed to keep on struggling for the causes of others while my own life is going by . . . I see Marian coming over there – I'd be glad if you don't tell them yet.'

In her heart she knows that they have veered away from each other.

118

BOOK TWO

One

EVERY MORNING WHEN SHE wakes up, she thinks perhaps Piet Sinksa will come today.

But he doesn't. Dirk Holtzman says he will come after Christmas, after New Year. Just be patient; he has spoken to Piet's sister, Piet will come.

She sells a plot by the sea. Elvin says the real buyers will come after Christmas, they know the owners are more willing to bring their prices down after Christmas.

After Christmas. After the flood when the waters have subsided. After the fever has subsided. Fortunately she bought the presents she had to buy long ago. She didn't buy anything for herself.

But the nearer it gets to Christmas Day, the more she feels that she is being dragged along by the tide. It's a fever beginning to take hold of her even though she knows that every window display, all the tinsel, all the decorations are simply a lure to entice the money from her purse.

When she goes out to buy bread, she sees the most beautiful dress or a carpet for the floor of her ark. Or a bracelet, or underwear.

When she gets home with the bread, she's moody, but she does not know why. Or she knows, but she will not admit it. It's Christmas. There's a God of heaven and a god of the earth; one of the two keeps on urging her to go and buy herself something nice. She doesn't know which one. All she knows is that she has to hang on to every cent until Piet Sinksa turns up!

The day before Christmas, the Saturday, it is as if the fever has risen beyond all bounds. The shops and streets are a crazy flood of people, apparently spending every last rand they possess in order to satisfy a terrible hunger. By ten o'clock in the morning, she needs every drop of her self-control not to run to the bank and withdraw all her money and go spending and spending until she is satisfied too.

When she wakes up again, it is – mercifully – Christmas morning.

She sits at the table and watches the mountain appear out of the night. Somewhere a wagtail pipes its incessant waking call. When the other wagtails do not answer, he seems to become annoyed. 'Wake up! Wake up!' he calls. Somewhere a Cape robin joins in, with its soft gurgling call and a sparrow begins to chirp . . .

As it gets lighter, every gorge on the mountain starts throwing a shadow to the west . . . when the sun comes out, the mountain sees it first. The warm yellow rays fall across its highest slopes and spread like a smile which is getting broader and broader.

'Happy Christmas!' she says.

'Happy Christmas!' it replies.

All is at rest. The fever has subsided. The birds are happy, the sky is blue; the earth spins quietly on its path round the sun with its tons of Christmas trimmings and presents, completing its daily journey of two million miles . . .

Something a lecturer once said during a geography class still makes her wonder sometimes . . . he said they mustn't forget that there is a group of top scientists who maintain that the earth is stationary at the exact geographic centre of the universe – that there is no proof of the 'proof' that we're spinning through the sky round the sun. The earth turns on its axis while the whole cosmos spins round it.

Everyone in the class laughed, except the lecturer.

Mountain, whether we're spinning or standing still, please see if Piet Sinksa's coming. Tell him to hurry up!

Two

SHORTLY BEFORE THE END of January she sells two properties: a house and a plot.

Frans de Villiers rings her twice to ask if he can come and visit her – after the second 'No!' he slams down the receiver.

And Piet Sinksa does not turn up.

Late one Tuesday afternoon there is a knock on her door and when she opens it, she sees Jan du Toit, Dirk Holtzman's partner. It's rather strange. If Piet had come, Dirk would have let her know himself. Or phoned.

'Good afternoon, Miss Rossouw. Maybe you don't remember me, but we have met before.'

'I do remember you. You are Mr du Toit.' He hasn't got any diamonds with him, she is somehow sure of it.

'I would like to talk to you for a moment.' He's uneasy.

'Come inside.' If it concerns property, he could have come to the office . . . 'Please sit down.'

'Thanks. To be honest, I've been trying to summon up the courage to come to you for some time now.'

'What about?'

'Do you mind if I smoke?'

'No.' She opens the window and passes him an ashtray. He has an honest face. His hair, his eyebrows and the hair on his arms are all exactly the same golden-red colour, it makes him look kind of transparent. She reckons he must be about forty and finds it strange that a man of his age can be so unsure of himself.

'Why did you want to come to me, Mr du Toit?'

'Please call me Jan.'

'Very well.' Perhaps it will put him more at ease. 'Why did you want to see me, Jan?'

'You won't believe me, but years ago, when my wife came here to George to teach, she lived in this very flat.' As if he wants to fence around and muster a bit more courage first. 'After a year, she found herself another place to stay – it's too cold here during winter.'

'It is. I won't be staying here much longer either. At least, I hope not.'

'I hope not, for your sake. I was working for the school board at the time. It was before we got married and long before Dirk and I went into partnership. That was after I inherited some money from my father, you see.' After every draw on the cigarette, he taps it to remove the ash, even if there is no ash ready to fall. 'It's actually a rather sticky matter I've come about.'

'Why do you say that?' He has no diamonds on him, she's sure of that.

'It's about Piet Sinksa.'

What does *he* know about Piet Sinksa? 'What about him?'

'To tell you the honest truth, I'm waiting for him too.' It sounds like an admission of guilt. 'You need not worry about Dirk telling me about what you did. You can trust us.'

'Trust you about what?'

'You know . . . I mean.' Tap-tap.

'I haven't the faintest idea what you're talking about, Jan.' If he wasn't so pathetic, she might have got cross.

'You see, what I mean is that I've asked Piet to bring me some as well. Diamonds. You know? So I'm waiting for him too. I've got the money ready and everything. But if my wife finds out, she'll divorce me. I had to take a second mortgage on my house to get the money: R10 000. I've got the money, as I said. But now this blooming Piet does not turn up.'

'You should be glad,' she says, coldly. 'For if, by any chance, you thought that I would sell diamonds for you, you made a very big mistake. I wouldn't have.'

'I'm sure you don't really mean that,' he says, sheepishly. 'I reckoned that if you were selling for yourself, you might as well sell for me too. Everybody says it is far more difficult to find a buyer than a supplier.'

'I don't like this. It's as if I had given Dirk Holtzman a key to my door, and now he has duplicates made for all his friends and partners.'

'I swear I won't talk.'

'We have nothing to talk about.'

'But I haven't told you why I'm here yet!' he says with urgency, stubbing out his cigarette. 'I can arrange something for us. I can get some very nice diamonds from another man.'

'Who?' The moment she asks it, she realizes she has been too eager; a tiny spark of hope had shot through her before she could stop it!

'Nick Wehland. You must have seen him around. He drives a smart red German number with a folding hood. He brings his pick-up to our garage for repairs.'

'I don't know him.'

'He's in town quite a lot. He owns a piece of land not far away, right under the mountain to the north.'

'Not my mountain.'

'I beg your pardon?'

'Just a slip of the tongue.'

'He wants to plant ferns for the export market.'

'So you told him I sell diamonds.'

'I didn't mention your name, I swear. We just had a chat one day. He said he comes from Koffiefontein, not far from Kimberley. Born and bred there. Just for a joke, I asked him . . . it was the week before Christmas when I

126

started to realize that Piet wasn't going to turn up. I asked him where you could get a few stones, so he said I could just say the word, he's got all the contacts up there, he could get me as many as I wanted. Good ones.'

'So you told him I sell diamonds.'

'He asked me how I was going to dispose of them, so I said I knew of somebody.'

Something doesn't feel right. She was waiting for Piet Sinksa. Now Piet is Jan-du-Toit/Nick-Wehland-Koffiefontein. A path that she thought was straight is suddenly full of bends that she can't see round.

'Mr du Toit – Jan – I don't think you quite understand my position. I was pushed into two situations where people in need had to get rid of diamonds. As it happened, I knew somebody that knew somebody that bought them. I got involved with something I know nothing about. Perhaps I'm naïve, but it never felt for a moment as if I was doing something terribly illegal. But what you're speaking of does.'

'Believe me, I know it's a dangerous business. But if we're cautious and keep quiet . . .'

'I hope I'm not included in your "we". I want nothing to do with it.'

'But you're waiting for Piet Sinksa too, aren't you?' he asks, obviously disappointed. 'I'm waiting for him. I swear that I've never even committed a traffic offence before. It's just that life has become so bloody unfair – I'm working my butt off, I'm paying through the nose to keep a roof over our heads. Everything they eat costs more every month and so does the bloody taxman . . .'

'Jan . . .'

'I promise you, I'm not a racist, but these days you have to be black if you want to have things your own way. If you're white, and you don't pay your rent or your water and electricity, they throw you out or cut off your supply. But if you're black, you only have to boycott everything, saying how oppressed you are, and nothing happens to you. They just put in the papers, now and again, how many millions of rands are owed in rent and electricity in the black communities. It's not that I don't feel sorry for these people. I know their argument is that they're taking what's been taken from them, but when are they going to stop taking?'

'Do you think R10 000 worth of diamonds is going to save you?'

'I didn't say that. But it can buy me a few nights' sleep.'

'And then go out and buy more diamonds, and come back to me, pleading with me to sell them? Sorry, I won't be here, Jan.'

'Nick Wehland told me only this morning that he knows of two chaps that are coming down from Koffiefontein with a load of sheep over the weekend; he can arrange something for us. Good stones.'

'Don't say *us*! If he can get hold of "good stones", he can surely organize a buyer for you as well? Seeing that he has such wonderful contacts.' She says it with her lips, while the tiny spark grows into a tiny flame inside her.

'But it's the buyer that's the problem! Nick says he's been waiting to do a deal himself for a long time, but he has no way of selling them. It's no use having diamonds if you can't get rid of them again. You know that yourself. Nick says, if you can get a couple of people to pool their resources and do a big deal, you take one chance and then you're finished with it.'

'I hope you succeed.'

'You couldn't just introduce us to your buyer? I mean . . .'

'Forget it.'

'Piet Sinksa's not going to come. I'm telling you. Dirk says so too. And Nick Wehland. He says if someone doesn't turn up, you can be sure he's been caught. Nick's no fool, he knows diamonds all right. He says it will take him a day or two to arrange everything – he'll get them here for us. Nice ones. Nick's our big chance.'

128

'Diamonds, Jan du Toit, are not playthings.' She knows these are Joop Lourens's words, but that is not how she means them. 'Diamonds are mysterious things, noble things.'

'Diamond have not been put on the earth for the Oppenheimers only, that's what I say.'

He did not understand. And a diamond would not be happy with him. Perhaps a handful of worker diamonds, but most definitely not wise ones or kings; perhaps that is why she feels jealous and wants to step in between him and them. 'I think you better make me an appointment with Nick Wehland; I want to meet him and talk to him.' Perhaps she should jump in before both of them – perhaps he is another Piet Sinksa.

'We can get in my car and drive out to his place right now. He said it's for me to say when I'm ready.'

'I want to talk to him alone.'

'Then you and he wangle things behind my back, and what do I get?' he asks indignantly.

'I only want to talk to him first, see what he looks like.'

'If we do it, we do it together.'

'Very well then. Make the appointment.'

'It could turn out doubly lucky for you – he's not married.'

'I'm not interested.'

Think nothing, hope for nothing, she tells herself over and over again.

But within her, the hope that had died – waiting for Piet Sinksa – quietly starts coming to life again. If she has to sell for two others as well as herself, so be it.

'ESCALATING VIOLENCE'

She has taught her eyes to look past newspaper headlines, but they won't always do it! It's as if they want to find something with which to stir up her sense of urgency. There are days when she feels like panicking, feels that she is in the grip of circumstances from which she may never

129

escape! Shortly after New Year, she had to have her car's exhaust system replaced, and when she went to fetch the car, the man said that the radiator had perished as well. The day after that, her hair-dryer broke. And one of her best transactions fell through: the building society would not grant the loan because they thought the purchase price was too high compared to the real value of the place. The seller refused to bring his price down, and the buyer didn't have the cash to pay the difference himself.

'TAMBO SHOCKS WITH ANC'S LUST FOR MURDER'

Elvin says that people from all walks of life are going to start grabbing what they can get while there's still time . . .

Her father wrote to her to remind her of the R250 interest she still owes him on the money he lent her. That's right. But in her heart she had hoped he would let her off, a sort of forgiveness.

Shortly after nine o'clock on the Wednesday morning Jan du Toit phones to say they have an appointment with Nick out at his place, at four in the afternoon. He will pick her up at the office at a quarter to.

Don't think, hope for nothing, she says to herself, but the whole day long a little spring of excitement keeps on stirring in her. Not even Major Harrington, a most irksome old Englishman, whom she takes out to have a look at property in Wilderness, can annoy her in the least. Nothing that's on the market is to his liking. If he sees something he likes the look of, he wants to buy it and when she tells him it's not for sale, he says, 'Everything is for sale at a price, young lady.'

At one o'clock he asks her to lunch, but it's more a command than an invitation. A command she obeys of her own free will, for he's actually only a big old lion that knows exactly where he wants to put down his big old paws. He no longer bothers about the conventions. When it's lunchtime you eat. When you want to ask a personal question, you ask it. If you don't like the answer, you say so.

130

She likes him. And after lunch she takes him to the large two-storey house on the lagoon that she has saved for last. But he is not taken in by her ploy. He congratulates her on her choice of trump card and says, 'It's a happy place.'

And the valley below Nick Wehland's smallholding is a happy place too. After they turned off from the highway, they took a dirt road through a pine plantation for about two kilometres, and then down a steep slope to the little valley covered with natural forest. One moment they were in a world of dry pine needles, the next moment in the green, damp shade of a place where fairies could live because man had left them a bit of old forest there. It had a brook running through it, and it was overgrown with the most beautiful ferns . . .

'Nick tells me he bought the place from a German chap.'

'When we come back, I want you to stop down here for a bit.'

'Why?'

'It's pretty.'

'I see.'

The road climbs back up a hill and back into pine plantation. At the top, in the open and against the slope of the hill, stands the house: a neglected house with a faded blue roof. Behind the house is an old corrugated-iron shed where four coloured women are busy packing huge fern leaves into cartons. Stacks of the dark green leaves are lying on wire frames waiting to be packed.

'Where's Mr Wehland?' Jan asks the nearest woman.

'He's gone to the airport,' she answers, stiffly.

'To the airport?' Jan reacts with surprise. 'But he's expecting us!'

'He's gone to dispatch the ferns.'

'Oh,' he says, relieved.

From the moment he picked her up he's been acting

guilty, long before he's done anything. As if he is looking over his shoulder to see if anybody's watching him take a step away from the straight and narrow. They had even driven out of town by way of the back streets, to avoid being seen by his wife with a strange girl in the car.

'Well, I suppose we better wait around till he comes, then,' he says, lighting another cigarette. 'I hope he doesn't take too long. I've told my wife I'm going to deliver a car, and I won't be late.'

'Are you afraid your wife?'

'I wouldn't call it that; it's just that I don't like to upset her – there's never been any trouble between us.'

'Where do they pick all these ferns?'

'Nick's got a team picking them down at Knysna in the forest. It's about half an hour's drive from here. He exports them.'

'Don't they die in the boxes?'

'No. They're called seven-week ferns – they're tough. I believe they're used for flower arrangements overseas.'

'Here as well.'

'Perhaps we should go and sit in the shade on those chairs next to the house. What do you think?'

'Yes.'

The mountain peak above the town looks much nearer from here. It stands like a colossal presence to the north of the house. It's a different mountain peak from hers, taller, but pierced by railway tunnels, and there is a tall metal structure high up on it like some kind of monster.

'What is that peak called, Jan?'

'I don't know. We call it George Peak. Have you ever crossed it by train?'

'No.'

'I took my wife and children over once. There are seven tunnels. In places the train runs so close to the edge of the precipices, it makes your hair stand on end. I hope Nick doesn't keep us waiting too long; I'm all keyed up.'

It's better in the shade. 'I sometimes drive up to the

lookout point at the top where you can see all the four passes that cross the mountain,' she says. 'It gives you courage to see where people used to go over in their wagons. They must have been extremely brave.'

'That's more than I can say for myself at this moment.'

'Would you leave the country if you could, Jan?'

'No. Actually, I don't know. Perhaps. Things are looking bad for us. They say the blacks are not only asking for one man one vote now, they're saying "one white, one bullet" as well. God knows what's to become of us. And our children. Where are we to go? What will it all cost?'

'A lot of money for a family like yours.'

'Exactly.' He sits up and points in the direction of the pines. 'Look, there's a pick-up coming now . . .'

Nick Wehland is like a big, clumsy dog with a moustache. Dark hair, thin at the top, curly and long round the ears. He does not look drunk, but he smells of alcohol; he's direct and rather blunt.

'Listen here, girlie, let me tell you straight out, I don't want any trouble.' He does not invite them into the house, but joins them in the shade. 'Jan reckons we can trust you; I say women are loose-tongued creatures and loose-tongues are to be kept away from certain goods.'

'I understand what you're saying, Mr Wehland.'

'My name's Nick. And first of all I want to know why a girl like you wants to get involved in something illegal.'

'For personal reasons.'

'I don't trust personal reasons. Are you in debt?'

'No.'

'Have you stolen money that has to be repaid?'

'I don't like the tone of this conversation; you're insulting me.'

'A man never knows what daft ideas you women might think up. Say, for instance, I arrange the delivery of the stuff and you go and report me to get the reward you're entitled to?'

'What reward?' Jan asks, nervously.

'Why do you want to know?' Nick retorts, brashly.

'I only asked.'

She takes him to be about the same age as Jan – perhaps not quite a worker's stone, more a yellow stone for a merchant or a farmer. 'I'm afraid,' she says, 'I don't think I'm interested in the so-called "goods" any more.'

Nick turns to Jan. 'How come she is talking like this now? I thought you said she could sell for us?'

'Wait, wait, wait – I said she only wanted to *see* you to begin with.'

Nick turns back to her. 'What do you see?' he asks.

'I don't know.'

'Then you better make up your mind. I can organize us a smart deal. There are two men coming down to Oudtshoorn with a load of sheep. They'll be there on Sunday.'

'How many can I buy for about R17 000?'

'Depends on what you want. Possibly four good ones. I would suggest – *if* I decide to trust the two of you – that you first make sure about your buyer. I don't want to sit with the stuff burning a hole in my pocket.'

'You won't.'

'Who's your buyer?'

'That's *my* business.'

'I don't want to eat the bloody guy! I only want to know where I stand.'

'Other people have trusted me. If I decide to buy, you will have to trust me as well.'

'If the two of you drop me . . .'

'No, man, we won't!' says Jan, throwing away a cigarette end.

'Maybe heaven knows why I should take your word for it, but I certainly don't.' He looks at them, clearly struggling with indecision. Then he says, 'OK, I'll phone. As soon as they arrive in Oudtshoorn, I'll drive over to check if everything's all right. Then I'll phone and you can come over early on Monday morning.'

'Why can't you buy them and bring them to us?' she asks.

'Seems to me you haven't got much in your head, woman. It doesn't work like that. Would you send someone else to buy you a pair of shoes?'

She can't help wishing that it was Piet Sinksa, not Nick. 'I'm not sure. I'll have to think about it first.'

'If you're not sure, you should drop it.'

'I need time to decide.'

'You have until tomorrow evening. I can't leave it later than that. My brother has to arrange everything up there.'

'It sounds as if more and more people are involved.'

'Listen, you either trust me or you don't. Say the word, and the deal's off.'

'Wait!' Jan steps in hurriedly. 'You two can't sit here fighting over everything. When we've given our word, we stick to it.'

'Listen, Jan,' Nick says with a grin, 'in this game you trust no one's word. Say, for instance, we buy the diamonds. That means you and I have to give ours to her to sell. Right? That means she can turn round and say her handbag got stolen or something. We have no law on our side, and it's easy money for her.'

'Forget it,' she says, getting up.

'No, wait!' Jan cries. 'Nick was only joking!'

The tunnel mountain is beautiful and green. Every rock on it is clear, every crevice. In the gorges, pockets of forest still survive, most probably because it was too high for the woodcutters to go.

Behind her Nick Wehland asks her to sit down.

'You know, of course,' he says, as she sits down on the edge of the chair, 'that once you've established a strong front *and* back door, no diamond detective will be able to get to you.'

'What do you mean?' Jan wants to know.

'If you have a safe supplier and a safe buyer, who is there to give you away? I know a man – he's stinking rich from diamonds – if a police stooge walks in, makes no difference how good he is, he phones the police right away and tells them there's a man trying to sell him diamonds, and will they come and collect him. Just like that. Because he has his supplier and his buyer, his front door and his back door. He is so safe, you won't find a crack anywhere at all.'

'Is that a fact?' Jan sounds very impressed.

'Yes. But it's not easy to get those doors in place. I tell you again, girl, I don't want any trouble. If Jan hadn't said that you already had a buyer, I wouldn't have been interested. However, should things work out, we could possibly think about setting up a little company . . .'

'I will not be part of your company, Mr Wehland, I won't be here.'

'And where, may I ask, will you be?'

'As far as possible from here.'

'Then be a sweetie and give us an introduction to your buyer.'

'No.'

'If I take a guess at his name, and I guess right, will you tell me then?'

'I might.' She is sure he won't know.

'A certain Venter chap at Mossel Bay?'

She does not answer.

Her own mountain is clear and very blue when she gets out of bed the next morning. Just once, she says. Just once. Please.

It's not that she doesn't trust Nick Wehland; it's different this time because it's a definite, planned transaction. Neither Jan or Nick will allow her to keep the diamonds for a few days. They don't understand that she has to play with them first, that Samuel Sundoo will not buy diamonds that are unhappy.

She did her sums during the night: together with all the outstanding commissions she has R20 500; the maximum she can spend is R17 000. She has to pay her rent and have money for petrol; she must eat.

But she has made up her mind she'll buy.

And she's come to terms with the fact that she will have to go over the mountains via Oudtshoorn to get away. How else could she do it? How much longer can she go on waiting in a flat that's not even an ark now, but a prison? No. She's done it for more than two years. Working. Hoping. Anticipating. Two years of struggling to get across a river, trying to grow enough feathers for her wings so that she can fly away. God knows why she had to be born in this country!

Her mother phoned her shortly after the beginning of the year. It's usually her father that phones. Her mother said, 'I am deeply shocked by this absurd decision of yours to leave the country, or rather to run away from the responsibilities that we must all face – as you did from university! A tree that bears no fruit is wicked in the eyes of the Lord ...' Squabble, squabble, squabble ... 'South Africa is still a land of milk and honey ...' 'No, Mother, of golden syrup and Cremora; milk and honey have become too expensive ...' 'Don't be cheeky! We, as your parents, forbid you to go ahead with this nonsense!'

Please, Mother, don't.

Two nights later, Marian phoned. 'Don't tell Mother, but Charl-Pierre says he's been thinking about leaving for a long time.'

Thursday. Friday. Saturday. Sunday.

Four days to wait.

It's hot. It hasn't rained for weeks. It's as if the year does not want to gather momentum. Everything is hazy, the mountain as well.

She had waited for Piet Sinksa for a long time and hope had gradually died away. She only has to wait for Nick

Wehland for a short time – but with all the intensity of uncertainty and excitement. Nick said he would phone on Sunday night between eight and nine to say whether everything was all right. Whether she and Jan should come to Oudtshoorn on Monday morning.

She goes to work. She goes home. She eats and sleeps. It feels as if her life has reached a closed gate, and she's waiting for the key. The key is Monday. And Thursday morning at eleven o'clock, when she has her appointment with Samuel Sundoo. She phoned him and said she was sorry to bother him again, but this will definitely be the last time. She told him that she might be bringing quite a few.

One thing she knows: when she walks away from Samuel Sundoo, she will not have much farther to go.

At the moment, however, Jan du Toit keeps phoning her every few hours to ask if she hasn't heard from Nick yet. He knows very well that Nick will not ring before Sunday evening and that he is down at Knysna with his fern pickers, but Jan wants to make quite sure.

On Friday afternoon, Elvin gives her a cheque for the amount of all her outstanding commission.

On Saturday morning, Jan walks into her office with a cake-tin under his arm. He does not speak normally, he whispers. In the cake-tin is a canvas bag containing his R10 000 in cash.

'A precaution, Araminta. Just in case. I can't take the money home – my wife will see from my face that I'm hiding something from her. She always does.'

'Don't you think I should go alone, Jan?' Diamonds won't be happy with him . . .

'Nick said we should each buy our own shoes. I can understand that you can't expect anyone to take risks for you. May I smoke?'

'Yes. And for heaven's sake, please stop acting like a child that's afraid to jump, but doesn't want to back down either! You'll make yourself a nervous wreck.'

'You're right. We must think positive. Be optimistic. I took a course in that once.'

'Wonderful. Apply it.'

'I told my wife I'm getting a lift to Oudtshoorn to fetch a car. It's true. So I must bring back a car, if you don't mind.'

'I don't mind.'

'And please don't phone me at my house on Sunday evening. I'll phone you when my wife's in the bath or something.' Tap-tap.

'You've told me that a hundred times already, Jan.'

'Do you think this is going to work out?'

'You've asked me that a hundred times as well.'

'I know. I'm sorry. It's just nerves . . .' Tap-tap.

'As long as you don't get on *my* nerves on Monday.' She doesn't want to be rude to him, but Jan du Toit would upset anyone. 'Go and buy yourself a sedative and take it early on Monday morning.'

'I wish I could be as calm as you are. Aren't you afraid that something might go wrong?'

'No. Because nothing is going to go wrong.'

'I'm a church officer. A man of faith. If only I knew whether it is proper to ask God's help when buying diamonds . . . What do you think?'

'You'll have to decide that for yourself.' In her heart she wonders if it's a sin to wish that he would have the runs on Monday morning . . .

Sunday.

She can't sit at home all day. She decides to go to Herolds Bay for a picnic and a swim.

An hour later, when she passes the airport, a huge, silver-bellied Boeing is coming in to land, so low above the road, she feels she could put out her hand and tickle it. As it nears the guard-fence, she wants to square her shoulders and say, 'Careful! Your wheels are going to touch the wire . . .' Then it's safely over and it lands smoothly on the runway like a big metal bird.

It's the omen she has been looking for, the eagle by the road, the harbinger that has come to say, 'It won't be long before I come and pick you up and fly away with you inside me. Faraway. To the land of the green valleys between the mountains with the snow on their peaks, where cows wear bells and moss grows on the slate roofs of the houses on the slopes . . .'

She's not stupid. Cows leave dung in the road. Roofs of slate leak and snow is cold. But in the land of the green valleys between the mountains you need not be afraid of a wall falling in on you, or of lightning waiting to strike you.

The tide is out. The sea is at rest, smooth and lazy. When she parks her car by the beach, she sees that someone has hacked down the sign that said 'WHITES ONLY/SLEGS BLANKES.'

Three

IF LIFE IS SEVEN storeys high, she must be climbing down quite a few steps to get to the diamonds.

In the end she sets out for Oudtshoorn without Jan. Nick Wehland phoned to say they must meet him at eleven o'clock at the hotel just outside Oudtshoorn. The 'goods' have arrived, everything's OK. Later, when Jan phoned, they decided that she would pick him up at the garage at half-past nine. It's just over an hour's drive to Oudtshoorn. At seven o'clock that morning, however, a most bewildered Jan du Toit was sitting with her in the flat: unshaved, his hair not properly combed, wearing one green sock and one grey one.

'Araminta, I tell you, I've had a hell of a night. I didn't sleep a wink. If something happens to me, what's to become of my wife and children? I don't know what is going to happen to them in any case, because I don't know how much longer Dirk and I can keep the wolves at bay. But at least I want to be with them. I know I can't expect you and Nick to buy for me as well, I don't expect you to take any risk on my behalf. Call me a coward if you like. I deserve it. But just before dawn this morning, I opened the Bible in my darkest hour, and the first words my eyes fell upon were: "*A prudent man foreseeth evil, and hideth himself.*" Just like that, as if Solomon was pointing his finger at me.'

She couldn't help feeling sorry for him. He was just a

big, frightened man who had realized that it was too high for him to jump down. Even his hands seemed too limp to hold a cigarette. She asked if she could make him some coffee: he said no thank you, would she just return the cake-tin ... When she told him to leave the tin, that she would buy diamonds for him and sell them and see to it that he got his fair share, he went down on his knees, asking her if he could kiss her feet. She told him not to be silly and to get up from the floor. He got up and said God would bless her for it.

At half-past nine she set out alone.

But she admitted to herself that she been hoping until the last minute that Piet Sinksa would still turn up.

It's cool. The mountains are in cloud up to their thighs. Long before she reaches the top of the pass, she enters the eerie white stillness of the mist. She likes it, it's peaceful. She actually woke up that morning with a feeling of peacefulness. Of completion. Like the morning she had woken up in the hall of residence knowing that that was the day when she would get up and start walking in a different direction. Because she had to. Because she realized she was a bird in a cage, but that the door was open, although she was still beating vainly against the bars.

She had got up that morning and started packing her belongings. Then she had taken a taxi to the station and gone home. Every possible reproach had been slung at her; they were pleading with her for hours – praying for her. In the end her father had threatened to take her back by car. She had told them she couldn't go back, she must start to earn money. She had to. The 'had to' was inside her. Like courage.

She had got the job at George, but from the first day she knew that it was just a bigger cage and she would have to stay in it for a while. When the man came and put six uncut diamonds on her desk, she had not realized it would turn out to be a short cut for her as well.

*

The higher the road goes, winding up the mountain, the thicker the fog gets and the more slowly she drives. Tiny drops of mist cling to the ferns in the rock crevices along the road; the mountain reeds look like long, ghost-like plumes. A cluster of wild watsonias makes a sudden splash of orange. It's beautiful. She wants to stop and walk in the mist to feel the droplets on her face, but she can't; women on their own on mountain roads get raped.

Jan du Toit had turned back because Solomon told him that a prudent man sees the approach of evil . . .

What evil?

She'll close her mind to it, grab the diamonds and run with them to Samuel Sundoo's. If the fog is still on the mountain when she returns, she'll stop and hold the diamonds out of the window so that the little drops can fall on them too.

It seemed to her that Samuel Sundoo had sounded a little friendlier when she phoned him to make the appointment. Almost as if he was glad to hear from her. She made the appointment for Thursday. On purpose. So that the diamonds could stay with her for three nights and two full days. She had given the African violet some plant food and cut out the old leaves. But when she goes to Cape Town, one little diamond will stay behind on a leaf.

In her skirt pocket is an extra R2 000 which she had withdrawn from the bank. Nick had said that the men had brought enough to make a good choice from. After the main transaction, she is going to buy a diamond for herself, to keep! Not as a talisman, but as a little magic stone which contains millions of years of light from all the stars that spin around the earth – or with the earth – through the sky. She will take it with her wherever she goes. And a little bag of African soil . . . for it to sleep in at night.

She had told Elvin on Friday that she is leaving. Not where she was going to, only that it would probably be quite soon.

143

He was shocked. 'Are you going back to university?'

'Why does everybody keep asking me that?'

'Do they?'

'Just about.'

'Could I persuade you to stay on with us?'

'No. I'm sorry.'

'Not even if I tell you that I've heard from a very reliable source that they're expecting extensive development here in the southern Cape, as a result of the oil and gas strike in the sea at Mossel Bay?'

'Oil and gas in the sea can't save us, Elvin.' She didn't want to get into an argument, she just wanted to add something. 'According to one of my clients, it's just another colossal and expensive gimmick to provide employment.'

His eyebrows gave a little twitch. 'It's funny to see you angry for a change!'

'I don't really get angry any more, but I get afraid sometimes.'

'What are you afraid of?'

'That things in this country might suddenly take a turn for the worse – before I've made enough money.'

'Strange, I always wondered whether you came to Carr & Holtzman to work or to hide – I never suspected that you suffered from the white fear syndrome. Not you, Araminta.'

'I don't have a British passport as you have, Elvin.'

'If it weren't for the Afrikaner's stupid, age-old dreams of the republican ideal and exclusiveness, you would have had one.'

'If it weren't for the Afrikaner's stupid dreams, we might all have had Russian passports now.'

'At least we would have been welcome in more places.'

'You don't really mean that.'

'I suppose not. It's been a bit of a shock to discover that you want to leave us. And I would never have suspected you of racism or ultra-conservatism.' From the twinkle in his eyes, she knew he meant it as joke.

'I'm not sure I know what that means. Words are walls

144

which I cannot see through. I don't even know what justice or injustice is any more; I no longer believe in either of them. What are the masses shouting for? Is it freedom, or is it simply the right to live in a state of anarchy?' She realized that she was taking the conversation in the wrong direction, but couldn't stop herself.

Elvin looked at her in astonishment. 'Are you telling me that you've been in a state of quiet revolt, right under our noses all this time, and that we haven't noticed it? That *I* haven't noticed it? I always know when Lizzie and Christel have problems. I help when I can, even if I'm just a shoulder to cry on. I was under the impression – as the others are – that our pretty, clever Araminta is getting over a love affair. Now I find out she's involved in a far more serious conflict than I would ever have guessed! It shows you we don't know one another. That is the whole problem in this country: we don't trust one another.'

'Don't jump to conclusions, Elvin. I'm not rebellious any more, but I still need to get it off my chest sometimes.'

'Stay with Carr & Holtzman; we don't want to lose you, Araminta.'

'Thank you for asking me. And thank you for having given me the work in the first place. I know Bernard had doubts about appointing a woman, that it was you that convinced him to give me a chance. Lizzie told me.'

'We've never regretted it.'

'Neither have I.'

'What are you going to do now?'

'I hope to have enough money so that I won't need to work for a bit – give myself time to decide where I want to live and so on. And then find a nice man,' she added, so as not to let him get too close to the truth.

On the other side of the mountain the sky is clear and the sun is shining. In the distance lies the next range of mountains: the Swartberg Mountains – 'black mountains', although they're always pretty blue.

She is scared. Not scared in the way that Jan had been. But scared that her car will break down and that she won't get there on time; that Nick will turn out to be another Piet Sinksa; or that the diamonds will not be right, that Samuel Sundoo will say he does not want them.

At twenty minutes to eleven, she stops at the hotel. It's hot. The shrill, incessant sound of sun beetles hangs in the air ... She sees Nick coming from the main building and gets out of the car.

'Where's Jan?' he asks abruptly.

'He couldn't come.'

'*What?*' he cries, taking a step back as if he wants to run away.

'He asked to be excused.'

'And you agreed?' He makes it sound as if she has committed a terrible sin.

'He got scared.'

'And you're so bloody stupid, you believed him?' He's raging mad, he smells of drink.

'Nick . . .' He frightens her.

'You've gone and got us into a fucking trap, woman! By this time he's reported us for sure. We'll have to cancel the whole bloody deal!'

'Nick, please ... I didn't realize it was such a bad mistake.'

'I said right from the start I don't trust no bloody woman!'

'You're overreacting! Jan is the last person that would want to get us into trouble. He gave me his money, I told him I'd buy for him as well. You're quite wrong.'

'Do you know to how much trouble I've gone to? If these people are walking into a trap because of your stupidity, there's going to be big shit, I tell you.'

She forces herself to stay calm. If he gets too upset, he won't see reason. 'Jan has a wife and children, Nick, he decided to get out for their sake. Please try to understand that.' He puts his hands in his pockets, takes a few steps to the left, to the right, looks up in the direction of the entrance to the hotel grounds, watching the car that has turned in and is coming towards them. He keeps watching. The car stops, a man and a woman get out and walk into the hotel. 'Jan will not land us in trouble, Nick. You've got to believe me.'

He seems to be deciding whether to run or to stay. At last he says, 'Come on then.'

It's a country hotel: all the rooms are round thatched cottages. There are small goats and geese and ducks in a large enclosure. Peacocks on the lawns. She walks to the back of the car and takes out the cake-tin and the bag which holds her own money.

'Come on!' He hurries her on, a bit more composed. She follows him through the rows of cottages to one in the furthest row: number 12. He has the key. He opens the door and walks in ahead of her.

It smells of thatch. There's a jacket and a newspaper lying on the bed. It does not look as if anyone has slept there, unless they have cleaned the room already. The curtains are drawn.

'Sit down,' he says, closing the door. 'We must get the money sorted out.'

'I've counted Jan's money, it's R10 000. Mine is correct too.' She wishes that he would open a window so that more air could come in. It's hot and close.

'They're bringing quite a lot, so that we can pick and choose. To start off, we'll spend an equal amount: R10 000 each. That's what I've told them. If we're satisfied with the deal, I'll buy you the biggest bargain of your life from the extra R7 000 you've got – but keep quiet about it, we'll have to soften them up first.' He looks at his watch. 'We must get ready.'

She can't decide whether she should tell him about the diamond she wants to buy for herself. She's afraid of saying anything that will make him flare up again. For the moment, she only wants it to be over because she doesn't like the situation, but she's there because she has chosen to be there.

He opens the cake-tin and starts counting Jan's money. He does it with the practised skill of a bank clerk. There is sweat under his arms. She wants him to open a window ... He counts the money a second time. Then he takes her money and counts out R10 000; the extra R7 000 he puts in the inside pocket of the jacket and puts it on.

'Watch me,' he says; 'with this I'm going to buy you the biggest piece of luck you've had in your life.'

'Where's your money? Or aren't you going to buy any more?'

In answer, he pulls back the bed from the cane bed head and takes a canvas bag from between the two mattresses. Barclays Bank. He pushes the bed back in place before he shakes the money out on the cover. 'Have you made arrangements with your buyer?'

'Yes.'

'For when?'

'For Thursday, as I said.'

'Why you want to sit on the bloody things till then, heaven only knows.' He puts all the money in the Barclays Bank bag and then tucks it behind the pillows on the bed. He looks at his watch again.

'What time is it?' she asks.

'Ten to. I'm going to get myself a drink. Do you want anything?'

'You can't go out and leave me here alone, you said they'll be here at twelve!'

'I'm not getting the fucking drink from a shop in town, I'm getting it from the bar inside! Or do you want me to order room service and advertise what we're doing?'

'Please hurry up, then!'

'You don't open the curtains, you don't go out of the room, you wait right here for me.'

'Please hurry.'

*

When he's gone out, she goes and sits on the bed. It's quiet, nothing but the sound of the beetles comes through the walls and the roof . . . Next to the door is a window; if only she could open those curtains. A round place feels different from a square place. How do you build a round place with square bricks? If only she could open a window! There's a lilac and brown carpet on the floor; it looks as if the dirt has dried in large circles when it was washed . . .

Was that a knock at the door?

Surely somebody had knocked on the door. Softly. Perhaps it was Nick. She walks to the door; there's no one on the other side of the peephole. She must have imagined it.

But she's hardly got back on the bed when she hears it again. When she opens the door, they're standing close to the curve of the wall, hesitant and unsure: an elderly man in khaki clothes who looks as if he has just come from a sheep-pen. His trousers are held up by a string, his shirt is clean, but faded from too many washings. The younger man does not look much better.

It's them. She knows it. Relief, gladness, fear – because Nick isn't back yet – all go through her at once. 'Good afternoon,' she says, holding the door open for them.

'Is Nick here?' the old man asks, cautiously. His hat has left a furrow on his forehead; his hair is grey and has clearly been cut with a pair of household scissors.

'Please come inside, Nick will be here any minute.' They are plain people, but good people. The mouth of the younger one is hanging open – perhaps he's a bit retarded. 'Come inside.' They don't want to come any nearer. 'Please, come inside.'

'Why isn't Nick here?' the old man wants to know. He's suspicious.

'Nick's just gone to the bar to get himself a drink. My name is Araminta Rossouw. I'm with Nick, you can trust me.' The young one moves first. 'Everything's all right, you can trust me.' As if she were luring them in. When they're inside, she wants to close the door and lock it –

149

suppose Nick takes too long and they want to leave again? She must reassure them, put them at ease. 'Please sit down on the bed or wherever you want to. I'm sorry I don't have something cool for you to drink. It's hot, isn't it?'

'Yes.' The older one sits down on the bottom end of the bed, twirling his hat round and round in his hands. The young one looks around inquisitively and puts his head round the bathroom door.

'Hell, Pa, you should come and see how many towels there are!' he calls out in surprise. 'White. Like cotton wool.' He's definitely stupid. But sweet.

'We told Nick we'd be here at twelve,' says the old man.

'I know. He'll be here right now, I promise.' In her heart she shouts: 'Nick Wehland, please hurry up, they're going to go!'

'A man should keep his word.' The old man's getting angry.

'I agree, uncle. And I apologize. I really do.'

'He's gone drinking, Pa. Aunt Poppy says he drink a lot.'

'Nick said there would be three of you. He and another man and a woman.' The old man is getting uneasy . . .

'That's right. But the other man couldn't come any more, so I came on my own.' Please don't go, I know you've got the diamonds. 'You can trust me, uncle, really you can.'

'I said twelve o'clock. It's past twelve o'clock now. Tell Nick we've gone . . .'

'Wait!' she stops him as he gets up. She grabs the bag with the money from behind the pillows and holds it out to him. 'See, uncle, here's the money! It's R30 000, you can trust me.' He does not seem to want to take it! 'Please, I've *got* to have the diamonds!'

'What does a young girl like you want diamonds for?' he asks, warily.

'I want to sell them, I need the money for something that is tremendously important to me!' Please, please . . .

'Give it to her so we can get out of here, Pa.'

Thank you.

The old man takes the bag with the money. From his shirt pocket he takes a plastic coin bag: Standard Bank. There's a lot in it. Her hands are shaking; she has trouble getting it open. She sits down on the bench at the dressing-table . . . they roll out into the palm of her hand: the most beautiful little crystals . . . some are at least five grains of barley, more . . . a few are so clear she can see right into their depths . . .

She bends down and puts her cheek against them. Magic. A feeling of joy rushes through her and she gently closes her hand round them . . . But there's something wrong with them, there's no gladness in them.

Why do they feel so dead . . . Are they glass?

'Uncle?' There's a hand pressing down on her head, trying to push her under the water. 'Uncle, are you sure these are diamonds?'

He swings the bag with the money between his legs. 'What do they look like? Don't tell me you haven't seen diamonds before.'

She bends down and puts her cheek against them again: they *are* diamonds. But there's something wrong with them, there is no joy in them.

When she looks up, it's no longer the 'uncle' either. It's a different man. The younger one too. Their faces have changed. The older one gets up and puts out his hand as if he wants to take the diamonds away from her. 'Sorry, lady, playtime is over, I'll have to take them back and introduce myself: I'm Major Kruger of the diamond detective branch and this is my colleague, Lieutenant Botha.'

The hand pushes her head down, down, down.

'You are arrested on a charge of illicit diamond dealing . . . You are free to keep silent or to make a statement. Anything you say may be used in evidence against you . . .' It's the voice of the retarded one. She sinks lower and lower and lower.

Four

THERE IS AN INSTANT where the sense of shock stops and the fear begins. There is an instant where fear stops and a sense of powerlessness takes over, when you are confronted with the law that says you may not buy or sell or be in possession of uncut diamonds unless authorized . . .

You're trapped. You've gone down a one-way street and you cannot go back and make the wrong right. The nightmare keeps on repeating itself in your mind . . . over and over . . . You don't wake up, you *are* awake. You have fallen into a pit of mud and terror lives there. You're trapped within your own body; if you try to escape, you're dead.

Your way home is a grey, tarred road that rolls away from you, while the nightmare goes on and on repeating itself.

There is an instant where powerlessness stops and despair begins; when you weep but there are no tears.

The colour of fear is black.

It was a police trap.

You walk between them to their car. A white Cortina. The worst shaking is in your legs; you think you're going to fall. They carry the cake-tin and the bag with the money. The goats in the enclosure bleat at you, the geese laugh. You have to sit in the front, and they drive into

152

town with you. You are under arrest. There are many people in the streets, tourists in stupid clothes with cameras on broad, coloured straps round their necks like flat snakes. You don't want to be under arrest. They must stop the car so that you can get out and walk with everyone else in the streets. *Please, let me get out!*

You don't cry it aloud, you cannot say anything.

They're taking you to prison. You think they are. The one that was the old 'uncle' at first drives the car. Nick is also in the car, he sits in the back with the idiot. Nick is also under arrest. He came into the room, quite jolly and with a glass in his hand, greeted them with a cheerful 'Yes! Yes! How's it going?' When he realized something was wrong, he said, 'You bastards.' So they said he must come along too.

They drive you through tall iron gates. It's not a prison, it's a large, grey, modern building. At the back of the building there are large grounds; in the far corner stands an old house that has been neglected. The garden is overgrown. They take you into the house. The rooms are offices. No bars. Bare floors creak with every step; you cannot breathe properly. Heads peep curiously round door frames as if at something unusual.

It's definitely not a prison, the room they take you to has no bars either. The window is open. You could jump through it and run away. An almanac hangs on the wall; it says '*Kelly's tyres are tough.*'

Nick is taken to another office. You don't see him again.

Major Kruger and Lieutenant Botha are with you. They are very friendly; you are the bird they have caught in the gin, now they want to play with you. Give you tea. Want you to like them.

They say, 'Young lady, if you plead guilty, you will make it easier for yourself and get it over quickly. If you plead not guilty, it will be a long-drawn-out affair. Plead guilty, and we'll try to have your case brought before the court today.'

You tell yourself to say, yes, guilty. You make a statement, they help you with the words. You sign your name, but it doesn't look like yours.

They take you deeper into the house to a smaller room. There is a table. Lieutenant Botha squeezes sticky black stuff from a tube on to a flat, square tin and rolls the sticky stuff with a little roller to spread it out. He rolls and rolls. You begin to realize – the most terrifying, helpless realization. You cry: Please don't! On another flat surface he puts a white form . . . takes your fingers one by one and presses them into the sticky black stuff. He tells you to relax and make your hand limp. You can't. Every finger is printed on the form: then all four fingers together. Both hands.

You say to yourself: don't make such a noise, crying. You can't help it, they have robbed you of a secret.

They show you where to wash your hands with pink jelly soap from a cup without a handle. Everything round the wash-basin is black. Every crack in the basin, between the tiles above the basin; the taps as well. You wash and wash, but the ink will not come off – it's got into you.

They fetch you, walk you to the building in front – the police station! You're under arrest. One constable shouts to another: 'Hey! Come enter her in the cell register; I'm busy.'

Back to the white Cortina and out through the iron gates. You keep your hands tightly closed on your lap, you're afraid to see the ink. They drive you down the street and say you're in luck, they've got you in at the court. There are people in the streets – they are not under arrest.

You must wait in the quadrangle at the court building. The walls are made of blocks of stone. You stand with your face to the stone so that you won't see the people looking at you. You stay there till they come and fetch you for your case to be heard.

The courtroom is like the inside of a church. Except

that the Eye that watches you is not up in the roof, but on the bench, in the magistrate's face: pale green eyes that glare at you as if they can't stand the sight of you. He reads the charge against you, asks if you realize the seriousness of the charge. You nod your head. You cannot take in all the words, your head feels big and heavy ... The magistrate says bail is granted in the sum of R500 and the case against you will be heard in this court on Friday 7 March. You are to be present on that day at nine o'clock ...

There is R2 000 in the pocket of your skirt. You ask to be taken to the cloakroom: you wash your hands, but the ink will not go away. You count out the money for the bail, they show you where to pay it and give you a receipt.

Then you are free to go.

No, not yet.

The idiot takes you back in the white Cortina to your car at the hotel. 'Promise me you'll drive home carefully, especially over the mountain.' As if he's concerned about you.

'What's happened to Nick Wehland?'

'Don't worry about Nick, worry about yourself.' He leans to the back to get the cake-tin and puts it on your lap. 'Here is my telephone number; if there is any problem, or if you feel like talking, even if it's later tonight – remember, we can do a lot to have your sentence reduced. I'll come and visit you in any case. I know we can rely on your cooperation.'

You don't ask him what he means, you just throw down the piece of paper with his number on, get out of the car and slam the door behind you as hard as you can.

Five

SHORTLY AFTER HALF-PAST five, she drives into George and goes straight to Jan du Toit.

The moment she places the tin on the desk in front of him, she knows it was not him. In her heart she had begun to believe that his guilty conscience made him report her and Nick in the end. But it was not him. He's too glad to see her.

'How did it go?' Anxious, hopeful . . .

'It was a trap. I've been caught.'

For a moment he stares at her blankly. Then the truth dawns on him. 'Caught?' he asks, stunned.

'Yes.'

'You were *caught*?' As if it hits him a second time.

'Yes.'

'And my money? What about my money?'

'They took it together with Nick's and mine. It's confiscated.'

'Oh God, don't tell me that! It's borrowed money!' he shouts, ripping the lid from the tin. When he sees it's empty, he looks up, his eyes so filled with fear that she cannot bear it. 'I've got to pay it back!'

'I'm sorry, Jan.'

Some time during the night, she falls asleep, still wearing her clothes. When she wakes up, it's daylight and she wants to close her eyes and go back to sleep, but she can't. Her mouth tastes foul. She hears herself groan when she gets out of bed.

She does not open the curtains. She never wants the mountain to see her again.

She's dizzy, she must eat something. But she cannot cut the bread because the ink is still on her hands. As if she had been branded.

She has a bath and washes her hair. Standing over the bath, rinsing her hair, she slowly reaches the moment where rebellion begins. She asks herself, 'How did I get into this! How am I going to get out of it?'

With the towel round her hair, she walks to the window and jerks open the curtains. The mountain stands tall and serene over everything. 'Mountain,' she confesses, 'I've got into the most terrible mess.' He looks at her without a trace of reproof on his old rocky face, and lets her cry till the first, faint stirrings of courage begin to break through the panic inside her.

She must dry her hair, get dressed and go to see Nick. Thank God, the R7 000 was not in the bag, they didn't lay their hands on that. They'll give her the choice of a fine, they won't put her in prison . . .

Mountain, they will not send me to prison, will they?

A cloud comes over his face.

Friday 7 March. That's three weeks from now. A new wave of panic starts to engulf her. Somehow she will have to stay on her feet and get out of this! And get her hands clean. She mustn't think about tomorrow; she must take one step at a time and keep on going.

First she must see Nick.

She feels bad about Jan's money. Nick's too. But he hasn't got a wife and children, he can sell ferns . . . If only she had waited until he came back, if only she hadn't given the bag with the money to the man!

If, if, if. What's the use?

It wasn't Jan. Could it have been Dirk?

She must get to Nick.

When she gets to the valley where fairies can live, all the beauty has been drawn back inside itself, it doesn't speak to her. It hides behind a thick glass wall, because she has horrible black ink on her hands.

The same four women are packing ferns as she walks up to the shed. Nick stands with his back to her by the nearest packer. He seems not to hear her coming; one of the women looks up briefly, and then goes on with her packing.

When she's about halfway between the house and the shed, she hears Nick scolding the women. 'I can't turn my back for one bloody day and trust you to carry on on your own! I told you I wanted Saturday's and Sunday's ferns packed when I got back from Oudtshoorn! But if I'm not here you just spend the time bloody fucking and boozing and . . .' One of the women makes a sign with her head and he spins round. 'And what the hell are you doing here?' he asks, without drawing breath.

'I've just come to tell you that it wasn't Jan,' she says, shaking.

He storms right up to her. 'Listen here,' he hisses, with clenched teeth, 'I don't want to hear another word from you or Jan du Toit! So get into your car and get off my property!'

She steps back because she's afraid that he will strike her. Behind him the women look on without a trace of emotion. 'I'll go as soon as you give me my money.'

'What money?' He throws it down as a challenge.

She's scared, but she doesn't let him see it. 'The R7 000 you took from me in the cottage and put in your pocket.'

'Don't come here with a bloody shit story, I took no money from you!'

Nick Wehland is a dirty wall rising up in front of her. She knows she can't make it budge an inch, whatever she does. It will just make her hands even dirtier.

*

When she gets out of her car at the flat, Lieutenant Botha gets out of the white Cortina behind her. Another stone wall.

'Hallo, gorgeous!' he greets her. 'You never thought I would come visiting you this soon, did you?'

No, she didn't.

When she was in primary school they discovered a cat in the classroom one morning. One of the children had probably smuggled it in. A ginger cat. Someone closed the door and the boys started chasing the cat. Over the desks, under the desks, the teacher didn't come and stop them! The cat got frantic. There were red scratch marks on the boys' hands and arms, but they would not give up. When the cat starting clawing his way up the corner between the blackboard and the curtain, she started screaming. When the teacher came, the cat was so terrified he just crouched in the corner, a large wet spot spreading under him. At break-time he saw that the door was open, and he fled.

Ever since, whenever she thought of the cat – even after all these years – the most awful feeling of anguish would come over her.

As it did now.

He takes his time, browsing through her flat with his hands in his pockets, looking at everything. When he comes to the books on the shelf, he stoops down for a while and says, 'Clever girl, hey?'

She does not answer him. She did not invite him in, and she did not invite him to sit down.

He's a tall man. Light brown hair, no longer parted in the centre as it had been when he was pretending to be retarded. His eyes are blue. His nose must have been damaged long ago: a scar runs down the bridge and it makes his face look cracked.

'Do you like cats?' She has to know.

'I'm a dog man. Bull terriers.' He picks up the porcelain bowl that stands on the bookshelf and studies it carefully. 'Must be quite old, hey?'

'Yes.'

'One day, when you don't want it any longer, remember to give it to me. I collect old stuff.'

'It belonged to my great-grandmother. I was named after her.'

'I was wondering why they had given you such a silly name. Why didn't they change it to Ami or something?'

'It's none of your business.'

'Bit of a spitfire, aren't you?' He sits down on the chair at the table, his back to the mountain. She sits on the bed. 'Don't frown at me like that, young woman, I'm here to help you. I was only doing my job, yesterday, as you do yours: selling houses.'

'Couldn't you just have given me a day in which to recover from the shock?'

'Remember the saying: strike while the iron is hot? Do your family and friends know you've been caught?'

'No.'

'That's something in your favour; it increases your usefulness.'

'Your decoy, Nick Wehland, has stolen R7 000 from me.'

'Is that a fact?' As if it's a joke.

'He took it from me, pretending he was going to buy me an extra bargain at the end. Then he went out to get himself a drink, giving you people time to get me.' She had worked it all out: Nick Wehland had been acting as if he were surprised and shocked when he came back; they never said they had arrested him. They just said he had to come along too . . .

'You should be careful, making allegations like that, you know. Can you prove that he took the money?'

'No.'

'I suggest that you take up the matter with him then.'

'In other words, he not only gets the reward money from you, he also gets away with the money he has stolen from me.'

160

'You will have to take it up with Nick Wehland. I know nothing about him. I'm here to help you so that you can help yourself in the end.'

'How?'

'By being a little pleasanter, in the first place. By accepting that you've been caught, coming to terms with it and cooperating with us.'

'In what way?'

'If you help us to arrest a certain man, we'll tell the court of your assistance, which the magistrate will take into consideration when he has to sentence you.'

'Is that what Nick Wehland had to do?'

'Forget about Nick Wehland. Look after yourself. Only last week, a man got a sentence of seven years' imprisonment in Windhoek on a charge of illicit diamond dealing – his first offence. Without the option of a fine.'

She keeps her face as impassive as she can so that he will not see the fright he has given her. 'Did they catch him with a lot of diamonds on him?' She has to ask.

'I don't know. But I promise you it's the truth. And I'm not telling you this to scare you, I'm telling you because I don't want to see it happen to you.'

'What must I do?'

'I've told you: help us to catch a certain man.'

'Who?'

'Your buyer.'

'I beg your pardon?'

'Take us to your buyer.' It's a cordial command.

'My buyer?' She tries to sound incredulous in order to play for time. *A name you never reveal, even if they put a gun to your head.* 'What buyer?' she asks, as innocently as she can.

'Come now . . .' Coaxing. 'You know very well who I'm talking of. The man to whom you sold Dirk Holtzman's diamonds, to whom you would have sold the others.'

'He's dead.' She says it without thinking – it's all she can think of in her dismay.

161

'Ami . . .'

'That is not my name!' she snaps at him, still playing for time. Her hands begin to sweat.

'Very well, then. Let's say I believe your little joke – tell me who he was when he was alive. I could take some flowers to his grave.'

Trapped. Jan du Toit with his loose tongue would have given away everything to Nick Wehland! She feels she wants to scratch and spit like a cat. She must find a way to escape! *How?* 'Whoever told you that I sold diamonds for Dirk Holtzman was talking through his hat.'

'You're a damn good liar for a clergyman's daughter.'

'If you know so much about me, you should surely know my so-called buyer's name. I suggest you send Nick Wehland to him to lure him into a snare for you.' Something tells her: spit and fight, they don't know who you sold the diamonds to . . . 'I can assure you, Lieutenant Botha, that I have stolen nothing from anyone. I wanted to buy a few diamonds with the money that I had earned, but I was prevented by the law made specially to protect the interest of the mining magnates, which says: "Woe unto the man who dares to touch a diamond unless they, the magnates, put it on the table for him! Woe unto the man that touches the diamonds that their forefathers came lying and stealing for in this country."' She knows she's making a fool of herself. He is sitting there with his legs crossed, calmly swinging a foot; he knows the door is barred, the cat can't get out.

'Missy, you're ingenuous. You should never have allowed yourself to get into a situation like this. It's not for children.' As if he is really feeling sorry for her. 'And you're very pale – did you get enough sleep last night?' As if he's truly concerned about her. 'I'm not here to scare you, I'm here to help you. This is a game for sharks, my girl, no one's going to help you unless you're prepared to swim with the others. I suggest you go and lie down for a while, take a good rest and have a good think. Then I'll come back and we'll talk. We might even take your buyer a few nice flowers this very evening. Or early tomorrow morning. Then it will all be over. We will testify to your cooperation and show the magistrate you've done something to assist us.'

Talking to her like a brother.

He closes the door softly behind him when he leaves.

She's the bird in the snare, the cat in the corner.

They want someone's head from her. They think that it will be someone living near by – perhaps the man at Mossel Bay. They don't know about Samuel Sundoo.

Will an attorney know what she should do? How much does an attorney cost? Will Joop Lourens know? No, he must never find out.

Her appointment with Samuel Sundoo is for Thursday morning at eleven – the day after tomorrow. Is this coincidence? A door that's been left open for her to escape through? With which to buy a lighter sentence?

Everytime she hears or thinks the word 'sentence', it is as if a snake is striking her with its poisoned fangs. Seven years for a first offence without the option of a fine? Did he make it up in order to scare her? Surely they won't send her to prison. They have to give her the option of a fine . . .

Where will she get the money to pay it?

Mountain, I'm afraid!

Stay calm. Think. Would Samuel Sundoo hesitate to trample on her in order to get himself out of trouble? No. If you're an Afrikaner you expect to be trampled on anyway.

Is Samuel Sundoo a descendant of the Indians that Britain brought here by the boatload? To come and work for the British colonists in the sugar plantations in Natal, where the Zulu refused to work for them?

Does Sundoo know about that, or has he forgotten?

Most of them were recruited in the slums of Calcutta or Madras: Coolie No. 1, Coolie No. 2 – Coolie No. 200 . . . Coolie No. 100,000! Because their names were unpronouncible to the British, they were given numbers.

She goes and sits at the table, resting her head in her hands. She knows she will destroy Samuel Sundoo to save herself. She has to.

It wasn't for the Boers that the Indians worked at ten shillings a month. It wasn't the Boers that tormented them during the day and crowded them into mud and corrugated-iron shacks at night, with holes in the ground for toilets and dirty water to drink. It was the British.

If Samuel Sundoo came in at this moment, she would tell him that it wasn't in the parliament of the Boers that it was decided that they were not a 'civilized race', but in the parliament of the British colony of Natal. It was not Boer documents that stated that they had to be kept apart from the white colonists, that they had been brought to Natal like mules and oxen or machinery: to work. Suggesting that they be sent back when their work contracts expired, because they didn't belong here.

Few ever went back.

What else would she tell Sundoo? That they arrived in their thousands between 1860 and somewhere early in the new century, and quickly learned to hate the colonists. When their contracts expired, they went off and started little shops: today a pumpkin carried under one arm, tomorrow a home-made cart on wheels, the day after a little shack with a roof on.

It wasn't long before the news reached India that pumpkins were selling well on the toe of Africa. Suddenly a fresh throng started to arrive from India: businessmen of a higher station – with money and expertise. Perhaps Samuel Sundoo is one of their descendants?

They came, buying the others' shops and putting them out of business. Within five years they were prospering and putting their grievances before the Colonial Secretary

164

in London. They complained about the brutality of the colonial police; the injustice of the colonial courts; the curfew. They started agitating for political rights, civic rights . . .

The British colonists were getting worried. The 'coolies' were increasing at an enormous rate. At the same time, resentment was gathering in the hearts of the Zulu people. They believed that when someone fights you and wins, taking what's yours, you submit, and wait until you're strong enough to take him on. If you win, it's his turn to submit. The Indians, they said, fought for nothing and defeated no one, they came to the land of the Zulus as slaves for the colonists and now they were getting fatter and richer by the day!

So the Zulus started plundering them, burning down their shops, raping the women, killing the men. And the violence spread, like a fire burning more and more fiercely. Next the stupid white colonists were sending in troops of white policemen with guns – not to help the Zulus, but to save the Indians.

And in the end everyone hated the Boers.

When Lieutenant Botha comes back, it's almost dark. She tells him he may take her great-grandmother's bowl, if he still wants it. The man to whom she has sold the diamonds is dead. He says, 'Now you're asking for trouble, lady. Big trouble, because you're messing around with me now.' She just keeps quiet. He says, 'You better start praying – the bloody sun's gone down for you!' She says nothing. Then he takes the bowl and walks out.

She couldn't give Samuel Sundoo away – she had given her word to Joop Lourens.

Six

SOME TIME IN THE SMALL hours of the night – like a tiny bubble of air rising from deep down – she remembers a picture she had seen in a book once.

It was soon after the spitting episode, before she had realized that she would have to prepare to leave the country.

It was a picture of a leper walking through a deserted village at the dead of night. Round his neck was a leper's bell so that people could hear him coming and get out of the way. It was cold, it was snowing. He was walking with a stick, his back was crooked. With him was an old woman, leading him by the hand. Because she was with a leper, the people were avoiding her too. The only light in the picture was a ray of warm yellow light coming through a window, and the leper was standing in this light.

No matter how dark it is around you, the picture said, there will be a ray of light from somewhere.

When dawn begins to break, she knows that she has no choice: she will have to go out and buy herself light.

At half-past ten the same morning, she pushes open the glass doors saying Visser, Malherbe & Visser, Attorneys. She does not know any of them, but she knows that one of them is a friend of Elvin's.

Inside, it feels like a doctor's waiting–room. The woman

at the reception desk looks up over glasses fastened to a string round her neck. She could be trying to decide which illness you have.

'Can we help?' Businesslike.

'How much does it cost to consult an attorney?'

'Our usual consultation fee is R75 per half hour or part thereof.'

'I would like to see an attorney, please.'

'There are three attorneys here. Which would you like to see?'

'It doesn't matter.'

'If you tell me what your problem is, I can refer you to the most suitable one.'

'I should like to see the cleverest one.'

'All three of them are clever. Otherwise they would not have been lawyers.' Snotty.

'Anyone, then.'

'Well ... I can make you an appointment with Mr Malherbe for three o'clock this afternoon.'

'I want to see one *now*, please.'

'That is not possible. Mr Leon Visser is in consultation at the moment; the other two are not back from court yet.'

'I'll come back at three.'

'Name?'

'Araminta Rossouw.'

'I beg your pardon?'

'I'll spell it to you.'

Three o'clock. That means a wait of five and a half hours. She can't go home, for she's afraid Lieutenant Botha will come back. She has phoned Elvin to say that she wouldn't be in the office today. He said it's all right, he understands. Understands what? Has Jan told Dirk, Dirk told Bernard, and Bernard told Elvin?

What if she goes and asks Elvin if she can stay on at Carr & Holtzman and he says no?

How did I get into this?

How is she going to while away five and a half hours? What is she going to do if Elvin says they don't want her any longer? If word gets out, not even the opposition will want her. She could go and work at an estate agents in Cape Town . . . how much will it cost to move there, how much more will she have to pay for her rent in the city?

Seventeen thousand rands' worth of wing feathers lost at a go. Shit. How could she have landed in this mess?

No, she doesn't want to live in Cape Town. She does not want to live under an angry mountain. Table Mountain, backdrop to the mother-city, the beautiful 'castle in rock', is a very angry mountain because he can never sleep. They shine strong lights in his eyes every night so that people can look at his beauty in the dark as well. He calls out for help, he cries out in fury, with fire after fire, but no one hears. As a student she had never wanted to go into Cape Town with the others at night.

Where is she going to find feathers for her wings again? *I'll grow myself new ones.*

They won't put her in prison, will they? What if she can't pay the fine? She walks faster. She can't go and ask her father for money. Or Joop Lourens. Why did she have to do it!

Eleven o'clock.

Twelve o'clock.

She can't keep on walking like this. She must go and sit in a café, order a pot of tea and take as long as possible to finish it . . .

'SEVEN PEOPLE BURNED ALIVE – BLACK TOWNSHIP VIOLENCE', says the newspaper hoarding at the entrance to the café. 'MORE SANCTIONS', says the hoarding on the other side. She walks past them.

How much longer is it going to take her to get away now? What if she has to find other employment and can't? Unemployment's rising by the day. She can't go without money.

Two years' work in a canvas bag, given to two stoolpigeons! Plus R7 000 in the third one's pocket.

*

She knew there was something wrong with those diamonds the moment she had them lying in her hand. Samuel Sundoo would not have wanted them. Once anger has moved into a diamond, it is no longer good, no matter how beautiful it is . . .

'Once upon a time, there lived a very beautiful diamond,' she tells the plumbago hedge, the ash trees on the pavement, the stones, herself. 'It was the largest, finest blue diamond in the whole world – until they stole it from its setting in the head of a god in India. The diamond became very angry and misfortune fell on everyone that possessed it after that; one of its owners was devoured by wild animals. When Louis XIV, King of France, bought it, he had it cut and faceted, making it about half its original size. It was he who revoked the Edict of Nantes, which meant that the Protestants were persecuted once more, and some of them fled to the Cape where their blood was needed to make a new people.

'When the king died, it was of a strange and terrible illness. Perhaps it wasn't because of the diamond, though, but because of the hundred whores he had had as mistresses.

'Louis XVI inherited the diamond, and he was guillotined. After that a man by the name of Thomas Hope bought the stone and lost everything he had – which was a lot, because he was a millionaire. At last they locked away the diamond and its wrath deep in the British Museum.

'Anger that's locked in for too long gets worse and worse . . .'

Two o'clock.

How tired she feels!

There *was* something wrong with those diamonds; Samuel Sundoo would have noticed it. . .

There is something in diamonds, one can feel it. They radiate something. They say that if the sick drink water in which the famous Koh-i-Noor diamond has been dipped, they will be healed. It was 900 barley grains, that Indian diamond. But it was stolen too, and taken to Persia where its curse fell upon one shah after another. It took revenge on all its owners until it was taken back home to India. But by that time, Britain had won the struggle for power in the East and was ruling over India. And over the Cape. So the Koh-i-Noor was sent to London, where it was cut and faceted and polished and set in a royal crown, and kept behind a thick glass wall in a dark tower. Most of its anger had by now been cut away, for only 106 grains remained of the original stone.

How much is going to be left of her by the time she gets out of this mess? The question confronts her like a challenge; she tries to find it an answer, but cannot. All she feels is a growing sense of outrage within her.

She waits outside on the pavement in front of Visser, Malherbe & Visser's offices until it's three o'clock.

The woman takes her down a short passage; at the end is a door on which it says 'Koos Malherbe'. A warning in bold, black letters.

'Please be seated. Mr Malherbe will be back soon.'

Stacks of folders, bookcases reaching up to the ceiling, rows of uniform books like soldiers standing in line, guarding dark and complicated laws. Two enormous desks. Walls covered with paintings and certificates in narrow black frames; a robe thrown over a dumb-valet in the corner.

The room is filled with the fear that people have left behind, and she has come to add hers to it. It is a place where the guilty and the innocent come to buy hope. How many times had she opened the rectory door to someone coming to her father for help! Some cried even before they reached his study; others never cried. But on every face was reflected the anxiety or the hatred or the grievance with which they had come, and some of it always stayed behind when they left. It was a cloud that you could feel, but not see.

And Koos Malherbe when he enters seems to issue a warning, sending it out ahead of him, saying it with his body: 'I'm every book on these shelves, I am the law come alive, I can save you or let you drown.' He's not thirty, he's not forty. He is not exceptionally tall, but he looks as imposing as a tree: dark, attractive mouth, eyes that warn you anew. If she had to draw a picture of him, it would be with red crayons. When he walks round the desk and sits down on his throne of charcoal-coloured leather, she realizes that it is not a ray of light that is falling over her, it is the icy cold shadow of a rock in the heat of day.

'Araminta Rossouw,' he reads from the folder the woman has left. When he looks up, it is as if he were looking at sinner number 100, or 200, or 1,000 . . . 'What can I do for you?' he asks. Very professional.

'I'm in trouble.'

'What kind of trouble?'

'Illicit diamond dealing.'

He looks at her sharply, as if she had just changed into a different creature before his eyes. 'I beg your pardon?'

'It's true.'

'When?'

'The day before yesterday.'

'Where?'

'In Oudtshoorn.'

'Where do you live?'

'Here in George.'

'Do you work here?'

'I sell property for Carr & Holtzman.'

'I thought I'd seen you somewhere. I go and see Elvin at the office sometimes.'

'Elvin doesn't know that I've been caught. At least, I hope he doesn't. I want to know if they can send me to prison without the option of a fine because I've refused to cooperate with them. I want to know what they do to you if you haven't got money to pay the fine . . .'

'It's your first offence, then.' This is not a question.

'Yes. I don't want to go to prison.'

'Relax. It's not the end of the world. Tell me what happened, just tell me the truth and start from the beginning.' It's another warning.

For a moment she does not know where 'from the beginning' is. 'From the beginning' is when you're born, long before you're born perhaps. From the beginning can be tomorrow. It would be best to begin with the Shirleys.

'In October last year, a man and a woman walked into my office . . .'

When she's finished, he leans forward on his arms. 'Miss Rossouw. Araminta. If I put everything you've just told me together, there are a few things that make no sense. Unless I can make sense of them, I can't help you. In the first place your apparent stupidity does not fit with your obvious intelligence; also I would like to know where you got R17 000 to buy diamonds with.'

'I had another R2 000 in my pocket.' She says it on purpose.

'There's not much happening in the property market at the moment, so where did you get it from?'

'The market's not as dead as all that. I saved it out of commission that I've earned. I'm not a thief.' I'll sleep with you if you help me. Please.

'How old are you?'

'Twenty-five.'

'How long have you been with Carr & Holtzman?'

'Two years and two months.'

'How many young women of your age in this town, do you suppose, have been able to bank R19 000 over the last two years?'

'I didn't buy any clothes, I didn't buy anything for the fun of buying it. I've just bought the absolute minimum.'

'You'll gain nothing by getting cross with me. If I am to find extenuating circumstances for you, you had better help me.'

172

'Can I go to court without a lawyer?'

'We'll decide about that later.'

'If you get the option of a fine, but you haven't got the money, can you pay it off gradually?'

'That can be arranged. But don't get the idea that it's a dress account that gives you six months to pay. What's the date of the trial?'

'The seventh of March. I've got enough money to pay you for this consultation, but not for a court case.'

'What makes a girl like you decide to smuggle diamonds?'

'I didn't *smuggle* diamonds! I only wanted to buy diamonds in order to sell them at a profit, so that I could get money more quickly for a specific purpose.'

'What purpose?'

'To leave the country.'

It's a hit. She sees it in the way he sits back in his chair, in his apparent surprise at discovering for the second time that she hasn't got the disease he had thought she had.

'Why do you want to leave the country?'

'Because I cannot see how any political leader will ever succeed in getting thirteen different nations – depending on how you count – though any Rubicon in this country.' She knows she's reacting with the brashness of fear because she has no other weapon against his unrelenting rectitude. 'Even if Moses came and parted the waters for us, it would make no difference, for on the other side there would still not be enough money for everyone. And because there isn't enough money for everyone, millions live by stealing and plundering and murdering and lying and all sorts of things to get hold of money – and the rest pretend they're alive, while they're living behind stronger and stronger bars. I'm sorry if my answer was a bit longer than you have expected.' He looks at her as if she is a child who has been allowed to get something off her chest. He doesn't say a word. 'If you're trying to make some kind of diagnosis, I'll gladly tell you more!'

'What?'

173

'Have you got any idea, Mr Malherbe, of how many billions of rands the world has already given to the oppressed of this land? How many millions goes from us, the taxpayers, to them? How many millions are being sent by the Arabs to keep the revolution going in order to get a black government into power, so that they can obtain the uranium they need for the nuclear bomb they want to make in the Middle East?' She gets a feeling that she's not impressing him . . .

'But all the money that's pouring in makes no difference, it's still not enough. In the meantime the government governs less and less and the country's creditors more and more, while cabinet ministers and bureaucrats are filling their own pockets as fast as they can. The few really wealthy people are getting their money out to Switzerland in case they have to flee. On the one side of the stage stand those that are pleading for economic stability because it's the prerequisite for peace and good government; on the other side of the stage stand those that are asking for international sanctions and boycotts so that the money supply dries up, because according to them the state must be bankrupted if we are ever to have peace and stability. There was a time when I thought communism was the answer, that everything should be divided equally, but that works even less well. So I can't be bothered to worry about what's right or wrong any more. Right and wrong, truth and lies are concepts that have become so confused in this country that no one will ever get them unravelled again. I wanted to buy the diamonds so that I could go and live in another country.'

'Is that a fact?' Like an amen.

'Yes. And besides, Africa no longer wants white children, and the world can't wait to see the last of the Afrikaner.'

'Really?' Cynical, like a second amen.

'Yes!' Maybe she had been given the stupidest of the three attorneys . . .

174

'Where did you plan to go?'

'Probably to Switzerland. Perhaps Austria. I would have been packing at this very moment.'

'So what will you do now?'

'I must get out of this mess and start again from scratch.'

'Is that why you wouldn't give away your buyer? Because you're hoping to go back to him with more diamonds later on?'

'No.'

'Are you sure?'

'Yes.'

'Can you see yourself repeating this whole political diatribe in court, arguing that you needed the money in order to leave the country?'

'I'll say it on my knees, if it will help.' And I'll sleep with you.

'Suppose I'm the magistrate, and I say to you that it's a poor argument, given the fact that there is a wonderful future waiting for everyone in this country, provided that we are prepared to break down all the barriers, make sacrifices, reach out to one another in friendship and forgiveness – that running away is for cowards?'

'Then I'd say: "Your Honour, you are dreaming, you are just like my father." '

'Who is your father?'

'Ignatius Rossouw.'

'What's his profession?'

'Minister of the Dutch Reformed Church.'

'Where?'

'Bloemfontein.'

'Brothers and sisters?'

'One sister.'

'Occupation?'

'Teacher.'

'Your mother?'

'Organist in my father's church.'

'Excellent. You must bring up your father's standing as mitigation. Under no circumstances will you go and repeat this other story in court. Magistrates don't like emotional political recitals. Especially not when delivered by a woman.'

'It wasn't a political speech.'

'I don't care what you call it, just keep it out of court. You'll put on the oldest dress you have and do your hair in a plait. A single plait, not the latest ones with dozens of rows: a good old-fashioned one. You'll go without a lawyer because it will be to your advantage. I know the prosecutor, I'll speak to him in the meantime. The day before you have to appear in court, 6 March, I'll brief you here in my office to prepare you. You'll go and tell the court that you're sorry and promise never to do it again. Your father will tell you that the Bible says, if you land up in the power of another, it's best to plead and beg in order to save yourself. You've done a stupid thing, now you'll have to be clever in order to get out of it as best you can.'

'I'll do as you say.' Your Honour.

'In the meantime, when you have nothing else to do, reflect a little more on the so-called complexity of money – it seems to be a subject that intrigues you. You might even discover that it's actually far more simple than you suppose. Lieutenant Botha, or one of his colleagues, will probably visit you again; make sure that it's not out of stubbornness that you're refusing to give them your cooperation.'

'It's not.'

'Diamond detectives are not the kind of men that allow silly girls to play games with them. And, incidentally, you were a fool to give away your great-grandmother's bowl. When you go out, make an appointment for 6 March at reception.'

Telling you it's time to go.

But she feels better.

176

She has a little more courage with which to try and get on with her life. First of all, she has to go back to work as if nothing has happened. If they know, they know. If they don't know, she won't tell them.

They do know.

She realizes it the minute she walks into the office. She sees it in Bernard and Lizzie and Christel, beaming at her, over-friendly; she sees it in their eyes that don't lie. And it is all over Elvin's face when he calls her to his office.

'Major Harrington, your client for the Wilderness property, was here to see you yesterday. He wants you to cancel his option on the house, as he's going into hospital for an operation tomorrow.'

'I hope it's nothing serious.'

'At his age, any operation is serious.'

She had been so sure that that transaction would go through; the commission it would bring was her speck of hope, if she has to pay a fine . . .

Elvin picks up a pen and starts to make doodles on the desk pad in front of him. 'Araminta,' – he does not look up – 'don't you think there's something you ought to tell me yourself?'

'If I'm an embarrassment to Carr & Holtzman, I'll leave.'

'Then it's true?'

'Yes.'

'I'm sorry.' He puts the pen down and looks up. 'I'm sorry if I have been instrumental in this, if I started it when I told Bernard about the Shirleys. I can't tell you how bad I feel about this.'

'It was my own stupidity that got me into this mess; there is no need to feel guilty, Elvin.'

'In spite of what you say, I still feel responsible.'

'Who told you what happened?'

'Bernard. Dirk had to call a doctor to the garage for Jan; his wife must not find out. But what surprises me

177

most is that you could have trusted a man like Nick Wehland. He's the biggest fern thief there is – he even picks them at night, and they can't catch him. They say he's not only picking ferns, he's plundering and destroying the forest as he goes, and making stacks of money, selling and exporting them. You'll have to get yourself a good lawyer.'

'I have.'

'Who?'

'Malherbe of Visser, Malherbe & Visser.'

'Koos Malherbe can be tough as hell, but he's a good lawyer. Promise me you'll tell me if there's anything I can do.'

'Do you think I will be able to live it down in the town?'

'Of course. At the risk of overestimating myself, I might say that, as a member of the city council and chairman of the hospital board, I do have some influence that I can use to make things a bit easier on you.'

'Thank you. What I actually wanted to ask, is whether there's a chance that I could stay on at Carr & Holtzman's.'

'I was hoping you would.'

'That's decent of you, Elvin. Thank you.'

Seven

THE DAYS ARE STREAKED with light and dark: more darkness than light.

Darkness is Ralph Linde walking into her office on the Friday morning, closing the door behind him. 'They could have knocked me over with a feather!' he exclaims. 'Araminta Rossouw, you're the cherry on the cake! Why didn't you tell me you were looking for diamonds? I could have brought them to you on a tray.'

'Go away.'

'Never send away your good fortune. How many do you want? I've got an old black friend, he can bring us a cupful. Tomorrow. Minimum four-carat beauties. Where do you think Klaas Muller got the money from to start that paint concern of his?'

'Go away.'

'What I can't figure out, is how you got involved with a riff-raff like Wehland. You know that he spent five years in jail for diamond smuggling before he came here? What possessed you? The moment the dust settles round you, I'll arrange us a proper deal. The only problem is to get a genuine buyer.'

'Ralph Linde, I promise you, if you come near me with anything illegal, I'll report you immediately.'

As he gets up, he says, 'Well, when the magistrate clobbers you, as he will, you'll know where to find me. See you!'

*

A ray of light comes on the Monday night when Lizzie and Christel knock at her door, cheerfully holding up a chocolate cake and a bottle of champagne.

'I bought the cake!' says Christel.

'And I bought the champagne!' says Lizzie.

'I haven't deserved this.' It's the first time that anyone from Carr & Holtzman has ever been in her ark, and for the first time she's sorry that she hasn't got two easy chairs.

'Whether you like it or not,' Christel announces, 'we've unanimously decided it's time to make you come out of your shell. We're finding you a man as well.'

'Wait a minute . . .'

'You wait until you see our list of possibilities!' Lizzie cries, and starts to ease the cork out of the bottle. 'Let's get some glasses!'

'I really can't afford to get involved with a man now,' she owns up after they've toasted her. 'I've lost all my savings. I've got to start again from scratch.'

'Man-time's at night, when you *don't* work!' Christel states with determination.

It's like the old times, the night-time sessions when she was a student: talking, laughing, gossiping – eating. Then she had had to hide her confusion and rebelliousness from the other students; from Lizzie and Christel she disguises her uncertainty and fear, knowing that everywhere clocks are ticking off the minutes to 7 March.

She laughs with them, chats with them; they pour the champagne, they cut the cake. But the two of them are together, while she is on the outside. And the 'subject' is carefully avoided.

'We've put Herman Johnston on top of the list of possibles for you,' Christel confesses.

'Who's he?'

'An architect's draughtsman. He's already asked Elvin about you several times.'

180

'Is all this Elvin's idea?'

'What if it is?' Lizzie asks. 'You don't know what people are really like until things go wrong. You, for example. We always thought you were the quiet type, recovering from a disappointment – I mean ... who would have suspected that you were into diamonds and ...'

'Herman's a really nice man,' Christel interrupts, loudly and quickly. 'He's good-looking, he's the right age, everything. Elvin's planning one of his super three-yearly dinner parties, inviting us all – plus, of course, Mr Johnston!'

'I'm afraid there's only one man I'm interested in at the moment and that's Koos Malherbe.'

'That stands to reason,' says Christel. 'But that doesn't mean to say ...'

'Do you know anything about him?'

'He's a bastard,' says Lizzie. 'My mother's cousin worked for him and his wife before they got divorced.'

It was gossip time. 'They weren't married a year,' Christel adds, 'when he threw her out. Just like that!'

'Threw who out?'

'His wife.'

'And then?'

'She divorced him.'

'How long ago was that?'

'Don't know,' says Lizzie.

'Six, seven years ago,' Christel reckons.

'It's good to know ...'

'Please don't get involved with him.'

'I *am* involved with him; he's the only hope I've got.'

'Let's tidy up,' Christel says, getting up. 'I promised my husband I wouldn't be home too late.'

When the three of them are gathered at the kitchen end of the room, Lizzie's curiosity apparently gets the better of her. 'Araminta, if you don't mind me asking: are they nice? The uncut ones.'

'Take a cloth and help me dry, Lizzie,' Christel orders.

'I'm only asking.'

'Yes, Lizzie, they are nice. Very nice.'

'I've only seen them in pictures.'

'Pictures can never show the real magic of them.'

'I would like to have a two-carat set in white gold,' Christel admits.

'I would like one big one set in ordinary gold,' says Lizzie.

They don't ask her what she would like.

After they've left, she puts out the lights and opens the curtains. The mountain is a pale silhouette against the night sky. It is sleeping.

There is something she has to face and think through: Koos Malherbe. For the first time since Frans de Villiers, she has deliberately reached out to a man. With Frans she did it playfully, challengingly. Shall I or shan't I? Will he or won't he? Infatuation – first love – heaven on earth. When she reached out to touch Koos Malherbe, it was from something akin to revenge. Why? Was it a case of hitting out instinctively at someone who was looking down at her from above?

Yes.

And no.

Is it because he is untouchable, behind an impenetrable wall of glass, and not a Frans de Villiers that was there for the taking? Is there something wrong with her, do 'forbidden' men turn her on? Or is she simply the bitch her mother had said she was?

No.

Koos Malherbe can show her that her hands aren't too dirty for a man like him to touch . . . She needs to have his approbation.

How?

What if she does not succeed?

She has to.

*

182

Every morning when she wakes up, she fears that this is the day Lieutenant Botha is going to return. And every night there's one square less on the calendar before the day of reckoning. The urge to start running becomes stronger and stronger.

Every night she says to herself: Tomorrow I'll sell a house or a plot or *something* – tomorrow – tomorrow – tomorrow. Elvin sells three houses; Bernard sells one of the best farms in the district, but all she sells is a cheap plot on the wrong side of town.

Every morning she warns herself not to panic. Every night she goes to bed with more panic in her heart. There ought to be a law that says you must be punished on the day of your wrongdoing! Every day you spend waiting for your punishment is a slow torture that breaks down your very life, your dreams – a vulture tearing the hope from your flesh. It brings bitterness against Jan du Toit, Nick Wehland and the other two, pulling you deeper down into the mud.

They wait until it is nearly the seventh before they come, Major Kruger and Lieutenant Smith. Not Botha.

They don't come to her flat, they come to her office like two prospective buyers, and none of the others suspects anything. Major Kruger is wearing a suit; Lieutenant Smith is in overalls, as if he had just stepped off a ladder after painting a ceiling. Even his hair is speckled with paint. They're pleasant, polite; ask how she is, ask whether she has got herself a good lawyer, if there's anything she wants them to do for her. Can you get a cup of tea in this place? No. What about a little smile, then? Keep quiet, don't show them you're scared.

'Well, can we expect a little cooperation at least?'

'What sort of cooperation?'

'Something that will let us go and whisper in the prosecutor's ear, the day after tomorrow . . .'

'What sort of cooperation?'

'You know Klaas Muller?'

'No.'

'Come now; you don't forget an old lover as easily as that?'

How does one run away?

Do you know Klaas Muller that has the paint shop? Yes. We've heard that he's desperate to get diamonds. Perhaps we should do him a favour and take him a few? Most sardonic.

Don't do this to me, please. Don't let me do this to Klaas, don't take away the last of my self-respect. They don't hear her.

Lieutenant Smith takes a little plastic bag from his pocket . . . two, four, six . . . he shakes them out into his hand and holds them out for her to see. Six little crystals fit for a king and crying out to her to take them. She can't, the hand in which they are lying is the force that guards them. And her. They are just bait, containing the indignation she feels surging up in her, for she knows she's to be reduced to bait as well!

Don't think. Do what they want you to do. Do it blindly: swim with the sharks, swim with the stream in exchange for a magistrate's leniency.

Their plan is thoroughly worked out; Major Kruger gives the details and instructions. 'It has to happen fast. Muller must be up to his neck in it before he gets a chance to think. At a quarter to one, Lieutenant Smith walks into the paint shop: he's busy painting his house and has run out of paint. After five minutes, you walk in, Miss Rossouw. You tell Muller that the regular supplier you were waiting for has turned up with diamonds unexpectedly. Tell him the poor man came all the way from Upington by bus, that he's absolutely to be trusted, but you don't have money to buy. Tell him the diamonds are magnificent, the best you've seen – I promise you, the ones we'll show him will be even better than the ones we've got with

184

us. Tell Muller the man wants R25 000 for them, but you're certain you can bring him down to R20 000 ... You'd better take careful note of what I'm saying, miss, nothing must go wrong. Assure him that the diamonds will sell for at least R100 000. Play a strong suite. Soft-talk him, ask him to help you out, tell him you would hate to have to go to Dirk Holtzman. If he asks where the man with the diamonds is, say you wanted to bring him with you, but he's afraid of trouble. Push him. Say the man has to catch the three o'clock bus back to Upington, say you'll bring him after two o'clock. Don't leave before you have a definite answer from Muller.'

'And then?'

'At two o'clock one of my men will go back with you. With the diamonds. And don't even attempt to give Muller a warning. Lieutenant Smith is notorious for his eyes and ears, he'll be in the shop all the time, watching you. Help us to catch Muller, and you help yourself. Don't try anything you might regret.'

'What if he doesn't want to buy?'

'He'll buy.'

'Can't this wait until tomorrow?'

'No. You must do it now.'

'The moment we strike, you freeze right where you are. You don't utter a word, you simply pretend to be extremely surprised and shocked and leave the rest to us.'

'I know how to do that. I've seen Nick Wehland doing it.'

'Put Nick Wehland out of your mind. Help us to trap Muller, and we'll help you on Friday.'

'Couldn't it be someone other than Klaas?'

'Well . . . we'd still prefer your buyer, of course.'

'Forget it, he's dead.'

Don't think.

White Cortina. She's not under arrest, she sits in the back. People are walking in the street; they are not under

185

arrest. Klaas Muller will notice them when they come past with him . . . Mountain! The sky is grey, clouds are hiding him . . . Smith gets out of the car to walk the last few yards to the shop.

This is not happening, she says to herself; it's a bad movie I'm watching.

The white Cortina drives slowly round the block. When they get to the shop, an old truck pulls out of a parking bay, perfectly situated so that it's not right in front of the door. Did Major Kruger nod to the driver? Has that been planned as well?

'OK,' he says, switching off the engine, 'go in and clear the way for us.'

Don't think, get out, start walking – even a pool of mud has a bottom somewhere. Klaas is standing talking to Smith between the shelves at the back and does not see her coming. Smith sees her. 'Believe me, my friend,' she hears him saying as she gets close enough, 'I'm halfway through the last room and we have to move in. I've been to every paint shop in town, and not one of them has any Old Lace in stock.' He looks disappointed, completely at a loss. 'Do you have a colour that would match it?'

'The closest would be Ivory. Perhaps you should do the whole room with that.' Klaas tries to help, still not noticing that she's a few steps behind Smith.

'Perhaps I should think about it. Help the young lady first, I'll look around for a while.'

'Araminta!' Klaas says in surprise as he turns round.

'Hallo, Klaas.' I can't do this.

'You're the last person I expected to see – excuse me a moment, sir . . .' Smith has already disappeared round the end of the shelf; she knows he's in the next aisle, his ears and eyes lurking somewhere between the tins of paint . . .

'I wanted to come and see you to say I'm sorry – Ralph's told me. I couldn't believe it at first. What went wrong?'

'Impatience. Not holding out, not waiting for my regular supplier.' I can't do this to you. 'That's why I'm here. I don't quite know how to put this to you, but I'm in a difficult situation.'

'Say if there's anything I can do.'

Look at what I'm telling you with my eyes. 'As a matter of fact, it's to do with my supplier. He showed up unexpectedly from Upington with some beautiful diamonds and I'm not in a position to buy at the moment. I haven't got the money. He wants R25 000 for them, but he's hard up. I know he would come down to twenty. I was hoping you could help him.'

'Hell, you're pushing me into a corner a little fast now,' he says, anxiously. 'How safe is this man?'

Where's Smith? How much is he able to hear and see? 'If I had waited for him, I would not be in the mess I'm in right now. He's safe.' Look at my eyes!

'Can I come and see you tonight?' A hint of eagerness has crept into his voice.

'That's part of the problem. He's catching the three o'clock bus back, and I don't want to take him to Dirk Holtzman.'

'Hell . . . this is a bit fast. Where's the man?'

'I can bring him to you.'

'Has he got the diamonds with him?'

'Yes.'

'You say they're good ones?'

'Very.'

'What do you think I'll get for them?'

See what I'm trying to tell you! 'A hundred thousand.'

'Wow!'

He sees nothing, he's already buying. 'I'll have him here at two o'clock.' I can't go through with this, I'll somehow have to make a plan . . .

She sees Smith coming round the end of the shelf. 'My friend!' he calls out to Klaas, 'I'll have to take your word about the Ivory – excuse me, lady. I'll tell my wife the Old Lace is a bit faded!' Ha-ha-ha.

Silly schmuck.

*

187

They pick Smith up in the next street, carrying the tin of paint under his arm. They laugh, they say she's the actress of the year, she's earned the longest drink in town.

Sit quiet, she tells herself, sit very quiet . . .

They don't drive her back to the office, they drive out north of the town. She asks, 'Where are we going?' Smith says, 'Unfortunately, we can't go and buy you a drink because you might be seen with us, but we do have a couple of beers in the car.' She says she has to get back to the office. It is absolutely essential. She has an appointment with a very important client who is coming at two o'clock, and she must go and make the arrangements. She cannot afford to lose the transaction, she needs every cent. She pleads with them, tells them they can go with her, stay with her, guard her if they wish.

They take her back and hurry her into the office.

Elvin and Christel are out at lunch, Bernard is probably in his office, Lizzie is at the reception desk.

'Lizzie . . .' she says very loud, praying that she will look at her eyes and catch on, 'my appointment with Dr Harrington is at two. Will you please phone him and ask him if he can change it to three o'clock. Explain to him that I haven't finished with these two clients. And could you get us some tea, please?'

'I was wondering if you had forgotten about old Dr Harrington,' says Lizzie, reprovingly. She has grasped enough. 'I'll bring you some tea right away.'

'Bloody white for a coloured girl, isn't she?' Smith remarks when they get to her office. 'Pretty too.'

They watch her, baby-sitting her. She has to put them at ease, she does not know quite how . . . 'I'm sorry you had to bring me back, but it's a really important client.'

'At least it's cooler here than outside. We would have brought you back to fetch your car in any case. This time you will go on your own and park right in front of the shop.'

'Who's going back with me to Klaas Muller's?'

'One of our other men. Smith will go with you and show you where to pick him up.'

'Will I be showing the diamonds to Klaas, or will he do it?' Win their confidence, if you can.

'It doesn't really matter.'

'Don't you think it would be better if I showed them to him?' Don't insist on it too much.

'Probably. We'll leave it to the other man to decide. He's the expert.'

Behind them Bernard walks up and down past the door like a watchdog. Lizzie would have told him that something was going on. 'If that's the best way, it's all right with me. Just promise me it will be over quickly.'

'Chop-chop.'

She says to herself: I'm scared, but not of them. It's not quite true, but it helps to keep her courage up. If Klaas Muller uses his eyes and his brains, she can help him, otherwise he will be in trouble too . . . Lizzie, please bring in the tea, she cries in her heart.

Lizzie arrives with the tea.

They drink up and talk about some wild party they went to the night before. They brag about how fast they drove over the mountain from Oudtshoorn that morning.

'Do you live in Oudtshoorn?' she asks. It's a quarter to two.

'No. We're not ostrich boys.'

Ten to. When she looks down, she can see her blouse moving with the beating of her heart.

Five to.

'I think we should make him wait until about ten past,' says Smith. 'Let him work up a good appetite.'

At last Major Kruger gets up and says, 'Come on!'

She takes her handbag and asks if she can go to the cloakroom first. The moment she has said it, they're on the alert, glaring at her suspiciously. She laughs and tells them not to worry, it's not outside the building,

189

and there's no telephone or even a window to jump through.

The man she has to pick up is waiting under a tree in York Street. A coloured man. The clothes he's wearing are old; the jacket is too big, his shirt is buttoned to the top. He looks kind and bewildered as if he's come from the backveld to bring a sick child or wife to see the doctor.

'Lieutenant Rensburg,' Smith introduces him as he gets out of the car.

'Pleased to meet you, Miss Rossouw. Let's go.' Professional. Strict.

'Where are the diamonds?'

'In my pocket. For the duration of this transaction, my name is Moses September. You will walk ahead of me. Don't try and give the man any hidden signs – I have men planted in the shop to watch you closely. We don't trust you.'

'If you don't trust me, why are you dragging me into it?'

'Don't give me any of your cheek. You need us more than we need you, because you have two problems on Friday: a formidable magistrate and an even more formidable prosecutor ... Put on the indicator when you are turning – keep your mind on what you're doing!'

Mountain! She can see it at the bottom of the street between two buildings for a moment; the wind has frayed the clouds round it. It can hardly see her through the haze.

A yellow Cortina pulls out from right in front of the shop, giving her the ideal place to park. And Lieutenant Rensburg is very crippled when he gets out of the car: one of his knees buckles alarmingly and she realizes that she is on stage with some very clever actors.

Klaas is standing inside the door; it's clear that he has been worried. When they enter, he gestures to them to follow him to his office. There are quite a few people in the shop, she notices. Don't look to the right or left, she says to herself, just keep on walking until you get to a chair so that you can sit down. Every drop of courage has left her since she picked up Lieutenant Rensburg. She's afraid that she might open her mouth and start screaming like the day the cat got into school; that the screams will come from her mouth involuntarily . . .

'Good afternoon, master.' It's Moses September, the humble coloured. 'My name is Moses.'

'Good afternoon. Hallo, Araminta. Please take a seat.'

Moses, the nonentity, sits down respectfully on the edge of his chair. She sits down on his left, Klaas on the other side of the table. He's tense.

'I believe you've got something to show me, Moses?' says Klaas.

'Master . . .' Troubled and beseeching. 'I was under the impression that everything would be ready when I got here. It's dangerous to try to sell these things like this.'

'That's true.'

'I didn't know about Miss Arri, I was only told when I got here.'

'I understand.'

'The master at the garage, Baas Dirk, bought from me some time ago, but now he wants to buy dirt cheap. I'm in a bit of a fix, master. Life is hard, I have two children in high school; I say to them, "If you don't get learning, you end up like me, hardly able to write your own name."'

A chill is creeping over her; but she is not going to scream, it's not the day of the cat. It's the day that Araminta Rossouw says, 'Do whatever you want with me, punish me as the law decrees; I can fall no lower. Not any more.'

'Show the master the diamonds, Moses,' she orders.

He has them loose in his pocket. They're unbelievably beautiful; one is almost bottle green and the others are clear and white. He holds them out for Klaas to see, an eager, captivated Klaas. She leans over and takes them from Moses's hand with the fingers of her left hand. She holds them tightly for a moment: there is no hatred in them. Nothing. Only sadness.

Then she swiftly rolls them over into her right hand and holds them out to Klaas. 'I told you they were beautiful, didn't I?' She counts to three. Then she puts them down in front of Moses September.

She does not look up.

'The green one is an unusual one, master. Rare,' Moses says. 'I can't take less than twenty-five for them.'

'Mr Muller said he'd give you twenty,' she says, sharply.

'Wait, Araminta!' Klaas interrupts. 'I'll give him R25 000. That's his price. I'm in business myself.'

You stupid fool!

'Thank you, master. Thank you.' Gratitude dripping from his lips.

'Not at all. The moment I manage to sell them, I'll send you your money, Moses. Just leave your address with me . . .'

'I don't understand, master . . . the rules say cash. Hard cash. It doesn't work otherwise.' Moses is a little at a loss. 'You can't do this to me, master. I'm a poor man.'

'Now don't get upset . . .'

She gets up. 'While the two of you are fighting this out, I'll go back to work.' She does not look to right or left, she keeps on walking.

Klaas Muller had seen what she had said; he's playing with a pigeon for his own amusement.

Eight

At twelve o'clock, the next day, the sixth, she tells Koos Malherbe he need not worry; she no longer has any intention of getting him off his pedestal or into her bed. Nor will she attempt to touch him again. She says it to get it over and done with, but he can't hear her, because he's not back from court yet; she was told to wait in his office.

She waits.

She has her oldest dress on, the white one with the little blue dots that she got in her first year at university. The colour is already faded. Her hair is plaited, as instructed.

Common sense tells her they won't send her to prison, but just in case she has put the violet on the desk in her office. Lizzie takes care of the office plants, and she'll water it for her.

Klaas had made her agree to go out to dinner with him the night before. When she got home afterwards, she threw up, because the fear is in her stomach now, not in her head any more.

Klaas wants to go to Oudtshoorn with her tomorrow; Klaas wants to have her flat painted for her; Klaas wants to buy her a second easy chair. Klaas wants to go and pick her a star. He says he would certainly have bought those diamonds if it hadn't been for the word 'DON'T' written on the palm of her hand when she held the stones out for him to see. She told him that she had had no idea of how or when she would be able to write it, with them watching her as they did. That she had not even been sure that there was a pen in her handbag.

When she got back from her 'business' with Klaas, the others at the office wanted to know what was going on, why she was looking so dazed. She told them it was because she had just been to the most ridiculous concert.

Hardly five minutes later, a deeply shocked Joris Oosthuizen, her father's friend, walked in. His voice was filled with emotion when he said that he had just heard that she had been caught for illicit diamond buying. Surely it couldn't be true? It is. His eyes growing glassy with horror, he said, 'How could you have done such a thing? Don't you realize what this is going to do to your parents?'

'Yes, but fortunately they don't know, and should you dare to tell them, I'll kill you myself.'

He said he had no intention of telling them – he would only pray that they would be spared this terrible humiliation.

She hears Koos Malherbe coming down the passage: whistling, faultless; self-assured.

The moment he enters the room, the shadow of the rock falls across her once again: cold, but safe.

'Good day,' he says. 'How are you?'

'If I could, I would run away.'

'Don't try to.' He hangs his robe on the stand in the corner. There is an air of great manliness about him that seems to emanate from his shoulders and his back . . .

'This the oldest dress I have and I have done my hair in a plait.' Please, be just a little kind to me.

'It looks good.' He comes and sits down on his throne. 'I now want you to go and stand over there at the window and let your hands hang at your sides.'

She gets up and does it. 'Like this?'

'Yes. That is how I want you to stand in court tomorrow. Don't fidget. Don't do anything that may irritate the magistrate. Remember that it's difficult for him to have a defendant in court without an attorney.'

'Why?'

'It means that he must do most of the work himself. Explaining your rights to you, protecting you from any injustice from the prosecutor. All sorts of things. Make it easy for him. The prosecutor will read out the charge and ask you how you plead: guilty or not guilty. Say guilty and *look* guilty. Not contemptuous, as you're now doing!'

'I'm not contemptuous.'

'Don't talk back!'

'I'm sorry.' Your Honour.

'The magistrate may put certain questions to you in order to satisfy himself that you indeed understand the charge and if you admit to the accusations thereof. He will probably ask if you were aware that you were doing something illegal when you bought the uncut diamonds.'

'I never really thought about it like that.'

He slams his hand down on the desk so hard that her whole body recoils from the shock. 'Whether you thought about it like that or not, you can't go and say so in court!' he shouts at her. 'If you do, the magistrate will put aside your plea of guilty, which means you'll have to plead not guilty. And your perverse line of argument won't get you out of that mess.'

'I'll say I knew it was illegal and wrong, and whatever else you want me to say!'

'Keep your hands still; stop screwing up your dress like that.'

'Stop shouting at me, I'm not deaf!' she yells back. 'I've admitted that I'm guilty, what more must I say? Why can't I be sentenced so that I will at least know whether I am to go to prison or not! If it please Your Worship to give me a fine, I don't know where I'll get the money from to pay the state, because the state has already taken R10 000 from me!'

'Come and sit down, you're hysterical.' It's an order.

'I don't want to sit down. I'm tired, I want to get it over with.'

'Come and sit down.'

She goes and sits down. 'I'm sorry.'

'The magistrate will say that the court finds you guilty. The prosecutor will say that you have no previous convictions, and then the magistrate will ask if you want anything to be taken into consideration in mitigation. Tell him that your father is a minister of the Dutch Reformed Church – speak clearly and humbly – say you love your father very much and that you feel infinitely sorry for what you're doing to him. That he is a good father, that he does not deserve this from his child . . .'

'My father doesn't know what I've done.'

'You'll say it as if he does!'

'I'll say it as if he does.' Don't bite my head off.

'When the magistrate is deciding on the appropriate fine for you, he'll ask how much you're earning and what you own. Don't make up stories. Tell him.'

'When does he sentence me?'

'After this.'

'When do the decoys testify against me?'

'There is no need, since you will be pleading guilty.'

'When will they say that I didn't want to disclose the name of my buyer?'

'The magistrate will not be interested in that.'

'Then they were lying to me?'

'They have their methods. You deserved it.'

I wouldn't sleep with you even if you begged me to. 'What do you think my sentence will be?' The bastards, they lied to me!

'If I were sentencing you, I'd give you a fine of R6 000 or six months' imprisonment.'

'I thought you'd have chosen the death penalty!'

'I would advise you to leave your sauciness at home tomorrow!'

'When do I ask if I can pay off the fine in instalments?'

'After you've been sentenced. In a place like Oudtshoorn, the magistrate will decide on the amounts of the instalments himself, and on how they are to be made. As a rule, the first payment is the largest.'

'Must I pay it immediately?'

'Not necessarily. You will most probably be allowed to start paying from the end of the month.'

'And if I can't?'

'Then you'll have to go to prison.'

Once upon a time, there were four little bushmen. They lived in a land called Botswana and one day they killed a man. Someone came and told her father about it one Sunday, after he had preached a sermon on justice and injustice. The British South African Police arrested the bushmen and charged them with murder – Botswana was still Bechuanaland then, the foster-child of Britain. The four bushmen were taken before the assizes and asked if they had in fact killed the man. Yes. The prosecutor and the judge did everything they could to make them understand that they should say yes, and then add that they had not killed him in cold blood, they had done it for such and such a reason. The bushmen, however, kept on saying they killed the man because he had to be killed – bushmen don't know about lying or swearing.

So the judge sentenced them to hang.

The four bushmen were then put in prison to await the arrival of the gallows. Bechuanaland had only one gallows and this was on the back of a lorry, which went from village to village to hang whoever had to be hanged. It was a vast country, the roads were bad and the lorry drove slowly.

At the end of the first month one of the bushmen died and the others looked pretty bad.

The head of the prison called in a man who knew everything about bushmen and asked him what he should do. Before another month is out, said the man, the other three will be dead too because bushmen must go to the veld to graze. So he suggested that he should come on Sundays and take them out to graze.

Every Sunday morning for three months, the man came and took them out into the veld. He said to the wardens, you need not fetter them, they will not run away. When they got to the veld, they clicked and clacked in their funny language, merrily digging up roots to eat and running around; stalking, playing, dancing, making fires and cooking little birds. When the sun went down, the man took them back to the prison.

At last the lorry with the gallows arrived. When the little bushmen were hanged, they were nice and fat.

She closes her eyes and says to the mountain: Please, let me graze on your slopes, let me sleep in a gorge until tomorrow. She climbs, she stumbles, she smells the wild herbs in the brush, she puts her face against the moss on the shady side of the rocks, she kisses the petals of a blood-red lily – she watches the mountain's eagle returning to its nest.

When she wakes up, it is Friday, 7 March 1986. Four hours later the magistrate sentences her to six months' imprisonment or R6 000.

That same afternoon, someone pays in the full amount of the fine. Koos Malherbe has to tell her a second time before she grasps it.

'Someone paid my fine?'

'Yes.'

'Who?'

'It was done through an attorney. I was simply asked to inform you.'

'Who was it?'

'I don't know.'

He's lying. She knows he is.

It's a warm, yellow, merciful light that falls on her from someone's window. It could be Klaas Muller. Elvin. Dirk Holtzman. Even Koos Malherbe, although he's the last person she'd suspect.

Nine

SLOWLY, DAY BY DAY, she begins to recover. Little by little, she begins to move forward again.

'UNREST FLAMES UP.'

Her rent goes up by R100 a month.

'MANDELA DEMANDS FREEDOM WITH MATCHES.'

It feels as though an ominous cloud is steadily gathering over the country; the lightning flash absorbing energy: here a spark escapes, there a stray bolt; bombs, knives, shots, sticks, stones. People roused up to a frenzy; people maimed, people murdered; people frightened.

Every morning the sun comes up and calls the people from their houses. People ride in cars, in buses, in taxis – or they walk; people go to work, talk, laugh, eat and drink.

When the sun goes down, the fear increases: doors and windows are locked, alarms turned on, dogs bark – people listen, people wait. Whose turn is it tonight?

The trees start to shed their leaves. The days grow shorter and cooler, the mountain is a deeper blue and the old restlessness begins to stir in her again.

At the end of April she sells the most expensive house on the market at Wilderness. She sells it to a remarkably recovered Major Harrington. Early in May, she sells two houses above the hospital to two brothers from Pretoria.

'The Great Trek is turning back, miss, the white people have started moving southwards,' says the elder of the two as he writes out the cheque. 'My late father predicted it years ago: he always said we would have to return one day, south of the Orange River and west of the Fish River where our boundaries lie. I thank God that I am here now for it's getting dark up north.'

Bernard sells one house and a gift shop. Elvin sells two houses and a smallholding. All to buyers from the north. She does not care if they came from the North Pole as long as they keep on coming. Elvin reckons it is the talk about oil and gas in the sea at Mossel Bay, fifty kilometres away, that's causing the upswing in the property market.

'ELEVEN KILLED IN UNREST – SEVEN BURNED'

Bernard has started putting his newspaper on her desk every day when he's finished with it. She takes it and throws it in the waste-paper basket, but she can't help seeing the headlines.

'BLACK POLICEMAN BURIED ALIVE'

Her stove breaks down. It's cheaper to buy a hotplate than to have the stove fixed. She will simply have to get along without an oven.

'700 SQUATTERS' SHACKS BURNED DOWN – FACTIONS FIGHT'

Christel's eyes are red and swollen from crying: she has discovered that she is pregnant. She says they'll never survive without her salary, even without a child. She didn't want a child yet. It will have to be put in a day-nursery . . .

Lizzie says, 'Don't worry, Christel, Araminta and I will help you make clothes for it, and for the first few months we can take care of the baby here in the office kitchen.' Christel says, 'I don't even know whether it's right to bring a child into this world; the pastor of the church says the devil's aim is chaos and perversion, and he's certainly getting his way in this country.' 'Don't worry,' says Elvin,

200

'it's the same all over the world.' Carr & Holtzman will give her maternity leave.

Was it Elvin that paid her fine? He denies it.

There is a stronger bond between Christel and Lizzie and herself since they visited her that evening. She likes it.

'BLOOD FLOWS IN FLAMES.'

ANC: 'Let us take up our weapons – our necklaces, our hand-grenades, our machine-guns, our AK 47s, our limpet mines and everything – and let us fight the keepers, the police and the army . . .'

She must get away.

June. She sells a beach house at Herolds Bay and four large plots in town. She has no outstanding debts, her car is paid for and if she adds up all her outstanding commission, she now has R22 000 in the bank.

Frans de Villiers's wife is back with him; she saw them together in church. Elvin says Bernard and he will have to think seriously about appointing another agent before the end of the year; there are rumours that an enormous refinery is to be built in the area . . .

Again she begs with him to wait until the following year before appointing anyone. If the rumours about oil and development for the Southern Cape are true, if the property market holds up, she'll not only recover from her own stupidity much faster than she had thought possible, she should be able to be out of the country in another year or so . . .

'VIOLENCE CLAMPED DOWN.'

'STATE OF EMERGENCY DECLARED.'

'RESTRICTIONS ON PRESS.'

Koos Malherbe. Suppose a miracle happens and he phones her and asks her out to dinner or something. Just once. Say an even greater miracle happens and he asks her to have a relationship with him . . .

She needs to be honest with herself, because she still

has a lurking feeling about him. It's not like being in love. It's more like a persistent hope that he might still stoop to touch her. Really touch her. Just once. To make the ink on her hands go away.

No, it's more than that. Koos Malherbe is the weight she needs to put on the other side of the scale: emigrate, or stay for a man like Koos. She asks herself which she would do – and knows if she lies to herself it will be like taking the wrong road for ever.

Emigrate.

Koos Malherbe is just the moon in the sky, the balm which she needs to mend her shattered self-esteem. If he had wanted to reach out a hand to her, he would have done it when she came back from Oudtshoorn. When she stood at his desk in utter desolation, crying out to him: Please take my hand! But he did not hear her. He had sat there on his throne like a judge, he had not even asked the old witch at reception to bring her a tissue or some toilet-paper for that matter. She had had to wipe her face with her hands and arms. He just went on telling her that the fine had been paid.

When he comes to see Elvin at the office, he greets her as he passes her door, his whole attitude saying: You haven't perhaps broken the law again, have you?

She sells a minimarket. Elvin sells a bottle store and Bernard a block of flats. All to buyers from the north.

Either it is coincidence or it is a little strange.

It does not matter. She is concentrating on reaching the opposite bank of a very important river! Better and stronger wings are growing on her back and somewhere waiting for her there is a green valley, between mountains with snow on their peaks and peace at their feet.

'CAR BOMB. THREE WOMEN KILLED – one about to emigrate to the USA.'

She tries to dismiss it, but she cannot forget the words. She thinks: I won't let it upset me, it happened in Durban,

202

it's still a long way from here. She throws the paper into the waste-paper basket, but the words keep jumping out at her.

She must get away.

She must get away as soon as she can. A friend's sister took care of old people in England for three years and earned a lot of money. It's the kind of work you can do without a permit. She must phone and find out about it. 'One about to emigrate to the USA' – is it a message telling her to hurry up?

'Good afternoon.'

When she looks up, he's there, standing at the door. Koos Malherbe. 'Good afternoon,' she says.

'How are you?'

'I'm fine, thank you. How are you?' I must get away as soon as possible . . .

'Well, thank you.' He does not walk past, he comes in and sits down as if he has a natural right. 'Elvin's busy with a client, Lizzie will call me when he's finished. How are your plans going?' As if he's in a hurry for her to leave.

'I've just decided that I must get away as soon as I can.'

'As long as you don't try doing it the way you did last time. Remember, next time they'll lock you up.'

'Mr Malherbe, how long are you going to look at me and talk to me as if I were a criminal?' She asks it straight out.

'I don't see you as a criminal. I see you as a typical example of someone with a good brain who cannot see the simple truth.'

'I saw the truth long ago: money. Although you and the law books may not agree with me.'

'Perhaps that's why I'm rather interested in you: because you seem to have succeeded in getting on the track of the truth by yourself. Unfortunately you then did what asses do: you built a bridge over it.'

'I beg your pardon?' You say I interest you . . .?

'Some asses need bridges to be built for them so that they can reach the truth. Other asses build their own bridges across the truth – to help them *avoid* the truth. Every bridge we build to avoid a truth collapses sooner or later. You survived the first crash; now beware of the second.'

'I promise you, there won't be a second one.' You say I interest you?

'I'm glad to hear that. Elvin says you've done a few good deals lately. When are you planning the big step?'

'Elvin seems to have a habit of discussing me with other people.'

'He did not discuss you. I asked him.'

'What for?'

'Because I think if you earn enough, you might not be tempted into doing something illegal again. I'm interested in your plans, because I hope you will manage things better this time.'

I don't really interest you at all. 'I'm leaving on 15 December.' She hears herself saying it – as if it had been decided already, inside her, without her knowing it. It's suddenly a reality. A specific date, the date of the birth towards which she has been struggling for more than two years: 15 December. There's sense in the date: Marian is getting married on 13 December and has asked her to be her bridesmaid.

'That's six months from now,' Koos Malherbe remarks. 'So see to it that you keep straight till then; don't be tempted to stray off after those shiny little stones again.'

'I won't.' In her heart she adds: the only foolish step I might be tempted to take between now and then is in your direction. Somehow, you are still an obstacle I have to surmount . . .

She no longer denies it.

'TWO BOMBS EXPLODE IN JOHANNESBURG'
July comes and goes without a single successful transac-

tion. It is cold and wet. The mountain is covered in mist for days on end.

'MOTHER'S ANXIETY FOR BABY AFTER BOMB'

Christel says they will have to sell their car to afford the things for the baby. Lizzie says she has ordered a book that will solve their problems. What book? *Your Money Problems Solved in the Ancient Way.* Lizzie herself is having money problems, for she borrowed R200 from her, Araminta, to pay into her account at Foschini's so that they would not take her to court. Bernard says he can't wait for Lizzie's book to come; he'll pay her R10 for every secret that works. Things are bad for Dirk and Jan too.

'44 PEOPLE LEAVE SA DAILY IN MAY'

She phoned her friend; her sister was looking after two wonderful old people in London. Very rich. A hundred pounds a week. That's more than R400. She promised to send her the address of an agent in London.

If it should turn out that she must go and work in England for a year or so, she'll come to terms with it.

Anything.

August. The month of dry leaves and wind storms. Life consists of getting up in the morning, going to work, hoping for a transaction, going home. Sometimes Klaas Muller comes and takes her out to show his gratitude. Sleep, get up, go to work. As when you dream that you're running, but you can't run fast enough to go forward.

'SOWETO UNREST CLAIMS 13 LIVES'

'RED BOMB IN SHOPPING CENTRE'

September.

Everywhere in town the trees are in bud. It's blossom time. It's spring.

One Wednesday afternoon there is a man waiting in the rain at the bottom of the stairs that lead up to her flat. A black man. His raincoat is a plastic dustbin bag with holes for his head and arms; the rest of what she can see looks like a scarecrow.

'Madam . . .'

Her first thought is that he wants to beg, but then he opens his hand and on his pink-brown palm lie four magnificent diamonds, on which the raindrops fall like little pin-head lights. He says nothing, he just stands there. Cars drive past behind them on the wet road. The sound of typewriters comes from the office at the corner of the building; the rain drips from her umbrella. She does not know what to do, she just stands there, bewildered.

'The man at the blue office said I must come and show them to you.'

'What's the man's name?' His act is even better than Moses September's.

'The man with the light brown hair and the glasses. I think his name is Linde.'

'Ralph Linde?'

'Yes, madam. I'll take R10 000 for them.'

'Where do you come from?'

'I work at the mines at Koffiefontein. Up north. We fly them out with pigeons.'

'Is that a fact?'

'Yes, madam.'

He does not stop her when she reaches out to take them. 'They are very beautiful,' she says when they're lying on her hand. They want her to keep them, they want to stay with her, they are nice and friendly. They're little holy stones. She stands there holding them, knowing she should be afraid, but she's not.

'The man said madam could phone him.'

'I'm sorry . . .' She says it to the diamonds. She wants to bend down and kiss them before she gives them back, but she doesn't. She lets them roll back into the man's hand and says, 'I'm sorry, I can't buy them.'

But her hands are shaking when she unlocks the door.

She makes herself a cup of coffee, she irons a dress and a blouse; she's restless, she's upset. Something tells her it wasn't a trap. He had an odour of old, stale sweat around him; his nails were dirty and broken. If it wasn't a trap, she had sent away the biggest chance of her life! But how could she know?

How? She could have phoned Ralph Linde. And then find out afterwards that it had been a trap after all? A clever one. With Ralph Linde acting as another Nick Wehland . . .

It wasn't a trap, she could almost swear to it. The diamonds were not angry, they were good and beautiful, Samuel Sundoo would have bought them!

It's almost dark. Should she get into her car and go and look for the man? No. Where would she find him? Go and *look* for him. Go to Ralph's house – maybe he's there.

Please, mountain, say yes.

No, says the mountain.

'EEC SANCTIONS'

She sells a plot.

'JAPAN IMPOSES MORE SANCTIONS'

She sells another plot.

'DISINVESTMENT WILL KILL 400,000 IN SA'

She must get away.

'SANCTIONS AGREED – DEFEAT FOR REAGAN'

She wrote to the agent in London.

'KODAK PULLS OUT – GM, IBM, COCA-COLA NEXT?'

October. The trees are covered in new leaves, the gardens are in bloom and the sky is blue; she wants to go out into the country, she wants to go climbing up the mountain . . .

Five clients in a row. Four turn away from every house she takes them to: the prices are too high. The fifth one buys Bernard's caravan in despair. 'They say it's OK in the caravan park, miss.'

Less than three months left until 15 December.

Koos Malherbe comes to see Elvin twice running when

she's out; as far as she can gather, he didn't even ask about her.

Get up in the morning, go to work, go home. Day after day after day . . .

Early in November, Lizzie's book of miracles arrives. It provides fun for everyone at tea-time. ' "Never pick up a button and put it in your purse or your bag," ' Lizzie reads from the cheap yellow pages. ' "Buttons button up your luck because they fall under the protection of Saturn, which is in itself restricting." '

'Lizzie, isn't that New Age stuff?' Christel asks, with distrust in her voice. 'Our pastor warned us to be very careful of anything to do with New Age. It's dangerous.'

'Read on, Lizzie!' Bernard prompts.

' "Make sure your money-box is made of tin and not plastic. Jupiter guards over things made of tin and Jupiter is the planet of money." '

'It definitely sounds like New Age,' says Christel.

'Don't be silly,' Lizzie says. 'It's exactly the opposite: "ancient" secrets.'

'Get rid of it, I tell you.'

Lizzie and Christel argue; Bernard tells her to read on; Elvin says it's baloney, the best he's heard in a long time – apart from the present political talks.

' "Should you need money urgently, wrap the scales of a herring in a piece of tissue-paper and put it in your purse or your pocket." Where do you get herrings?'

'Take any old fish,' Bernard suggests.

' "Plant a purple lilac at your front door; plant it on a Thursday . . . the best day of all, however, is 4 November, whether a Thursday or not, for that is the day of money.'

'I started working here on 4 November,' Araminta reminds them.

'Did you?' asks Elvin, surprised. 'I knew from the start you would bring us luck.'

'Do you still think so?'

'Of course I do.'

'"If a purple lilac is not available, morning glory will do."'

'Buy a purple lilac in a pot and put it right at the entrance to the office,' Bernard proposes. 'I'll get one for my brother too.'

'Here comes a good one: "Put a silver coin on your hand, bow three times to the new moon and say: 'Money in my hand, multiply in my land!'"'

'Send that tip to the Minister of Finance immediately!' Elvin suggests with a snort. The phone rings. Christel gets up.

'"When you move into a new house, sprinkle salt on the doorstep and you'll never be in want for as long as you stay there."'

'Araminta!' Christel calls from the switchboard, 'it's for you, I'll put it through to your office.'

Ten

It is Piet Sinksa's sister.

It is Piet Sinksa's sister!

She says her name is Angeline, and she got the number from the man at the garage. Baas Dirk. She knew that she had been waiting for Piet earlier. Piet had been in a very bad car accident. Yes, madam. Both his legs were broken. No, madam, I was in Windhoek with our mother at the time. Piet is much better now, thank you, madam. He asked me to phone and tell madam, if you're still interested, he's back in business again. He's got good ones. Big ones. The only problem is, he can't get down there, madam. He bought himself another van, but it's an old thing, it gives him more trouble than anything else. He asked me to phone and ask if madam could possibly come up to Kimberley. Yes, madam, Kimberley. Yes, madam can talk to Piet himself. I'll give you our number and if madam phones at about six o'clock, he should be home from work. Yes, madam. Thank you, madam.

She puts down the receiver and gives it time to sink in . . . Piet Sinksa's sister . . . Tidings from the blue. The old hope suddenly flares up from the cold ashes, sending a flush of shock through her. It was a chance she thought she had lost for ever; luck, which seemed to have passed her by, returning. It's the coin with which to pay back Nick Wehland and the two decoys, even if they never know it!

She tries to find in herself a sense of wrong, a twinge of conscience, but she doesn't. All she finds is a faint and wonderful feeling of relief and happiness.

'Araminta!' Lizzie calls from inside, 'when you're finished, come and listen; you're missing the best of all!'

'I don't want to hear any more.' she calls back.

It's a dream she would not even have dared to dream. It's deliverance. It's Piet Sinksa's sister.

Later, when Bernard comes and puts the paper on her desk, she asks him to take it back for she never wants to see a paper again.

'I don't blame you,' he says. 'Things are looking bad; God knows what we're heading for.'

In her heart she says: I know where *I'm* heading.

Elvin comes past and wants to know if something is wrong. Why is she sitting with her face in her hands?

'I'm working something out, something very important.'

'Can I be of help?'

'No, thank you, it's personal. Please, don't look so worried, I'm fine. Really fine.'

She waits until two o'clock and rings up Dirk Holtzman to ask if somebody had asked him for her telephone number. Yes. Piet Sinksa's sister. Did the woman specifically ask for her number? No. She actually phoned to ask if he was interested in buying again. He told her that if he had the money, he would certainly have been interested. So then she wanted to know about the lady Piet was supposed to contact.

'I only wanted to make sure.'

'Are you going to buy?'

'I just wanted to know how she had got hold of my telephone number. That's all.'

She has the strangest feeling of reliving a situation she's

been in before. Like a forgotten dream. Not quite. As if she is heading for something that has been put in her way a long time ago. Something inevitable. A paradox: she knew that she was on her way there, but she just didn't realize it.

She cleans out the drawers of her desk to keep herself busy, quelling her increasing anxiety. She goes to the chemist for Christel. She comes back and starts dusting every leaf of every plant in the office. 'ANC'S TO MURDER FARMERS, SAYS WITNESS.' She didn't want to see it, but the paper is lying on the cupboard in the corner of Bernard's office as if some joker had known she would be coming to dust the plants. Even the words in the heading sound like something that's been buried deep inside her for a long time. A hundred years, two hundred years . . .

She stands with the cloth in her hands, staring at the wall while old pictures appear from deep inside her. Between the first and second British occupation of the Cape, the Dutch had another go at governing the foot of Africa. When Governor Janssens asked the Xhosas on the eastern border why they were murdering the Boers and burning down their farms, they said the English told them to do it because they were coming back.

It does not matter any more! she tells herself, turning away from the wall. Piet Sinksa has come. A wave has come, it's picking her up and carrying her with it to her destination. Straight there, without her having to go and wash up in England first.

It's a long, restless afternoon, waiting for six o'clock to come. One thing is clear in her mind: if she must go to Kimberley, she must go right away. Or as soon as possible. With outstanding commission, she has R27 000 in the bank, of which she can use at least R25 000 for the diamonds. She will have to ask Elvin for an advance again, which might be a problem. What if he asks her what she wants it for?

Eight minutes to six. Wait until after six, don't give the

212

impression that you're over-eager. Tidy the bookshelf . . .

Why Kimberley of all places? Can it be coincidence? She has always wanted to go to Kimberley to see the land of Prester John for herself . . .

Tomorrow is Friday; she will have to have her car serviced just in case, and the garages will be busy. She hasn't got an appointment. If she leaves on Sunday, she can come back on Tuesday; perhaps she can come back via Bloemfontein and stay the night with her father and mother . . . What will she tell Elvin if he asks what she wants to do with the money? She'll say she can do what she wants with it, she's not a child. She'll tell him she wants to go away for a few days, she won't say where to. No one need know.

Six o'clock. From sheer nervousness she dials the wrong code and has to start all over again. On the other end a man says cautiously, 'Hallo.'

It's Piet Sinksa.

He says he would like to come down himself, but the old Combi he has bought is as useless as he is. How is Baas Dirk? Shame. Yes, madam, things are bad for us all. My sister said madam wanted to speak to me personally. Yes, madam, don't worry, I understand. Nice ones. Ten. But madam would be under no obligation to take them all. I had some very nice ones last month as well, but before I could let madam know, the man that buys for the man at Mossel Bay came and took the lot. The smallest one I have at the moment is about . . . about six carats, madam. Very good ones, all of them. It's difficult to fix a price over the phone, madam, but don't worry, I won't rip madam off . . . As soon as possible would suit me too. Monday's fine. Just tell me where I must meet madam. The best hotels are the Savoy and the Kimberley Sun. Yes, they're more or less in the centre of the city. I would appreciate it if madam would give me a ring the moment madam gets here . . . and, madam, drive carefully – it's a long way . . . A little over eight hundred kilometres. The best route is via Beaufort West and De Aar and then on to Kimberley . . . It's a pleasure, madam, and my sister sends her regards.

She's not stupid; she knows it could be a trap that is being set for her; she's aware of it all the time. Even if Piet Sinksa sounds friendly and decent, even if Dirk said he could be trusted absolutely, she will have to be on her guard every moment and somehow think up a way of making the transaction as safe as possible. Just in case.

And this time she will wait until she has got the diamonds home before making an appointment with Samuel Sundoo. This time she'll let them stay with her as long as she wants to, and she'll keep one to take with her.

Early on the Friday morning she has her car serviced. She goes to the bank and withdraws R18 000 of the R19 000 she has there. Later in the morning, she helps Lizzie in the front office because Christel has had to go to the doctor's. The fact that she must go and ask Elvin for the rest of the money is worrying her. What if he says no? She cannot go all the way to Kimberley to take the biggest risk of her life with only half an egg in her hand!

When she woke up that morning, she told herself to think it over carefully before getting out of bed. To change her mind while there was still time. She asked herself if she wanted to go on selling property in the hope of getting away some time during the next year or two? No. Does she want to go and work in England? No. Does she want to go to Kimberley? Yes. And if it's a trap? She'll simply have to be sharper than the trap. How? She'll ask if she can hold the diamonds before she hands over the money. She'll know if there's something wrong with them . . .

That's jumping off a roof, hoping you can fly, she warned herself.

214

She will put the money in the boot of the car and tell Piet Sinksa to take it out himself and leave the diamonds in its place. Then she will get into the car and drive off. What if they follow her? Who? Major Kruger and Lieutenant Botha. Don't call for trouble. Say everything goes well, and then when she stops she discovers it's pieces of glass? She will ask to see the diamonds first.

At half-past one, she summons up the courage to go to Elvin's office. 'I want to ask a favour.'

'Come and sit down. What can I do for you?'

'Could you please let me have my outstanding commission in advance again? Today.' She sees his eyebrows twitch. 'It's R8 000.'

'May I ask why?'

'I need the money.'

'I don't mind giving you the money, your transactions are secure enough, but you can't blame me for being a bit suspicious. When you asked me before . . .'

'I know. But you need not worry. I'm not involved with Nick Wehland again, and I'm not going to Oudtshoorn to walk into another trap, I promise you.' Please don't say no.

'Araminta, I often wish I knew what your real problem is.'

'My only problem is that I want to be free – to start really living my life.'

'What do you want to be free of?'

'Of living behind bars with the walls closing in around me. I need money to buy myself out. I want to go away for a few days – I am planning to go and stay with my parents at Bloemfontein.'

'Promise you won't get angry if I tell you something.'

'What?'

'Koos thinks you'll do it again.'

'It's not for Koos Malherbe to speculate about what I'll do or won't do. It's my life. And I've come to the conclusion that it is wrong to go on living in fear, for then you're not really alive. So it's time to pack up and go. That's why I need the money, Elvin.'

'Where are you going?'

'You once asked me why I came to work for Carr & Holtzman. I came to work here to make enough money to enable me to leave the country. That's why.'

'What?' He obviously didn't expect it. 'You're leaving the country? I don't believe it.' He sits there, staring at her as if he has trouble fully grasping what she means. Then he leans forward and looks at her closely. 'Or perhaps I do. That would explain a lot of things. Are you serious?'

'Yes.'

'Where are you planning to go?'

'Probably Switzerland. I plan to look around for a bit first though, to find the right place.'

'You are serious.'

'I am.'

'I have a sister in Switzerland, she's married to a Swiss. I'll give you her address – I'll let her know about you.'

'That would be wonderful.'

'This comes as rather a shock to me, although you're the third person this week to tell me they're leaving. Everyone can do as they think best, but personally I think people are in too much of a hurry to run. And this puts an even bigger question mark in my mind about giving you your commission in advance again. Why?'

'I promise you you need not worry.'

'I don't know about that. But I'll ask Christel to work out the correct amount and give you a cheque.'

'Thank you. I'll be back on Wednesday.'

'Don't do anything irresponsible, please.'

'I won't.'

Something feels wrong. All day Saturday she feels it. She knows that if she sits down quietly, she'll be able to get to the bottom of it, but she does not want to.

216

She tidies her flat, puts the violet in a basin with water, gets out a suitcase and puts petrol in her car. She makes herself something to eat. She counts the money for the third time and puts it in a plastic shopping bag: R25 000. Plus R1 000 in her handbag for expenses.

She tries to read.

When the sun goes down, she goes and sits at the window, watching the mountain slowly changing colour for the night . . .

She will not let her guard drop for a moment, she will not walk into a trap.

Going to Kimberley means more to her than just the diamonds. She can think of no better place to shed the last traces of bitterness.

The first star comes out above the mountain . . .

Maybe that's just an excuse. Maybe, deep down in her heart, it's also a journey of revenge, although she does not like the word. Perhaps she wants to go to Kimberley to climb over a forbidden wall, pick up a stone and hurl it through a window with all the force of her anger before running away . . .

When the first diamonds were found in the Free State, British geologists assured London that there could not possibly be any diamonds there. The Boers must have rigged it in order to attract capital to their wretched wilderness! 'Wicked inventions!' cried the London *Times*.

When Britain realized her mistake, they made a Griqua swear . . .

The Boers were persecuted with lies and deceptions, and she feels every turn of the screw in her own flesh, because she has dug too deep in her efforts to find herself.

Then there was the gold. While the Boers were being angered on this side, hatred was stirred up for them amongst the ordinary people in Britain, so that when it came to war over the gold, they would be willing to pay the taxes to pay for the war. 'They're a kind of Negro, cruel, and live on mealies,' the British newspapers wrote.

When Rhodes started smuggling firearms to the foreigners at the mines, Paul Kruger discovered that only four out of ten Boers possessed a gun, and an old-fashioned one at that. But for ever after the Boers are depicted as having had a Bible under the one arm and a gun under the other.

The knock on her door is so sudden and so loud that it makes her jump. When she opens the door, Koos Malherbe is standing on the other side of the safety-gate.

'Good evening,' he says. It's a warning rather than a greeting.

'Good evening.' I wonder if Elvin has sent you . . .

'If you're not going to ask me in, could you pass me a chair so that I can sit down out here.'

'Sorry.' She unlocks the safety-gate and invites him to come in.

He is a self-assured Noah entering the ark, letting his eyes wander slowly over everything. He's a relentless rock sitting in her armchair, looking at her as if she is a particularly troublesome case. 'Araminta Rossouw,' he says, 'I had to choose between letting you carry on with whatever you are doing, which would have saved me a lot of trouble, or coming here and trying to bring you to your senses.'

'Am I supposed to feel flattered because you have chosen to try to rescue me?'

'No. Not at all.'

It's a slap in the face. For a moment her pride is shattered, but then she recovers and hits back. 'Mr Malherbe,' she says coldly, 'I once climbed over a passion-fruit hedge to get to a forbidden man, but I realized later that I had only reached the physical in him. The day I came back from Oudtshoorn I would have climbed over the highest barbed-wire fence for a little kindness from you, to hold on to until I could get myself together again. I realized then that you are too hard and dispassionate to be reached. So why don't you save yourself the trouble and go home? You do not understand me.'

218

'You're right. I don't understand what goes on in your mind. I've never come across a girl with a mind like yours.'

'Now that is a compliment.' He did not even seem to feel the irony. 'I can offer you coffee or tea, I don't have anything stronger unfortunately.'

'I don't think we should interrupt this conversation in order to make coffee. When you stop evading the issue, we might get somewhere.'

'Is it true that you turned your wife out of your house?' She knows it's a silly way of trying to get back at him.

'I never had a wife. But I did ask the person I was married to to leave my house and get her priorities sorted out. She did. She's playing golf in America at the moment.' Without a flinch.

'Did Elvin send you here?'

'Elvin phoned to tell me that you had asked for an advance on your commission again.'

'That's right. I did.'

'To buy diamonds?'

'To go on a journey of revenge.'

'Answer my question: to buy diamonds?'

'If I say yes, it's not the whole truth; if I say no, that's not the whole truth either.'

'One moment you speak absolutely frankly, the next moment you play games. I'm not your rescuer, no one can rescue you except yourself. Had you been a common little lawbreaker, I would not have gone to any trouble. You think you're smart. But let me tell you, you're playing with fire without realizing how hot that fire can be. If you are caught again, you will go to prison. If you think prison is like what you see on television or in films, you're making a mistake. Prison is hell, a women's prison: the lowest circle of hell.'

'This time it's different. They won't catch me.'

'Even if they don't, the unwritten law will, even if it has to pursue you across the globe!'

219

'What law?' she asks.

'I did not come here to give you a sermon. I'm here to appeal to you not to try and buy diamonds again.'

'What law?'

'A law that is not written in any of my books, as you would say. An unbending law that brings its victims into my office every day: ninety-nine per cent of the people that come to me are there because they have tried to build a bridge avoiding this law of laws! They're there because their bridges have collapsed. As you yourself came, and as you will again if you don't start thinking.'

'Laws are made by people, Mr Malherbe. Maybe they are the supports of the bridges you're talking of.'

'I'm talking about a law not made by man, the law that says we get nothing in exchange for nothing.'

She laughs. 'I would never have suspected you of such naïvety, Mr Malherbe.'

'Nothing for nothing,' he repeats, quietly. 'If your father had made you read the Bible more often, you would have known that it says you'll be despised and punished when you steal, even if you steal because you are hungry.'

'I did not steal!'

'Nothing for nothing. Weigh that against all the clever arguments you put forward about money in my office that day. Use it as a watch word in all man's affairs if you wish. We get three basic things: food, shelter and clothes to cover our nakedness. The rest we must earn.'

'Unless you are one of the millions of unemployed; then the state will look after you,' she objects with a sneer.

'Yes. But remember, the state's bridges are often the highest, and that's why they fall the hardest when they do.'

'I wonder who paid my fine . . .' She puts it down like a trump card.

'You must have earned it somehow.'

'I sold Dirk Holtzman's diamonds for a Sunrise toffee box full of money . . . was that nothing for nothing?' She tries another card.

'He must have earned it somehow.'

'I don't believe you're saying this.'

'Every good you do is multiplied by seven and placed to your credit. Everything you squander, money as well, is multiplied by seven and taken away from you – your father should have taught you that as well.'

'Does this law apply to everyone, or just to some?' she asks, mockingly.

'To everyone.'

'I'm afraid I have bad news for you, for your laws and your bridges. I'm going away tomorrow, and I'm going to stand on one of the best and soundest bridges in the world; when I'm there, I'm going to spit out the last of the poison that is in me. Then I'll turn round and walk away from this country, taking with me money that I have not stolen from anyone.'

'Where are you going tomorrow?'

'To the land of Prester Johannes.'

'Who's Prester Johannes?'

'A descendant of the Wise Men from the East who took gifts to the baby Jesus.' She plays with him. 'You may know him by the name of Prester John. He had a great kingdom in Africa which remained undiscovered for many years.'

'If I'm not mistaken, they came looking for his kingdom in Africa after they failed to find it in India.'

'You surprise me, Mr Malherbe.'

'Tell me where you're going tomorrow.'

'I told you. To land of Prester Johannes. They say there's a copy in the British Museum of a letter he wrote to the Byzantine emperor in Constantinople in which he describes his peaceful kingdom and the wonders to be found there. Of the river full of precious stones that flows through his land; of the earth strewn with gold. There were no poor in his kingdom, no one stole or lied or committed evil deeds – I assume they knew about the law of nothing for nothing.'

'Why didn't you finish your studies?'

'Because I decided to make a life for myself elsewhere. The early Portuguese explorers were instructed to keep a lookout for the land of the Priest and to win him over in the name of God and for the profit of Portugal, Mr Malherbe.' I'm enjoying this. 'Something like two hundred years later, Jan van Riebeeck arrived at the Cape and soon the powers that be in Amsterdam were giving him hell for not making contact with the lord of the land of diamonds and gold.'

'Where are you going tomorrow?'

'Do you know about the letter that Van Riebeeck wrote to the magnates in Amsterdam after ten years of never-ending pressure to find this elusive kingdom?'

'You're going to walk into a trap.'

'He said that he had studied the old Portuguese maps and had come to the conclusion that the land of precious stones and gold lies, not to the south, but to the north. And to get there you had to overcome many hardships: desert and heat and thirst. You had to travel to the river of the elephants, through the vast grazing areas of the Koikoi, and everywhere the Koikoi tribes were at war with one another over cattle and women. Beyond all these dangers, you would get to the land of the cannibals, which was guarded by tame lions, and only then would you get to the land of diamonds and gold. Van Riebeeck's calculations were not far out, were they?'

'Are you going to Kimberley?'

'Yes,' she admits, defiantly.

'To buy diamonds?'

'Yes. And to spit.'

'Why is a girl like you so very bitter?'

'Because something made me fight against a fate that made us the only white tribe on the foot of the darkest continent on earth! We're not West, we're not East. We're south, in the middle of the day where there's neither dawn nor dusk, and for the sins of forty years we've been reviled as the most hated nation on earth. The world does not want us, Mr Malherbe. Africa does not want us – they can't send us to the moon, so what are we to do? Pack up and go while there's still somewhere to go to. I know there are fools that think we can get on to wagons again, take up our Bibles and our hymn books and . . .'

'If you're going to Kimberley, you're going to make an ass of yourself.'

'I must.'

'Why?'

'I once had a friend that I loved like a brother. He always said Prester Johannes is just the secret name of the great Spirit that lives somewhere between the south and the north. To me it's a place where a handful of diamonds is waiting for me, so that I can leave at last. And while I'm there, I would like to ask this great spirit why he never had pity on us. I want to ask him why Jakob Hart went north to join the ANC – and if it really was an accident that he was standing up in the lorry as it passed under the bridge that beheaded him.'

'I remember the Jakob Hart case; it was in every newspaper at the time. There was no question of foul play, and it's an established fact that he had joined the ANC as an agent of the South African government.'

'I know. It's just that I often wonder if we have angels that push us where we must go.'

'Maybe one goes of one's own free will.'

Eleven

SHE WAKES UP AT an unfamiliar noise . . . as if someone had wrapped a stone in cloth and thrown it against her window. A moment later, her alarm clock goes off and she wonders if she didn't dream it.

'Good morning, mountain!'

It's six o'clock. The first rays of the sun are already touching the highest cliffs with a deep, warm glow. She must get up. She must go to Kimberley. She closes her eyes and allows a feeling of excitement and anguish to seep through her. Excitement because she knows that when she gets out of bed it will be the start of the last lap. Something inside her is telling her so. The great spirit, the one that makes the sun to rise and the rain to fall, that sends the drought to make you get up and move on, has put it inside her.

Her anguish is the fear that something might get in her way and that she will not see it in time . . .

Suddenly she hears the noise at the window again. She sits up in bed and waits. There's nothing there. Just a speck against the sky that comes sweeping down and hits the glass with a resounding thud! It's her stone wrapped in cloth: it's a swallow.

Why does it do it?

She jumps out of bed and runs to the window to see if it is hurt and lying on the ground. There's nothing there.

224

But when she turns away from the window, he does it again! She pulls the curtains – maybe there's a reflection on the glass and he can't see the window.

It must have been that, because he does not come back.

Or perhaps it's the day of the birds.

For when she drives out of town, there is a most beautiful reddish-brown eagle with a spotted white breast sitting proudly on a telegraph pole. She winks at him as she drives past . . . a hawk or an eagle at the start of a journey is a good luck sign and it makes her feel better about the swallow.

The road starts climbing the foothills of the mountain; the air is still cool after the night. She listens for the little voice inside her telling her to turn back, but does not find it. But she does not find the excitement with which she had woken up either, because the memory of the last time she drove over this very same mountain haunts her like a ghost. It was foggy that morning, and she drove into the trap almost jubilantly.

No matter how often her common sense tells her that Piet Sinksa is not a trap, she knows she'll have to be wary and alert as never before in her whole life.

Just before she left home, she phoned to make sure that the arrangements are unchanged. Angeline answered. Piet was still asleep, she said, but she could go and wake him if madam wanted her to. Please don't. She only wanted to check before setting out. Not to worry, madam, Piet is a man of his word, he walks a straight line and so do I. By the way, if madam would like a cat, bring a box – there are six kittens here that we must find homes for.

One of the first things she is going to do when she has settled down in her new country is get a cat.

Nothing for nothing . . .

She's not getting the diamonds for nothing, she's paying for them. Koos Malherbe's philosophy is paradoxical. What about the money people inherit or win – or welfare money? What about gifts? Or are these conveniently included somehow in the category of money that has been earned?

Koos Malherbe. One thing she knows now: no woman will ever dare to climb over any of his fences. But it makes her feel good that he had come, evidently thinking that he would be able to stop her. It means he must have cared a little. The only thing she had promised him before he left was that she would turn back if she had any doubts along the way – even if she was only ten kilometres from Kimberley.

Should she turn back?

No.

It's hot and dry on the Karroo side of the mountains. If all goes well, she will be in Kimberley between three and four o'clock . . .

She'll work until the end of November. That will give her time to sell the car and furniture and pack.

She waves to a little grey hawk with black shoulders sitting at the side of the road. Funny, she can't remember a single hawk or eagle along the way on the morning she went to Oudtshoorn . . .

Nothing for nothing.

It's not always true.

They say you must never wait for opportunities in life, you must look for the opportunities that are there already and grab them. Fine. She had taken a chance to go and sell diamonds for the Shirleys and Dirk Holtzman; now it's her turn.

Money. They say it's a sin to be poor, for if you're too poor for too long you lose your courage as well as your morals – it sounds like something from Lizzie's book. To be too rich is not good either, for then you become mean or bored to death.

Money, money, money.

If Koos Malherbe had said there should be a law that forbids you to have more than you really need, she would

226

not have argued. Except perhaps to remind him that even the communists had not managed to make that work in practice. On the other hand, the capitalists would have the horrors: for capitalism depends on people wanting all the nice things that can be bought – preferably on credit, for then you have to work in order to pay off the money before you can buy the next thing and start paying off the money for that . . . Is that how people are kept working? She has never thought about it like that before.

Nothing for nothing?

There's a God of heaven and a god of the world. Perhaps the god of the world is too smart for the people of the earth?

Think about something else.

Prester Johannes had three magic stones: one that could make you see the unseen, one that could make you invisible and one that made light in the dark . . .

On the other side of Oudtshoorn, although it's not quite half-past eight the heat already runs in waves across the veld. Ostriches peck about in bare paddocks on both sides of the road. They have wings but they cannot fly. Hundreds of ostriches. Thousands of ostriches. In places it seems as if they had eaten the earth itself . . . They say that there was a time when ostrich feathers sold so well that the farmers and merchants of this district wallowed in money. They built themselves mansions of dressed stone and ordered shiploads of luxuries from Europe to put in them and lived like kings and queens.

When the price of ostrich feathers fell, they fell with it.

That's not what she wanted to think about. There is something about ostrich feathers . . . they're different from those of other birds. All the little plumes that grow from the central quill are exactly the same length – like truth and righteousness. The ancient Egyptians believed that when you get to heaven, your heart is put on a scale and weighed against an ostrich feather to find out how much wrongdoing you've brought with you. If your heart moves the scales even

227

slightly, you have to come back to earth and try again.

Hundreds of ostriches, thousands of ostriches, and most of their wing feathers have been clipped.

Perhaps that is why there are so many people on the earth: no one is getting it right?

Don't be silly.

On the other side of De Rust, the road begins to wind through an enormous gorge in the Swartberg Mountains. She's already some way into the pass when she sees the white police car ahead, waiting at the side of the road, the blue light on its roof flashing on and off. An officer steps into the road and puts up his hand to stop her.

There are no cars in front of her or behind her, which alarms her a little as she starts to put on the brakes. Why is she being stopped?

'Good morning, lady,' the man says as she rolls down the window. 'Will you please pull over on the other side of the bridge. There's been an accident a little further on and the road is blocked. It won't be long before we have it cleared.'

'Has anybody been hurt?'

'Nothing serious. Furniture van from Kimberley turned over; they come speeding through here, they think the signs warning of sharp curves have been put up for fun. If you would just pull over – thank you.'

A furniture van from Kimberley. Why did he tell her that? He was not supposed to tell her, was he? They never tell you anything unless you ask . . .

She pulls over on the other side of the bridge and stays sitting behind the wheel in order to calm down. There are quite a few cars waiting already, people are walking along the road in the direction of the accident. She tells herself not to be foolish, no furniture van would have been sent from Kimberley specially to come and block the pass to her.

And the swallow at the window? Birds know things people don't know.

The sexton's wife had been expecting twins once. Suddenly, one day, two swallows came flying into the window-pane where she was sitting sewing and that same night the twins were stillborn. Afterwards the woman said she knew the swallows had come to tell her something.

OK, the sexton's wife had been forty-five. But what about the two pigeons that suddenly fell stone-dead from the roof of the Governor's residence at the Cape one morning? Would it have even been recorded if it hadn't been seen as something supernatural? And shortly afterwards the most devastating smallpox epidemic broke out: within a month, more than a hundred of the settlers were dead and the Koikoi were dying like flies.

The birds had known.

She gets out of the car.

Perhaps the swallow had tried to tell her that the road through the pass would be blocked. No. Perhaps he was trying to tell her that Piet Sinksa is a trap that they're setting for her. Perhaps she's getting paranoiac.

What about the eagle she saw when she was just setting out?

Behind her, formidable cliffs tower into the sky – and on the other side of the road rises the opposite wall of the gorge. It's like being inside a mountain that broke in two millions of years ago. First a little river came and made a way through the crack, then man.

With her eyes she starts climbing the rock-face on the opposite side of the road: from ledge to ledge, from foothold to fissure, hanging on by her fingers – it's a game. She must get to the top without slipping and falling . . . higher and higher, calculating every move until she reaches the summit. When she looks up, three swallows are circling above her head . . .

Must she turn back? If she wants to, this is the place to do it: she's just over a hundred kilometres from home.

But what will she return to, her other self asks. Continuing to work, perhaps for years, while life goes by, day after day? Turn back and never know whether Piet Sinksa was a good deed multiplied by seven? Turn back and survive

229

behind bars for the rest of your life while hatred piles up around you because you're white and live in Africa? While the world weighs you with more untruths than truths for sins you have not committed, while political parrots with golden teeth keep on tearing your people apart?

It's a farce.

The white man on the foot of Africa does not have the money to buy himself free. Except a few perhaps. Except those who make plans and buy themselves free in time.

An hour later, when they've cleared the road, she drives north. The wreck of the furniture van lies along the road: GOODWILL REMOVERS, say the big red letters on its side.

At the end of the pass, there is a little brown hawk sitting on a post. She does not wink or wave at him; from here on she intends to keep her eyes on the road, rather than looking out for omens along the way.

Slowly the vast arid plains of the Karroo begin to spread out around her. It's no longer Africa's green, mountainous toe, but a hard, desolate, sparsely inhabited world.

It's hot.

She drives through Beaufort West without stopping. Hour after hour, a feeling of determination builds up in her, giving her strength and stilling the fear in her.

Victoria West.

Piles of rough, dark brown boulders are scattered like little mountains across the immensity . . . She sweeps away the road and the telegraph poles, the power-lines and jackal-proof fences, and imagines bushmen running across the plains like little yellow-brown ghosts. Their shelters nestle against the piles of rock; they hunt, they gather, they dance . . .

And they get up to leave when they have to.

Hour after hour she drives. It's hot. For long stretches at a time, hers is the only car on the road.

230

Britstown.

More and more thorn trees on the plains; tall grass between the scrub, and desolation everywhere . . .

Where am I going, she asks herself. Why don't I turn back? Because I'm three quarters of the way there already. Because it's the only short cut I can see . . .

Ages go by in kilometres and ghosts: the bushmen bands grow fewer – the Koikoi tribes with their horned cattle and fat-tailed sheep, covered with hair instead of wool, grow bigger and stronger, the tribal wars grow fiercer.

Far behind her the first ships round the Cape of Storms at the foot of Africa. More ships. Fleets of ships. In the bays animals are acquired for meat from the nearest Koikoi – and they in turn must barter or trade with the Koikoi deeper inland: ten head of cattle and ten sheep are needed for every fair-sized ship, five of each for the smaller ones, and at least forty head of cattle and fifty sheep for every East Indiaman – and that, multiplied by a few hundred years and hundreds upon hundreds of ships, results in the Koikoi becoming vagrants without cattle.

From the south came the wagons with the children of the children of the first white settlers, searching for another place to stay. As she is.

God in heaven, that is supposed to be in us all, is there a pattern we do not see or have you made us as a joke?

She cries it out from the depths of her being.

Shortly before three o'clock, she stops at Hopetown. It is eight hours since she has left home and according to her road map the Orange River must be just outside the town. From there it is another 120 kilometres to Kimberley.

She fills up her car with petrol. She washes her hands and face, buys a sandwich and a cool drink. For the first time since that morning, the feeling of excitement returns.

Ten minutes later she comes to the river.

The only other time in her life that she could not take

in the full wonder of what she was seeing was the day she saw the diamond in the sceptre in the Tower! As then, she cannot stop and look, because 'No Parking' signs forbid her to stop on the bridge; she has to keep driving and at the same time try to see as much as she can of the river, coming from the east and disappearing to the west. She drives more and more slowly . . . the car behind her hoots . . . It's a wide, formidable, yellow-brown mass of water that flows like blood through a huge open vein. It's a primeval force. It's a living thing.

It's a boundary.

When she gets to the other side, she wants to turn back and cross the bridge again, but there are cars in front of her, and impatient ones behind her. She has to keep going.

About twenty kilometres farther on, she begins to realize that there has been a gradual change since she crossed the river. The earth is speaking a different language. The air is different. It's not her imagination; she can feel it, see it. It's a different country. Humpbacked hills, pointed hills, flat-topped hills. Stretches of thorn trees like umbrellas with their feet in a carpet of long green grass. Farms, power pylons . . .

Is *this* the start of the Priest's land? She cannot decide whether she's disappointed or simply too tired to appreciate anything at the moment. It's beautiful, but in a different way, and it doesn't feel the way she had thought it would . . .

The traffic on the road is heavier, people are driving faster. A grey hawk with a red beak and red legs sits on a telegraph pole at the side of the road. She's never seen a hawk like that before. A little way further on is its mate.

An hour later, the road becomes a long avenue of pepper trees.

Kimberley.

Twelve

THE FIRST THING SHE does when she gets to her room in the hotel is to dial Piet Sinksa's number. The telephone rings and rings.

No one answers it.

She tells herself not to worry, they will have just gone out for a while. But it does worry her. They knew she was coming eight hundred kilometres to see them, they knew she was going to phone when she got here; the least they could have done was to be at home!

It is almost five o'clock. She unpacks her suitcase and puts the bag with the money in one of the drawers. After a shower, she dials the number again. Still no answer. She tells herself not to panic, but she does. Nothing is as she thought it would be. The air-conditioner in the room makes more noise than anything else, she's forgotten her comb, she feels cooped up between the four papered walls!

She turns the air-conditioner off and opens the window. There is not a breath of air, but at least it is less noisy. From where she is standing, she looks down on the backyard of the hotel: a row of garages with their doors painted orange. Not a car, not a soul. The rest of the view is roofs: red roofs, pointed roofs, tin roofs. Like hats, one can't see what's underneath them. A church tower, the purple tops of jacaranda trees. There are no mountains.

233

Only a tiny strip of veld in the distance and huge, white, bulging thunderclouds against the blue of the sky.

She's the only living thing left on the earth. Except for a rumbling somewhere up above, getting closer and closer until it turns into an SAL Boeing coming in low over the city, with its wheels out ready to land.

Nothing feels the way she thought it would . . .

She turns away from the window to dial the Sinksas' number again. Please be at home; please answer the phone!

Nothing.

The Sunday stillness is oppressive. The room is a concrete cell closing in around her. She lies down on the bed, gets up again; she sits down on a chair, gets up and walks to the door; she opens the door and looks down the passage. Nothing. Only a red carpet and a row of closed doors.

It is a quarter to six.

What if she has come all that way for nothing?

She goes back to the window and looks at the strip of veld on the horizon. It is something to hold on to, a last bit of land that has been left undeveloped, where she can go and burrow into the earth with a stick and find a handful of little stones with which she can light her way out of the darkness . . .

What if she has come eight hundred kilometres for nothing?

Mountain?

The mountain is too far away, he can't hear her.

The Priest is gone too. He left long ago. He walked away with his magic stones. Perhaps he made himself a raft of tree-trunks and carried it south until he got to the river – she thinks up a story, it helps her to feel better. When he got to the river, he floated down to the sea on his raft.

Then came the bushmen, the Koikoi, the black people from the north and the east; they came with their bows and poisoned arrows, their sticks and their spears, to wage a thousand years of war, because the Priest had taken the peace away with him. And the earth had to drink every drop of blood that was shed; it became a bitter place, and all the bitter places joined together into a large bitter stain that seeped into the very stones, as prayers seep into the walls and make churches holy places; as curses seep into the walls and make prisons evil places . . .

No, she says to herself, go over it again and go think it out better. Fortunately a river full of diamonds was flowing deep underneath the earth, and in every diamond was a speck of light it had got from the stars themselves. Yes. And so from the earth came millions of little lights to heal the bitter stain.

Then the Boers came with their wagons. Some kept on trekking northwards till they crossed the Vaal River. First they found the Priest's diamonds and then the gold, and then the earth had to drink a lot of blood . . .

Behind her the telephone gives an ear-splitting ring.

'Miss Rossouw?'

'Yes.' It is the girl at reception.

'Can you come down please; there's somebody here to see you.'

'Could you send them up to my room please?'

'I think it would be better if you came down.'

The woman is standing outside on the pavement at the entrance to the hotel. She's black. Her eyes are wary; her hands betray her nervousness. She's wearing a bright pink skirt and a white blouse; a red and white headscarf covers her hair; her shoes are old and worn.

'Are you Piet Sinksa's sister Angeline?'

'Yes, madam.' Cautiously.

'I tried to phone you, but there was no reply.'

'That's why I've come. Our phone's out of order. I said to my brother, madam will ring when she arrives. I went looking for madam at the other hotel, but madam wasn't there.'

235

You're either a very good person or a very good trap. 'Thank you. It was kind of you.'

'I just came to tell you about the phone.'

'As your phone is out of order, we had better decide now where we are going to meet tomorrow.' I will not make a single move unless I can see exactly where I'm going. 'If Piet and I can meet somewhere in the city, we can make further arrangements.'

'If you don't mind, madam, it is not a good idea to stand talking like this; it would be better if we walked along, pretending to be window-shopping. You understand?' She is very uneasy.

'Understand what?'

'Kimberley is a place with many eyes, madam. It's better if we walk as we talk.'

'I see.' They cross the street because there are no shop-windows on the side of the hotel. 'I thought if Piet and I could meet as early as possible . . .'

'He leaves home a little after six in the morning; he has to start work at seven. He asked if you could meet him at one o'clock. Madam can say where.'

The first window they stop to look at has a display of motor-car spare parts. 'If you don't mind me saying so, Angeline, I find this rather silly. And it may sound irresponsible, but all this secrecy makes no sense to me. We're not planning a burglary. It's a matter of Piet handing over certain articles, and me handing over whatever I owe him for them. Why can't we get into my car, go to your home right now and get it over with? It's still long before dark.'

'It's not safe for you to drive into the township, madam, and anyway Piet will not do business on the Sabbath. He's a man of the church, madam.'

I wonder . . . 'Fine, I understand. What do you suggest? Where should we meet?'

'It does not matter, it's your decision. As long as it is not at the hotel, if you don't mind. Hotels are dangerous places – Piet has never been caught. Neither have I.'

236

'Are you in it as well?'

'I just stand in for Piet sometimes. He gives me something for it. He had a man that helped him, but he went off with all the money one day. So we said never again. I think we should go on a bit.'

They come to a chemist's shop on a corner. She points down the side street. 'Tell Piet I'll park my car down there, shortly before one o'clock tomorrow. It's a red Datsun with a CAW registration number . . .' Something's wrong; there is open hostility suddenly on the woman's face and in the manner in which she pulls away. 'Is something the matter?' The woman stands there, glaring at her, challenging her. 'What's the matter, Angeline?'

'You've chosen an ideal place, madam,' she says sarcastically. 'We may be black, but we're not stupid!' she adds, with undisguised hostility.

'I'm sorry, I don't know what you're talking about. First you say we mustn't stand around talking, and now we are standing here arguing! Please, I'm tired, I've come a long way. If I said something wrong . . .'

'That place down there, madam, where you say you'll park your car, that bluish building – do you know what it is?'

So it was about a building lower down in the side street. 'I have no idea what you mean. I've never been in Kimberley in my life before!'

'That place, madam, happens to be the headquarters of the diamond spies. And you want to lure Piet there.'

'I'm sorry. I swear I didn't know it. I'll park my car in front of the hotel.'

'Can I make a suggestion? Park your car somewhere outside the city and let Piet bring the stuff to you there.'

'Whereabouts outside the city?' She's not stupid either.

'It does not matter. Madam can go ahead of us and pick a place – we're not cheats. We don't steal, we're only taking what has been taken from us and you're buying it!' Bitter and vindictive.

237

'Tell Piet I'll wait for him in my car under one of the last pepper trees on the road coming in from the south. I'll be there at one o'clock, and then I'll decide where we exchange the necessary.'

'I'll tell him,' she says, stiffly.

'Please, I've come a long way.'

'I'll tell him. He'll bring them.'

When she gets back to her room and lies down on the bed, total exhaustion gives way to relief: Angeline Sinksa – or whatever her surname is – is no police-trap decoy. She is quite sure of it.

When she wakes up and puts on the light, it's six minutes past midnight. She's hungry, she has slept right through dinner-time. It is a long time until dawn and an eternity to her meeting with Piet Sinksa. She puts on her nightdress and tries to go back to sleep.

Very well, she admits to herself, I wanted to romanticize this whole thing, see it as inevitable, something of a last pilgrimage. Now it's not. It does not even feel like a dream falling into place. It feels like nothing.

Perhaps it is like being happy; often you don't know you're happy, and it is only afterwards that you realize you've been happy at a particular moment. Maybe she'll feel better once it's morning and she can get out of this hotel room. Or once she has eaten. Then she'll take a walk through the centre of the city to kill time. She may even go and see the Big Hole.

It's not a trap that has been set for her. She knows she'll get the diamonds. They will go home with her and she will show them to Koos Malherbe before she takes them to Samuel Sundoo.

It is no use closing her eyes and trying to get to the mountain. It is too far away.

So is Koos Malherbe. She had tried to touch him, but couldn't. She accepts that. He probably thinks her hands

238

are too dirty for him. Perhaps he has other preferences, like Wilhelm. In any case, she only wanted to feel what he feels like, for the worst loneliness is when there is no one to touch you because you first have to make a new life for yourself somewhere else. That's why a man like Koos Malherbe could have provided a moment of comfort for the something in you that needs to escape and go playing sometimes. With a man.

Think about something else.

Are certain things put in your way, long ahead of time, without you suspecting it? Little things, big things. Do you walk right past some of them because you don't know they've been put there with a purpose? Sometimes you stoop down and pick one up simply because it holds some kind of fascination for you; you don't realize that it's been put there for you to find it much later . . .

Why was the river such a vivid moment? Why is she so aware of it?

You start learning about the Orange River almost as soon as you start school. So what? It's a river. Later on you come to realize that it is a particularly important river. Later still, when you begin to rebel against the fact that you were born in Africa, you notice that Africa gave its best and sweetest water to its black children in the north. To its white children in the south, it has given the most arid soil – and the Orange River.

One day, Uncle Joop called her over to his house; he said there was something he wanted her to have because Wilhelm was not interested in it. She was in grade nine. No. Grade nine was Frans de Villiers. She must have been in grade eight. He gave her three old books and she had to look as if she was pleased, because he was watching her reaction.

She walked home with the books. It was winter, and it was nice out in the sun. As she walked, she idly flipped the pages of one of the books through her fingers as you might kick a stone as you go along. As she did so, she noticed scribbling in a margin and quickly turned back to find it again: scribbling in a margin could be a secret someone had written there and forgotten about.

The person who had written it, had done so with a purple-coloured pencil; the handwriting was old, older than Uncle Joop's, and the words were: 'Often God's love manifests the greatest in the least of us.' With the same pencil, the person had drawn an intricate frame round an entry in the book – which was actually a diary, *Van Reenen's Journal*, for the year 1803. Fascinated, she sat down on the grass inside the front gate; as she read, she imagined the scenes she was reading about.

It described the day when Governor Janssens and his party arrived at the Orange River on their journey through the settlement at the Cape. The Orange River was more or less the northern boundary at the time. With some difficulty, they managed to shoot and kill a hippopotamus, which then, unfortunately, drifted down the river and on to the other bank.

There it lay. They thought up every plan they could to get the hippopotamus back across the river, because the Governor had never seen one in his life. A freed slave who was in the party, and a very strong swimmer, came forward and offered to take a rope over to the hippopotamus. It was winter and bitterly cold. He swam and swam, but the current was too strong. One moment he was swimming in the water, the next moment he had gone under. The river took him just as it had taken the hippopotamus, and threw him up on the opposite bank.

So now the slave was lying there too. Whether dead or alive, they could not tell.

When the six wild bushmen that had been following the party for days for meat and tobacco and beads saw the former slave lying on the other side of the river, they became frantic with concern. They ran up and down, they shouted and carried on; no one could calm them down. At last they got hold of a dry log, pushed it into the water

240

and, sitting astride of it, started paddling out across the mighty river with their hands, apparently quite unafraid of the water.

When they got to the other side, they made a big fire and dragged the slave to it; they took off their skin cloaks, and covered him with them, and slowly the slave started to revive. The next morning they made a fire again, and when he was warm, they put him on another log of wood and started back with him. Two of them swam across next to him, but it wasn't long before he was in trouble. The slave didn't know how to ride on a log – he kept falling off it. They stayed with him and held on to him. The current tried to take the slave, but they wouldn't let go of him. Little by little they struggled on. For hours they struggled to get him back and, the diarist said, if it had taken even another five minutes, they would all have been drowned.

She wrote many an essay at school about that incident afterwards. The pictures she had made herself of the river matched the river nearest to the village, the Gouritz River. Now, after all these years, she knew that her pictures were wrong: the Gouritz is just a little trickle compared to the Orange. For the first time, she knows why someone had written those words in the margin of the old book . . .

When she wakes up again, it's morning.

It's a new day. A normal day! There are people on earth again; they're talking and laughing down in the yard and a car is pulling out from one of the garages . . .

It's the day of Piet Sinksa!

Nothing, nothing, *nothing* must go wrong on this day. She says it out loud, at the same time becoming aware of sharp twittering noises somewhere outside . . . She recognizes the sound, but she can't place it immediately . . .

When she gets out of bed and goes to the window, she sees that the sky is filled with hundreds of swallows: flying and gliding like little black bats in broad daylight. Those that come diving down pass at some distance from her window; behind them in the clear blue sky is the long white trail of another jet, like an omen.

She stands there at the window, and can find no sense of wrong or fear, or any desire to turn back, within her. She finds only a wonderful feeling of peace, as when, after a long journey, you suddenly find yourself in a green valley between mountains with snow on their peaks . . . it's just a matter of getting there. And picking up a handful of magic stones on this side of the river to light your way out of this land . . .

Is it wrong, she asks herself for the last time.

No. Africa does not want white children. Not even at his feet does he want to make room for you if you have a white skin; when your father no longer wants you, you leave.

The last part of her journey out starts today. She knows it. She'll ask them to get her account ready at the reception desk, she won't stay another night. It won't be necessary. Her 'task' will be completed early enough for her to be able to drive home, even if she gets there after dark. Straight home. Not via Bloemfontein. Not now. Bloemfontein is for later, when Marian gets married and she has to go there to say goodbye.

Always, no matter how much she clung to her dream of the valley between the mountains, a little pool of lingering doubt and uncertainty had remained. Now it had gone.

What if Piet Sinksa is part of a trap? The question does not come from the pool of doubt – she asks it herself, on purpose. Like testing a stone before you step on it to see if it's quite firm.

It is.

She has a shower, gets dressed, packs, takes the bag with the money and goes down to breakfast.

For an instant, as she's going down the stairs, she has the strange feeling that she has been here before. Not on the stairs; somewhere else where it felt the same. Like a film stopping to reel back, but gets stuck. Then she's on the stairs again, knowing it's probably the Oudtshoorn incident that has come to haunt her.

The foyer is bustling with people and so is the dining-room; mostly men in suits with briefcases beside their chairs, like members of a congress or something. Nice men. Clever men. Two are black. The dining-room has no windows; heavy curtains, draped over the walls, create an impression of windows, and air-conditioners blow a soft breeze across the room.

She takes her time over breakfast – it's a long time until one o'clock. When she's finished, she'll check out and go to the shops. She might even buy herself a new dress. Why not? For months now she's had this desire to throw away all her clothes and buy herself new ones. In the meantime, she'll treat herself to just one new dress.

But it is an impossible city with impossible streets! If it's not 'One Way' signs sending her circling round the block, it's a creep cutting shamelessly in front of her and taking the only empty parking bay. Twice it happened. And it's hot. And no matter which way she turns, at the end of the street there's a board with an arrow saying 'Big Hole'. When it happens for the umpteenth time, she turns and follows the arrow out of sheer frustration. In any case she had planned to go and see the hole if there was time.

At first she thinks she has taken the wrong turn again, for it is not outside the city as she thought it would be; it's down an ordinary street with industrial buildings on one side. Another arrow shows her where she should park her car. Perhaps she should go back and buy the dress first – it's too hot to be out in the open. Fortunately someone, long ago, had the sense to plant the parking area with pepper trees. An enormous luxury coach has taken up a whole row.

As she gets out of the car, she stops dead; the very first

243

sound she hears is the long, lamenting call of a didric cuckoo: dee dee deederik ... dee dee deederik ... It's a mocking sound, a memory, a call that says something to her – it's the bird that lays its eggs in the nests of other birds. It's strange to find him calling here ...

She locks the car and follows the path up the slope to the top where a group of tourists are queuing to buy admission tickets at a window. It's hot. The place is making her feel irritable. Perhaps it's the heat. A board says: 'Big Hole and Open Air Museum'. Perhaps she should turn back; if she has to wait till all these people have been attended to, it may be too late to buy the dress ... dee dee deederik ... But the group starts moving towards the entrance; the tour leader must have bought one ticket for all of them.

Then it's her turn. She asks the man if she has to pay separately to see the hole and the museum. No. She gets her ticket, but does not know which way to go. She's thirsty, she must find some water to drink ... She's in a little village; it's a replica of Kimberley when it was an old mining town: narrow, dusty streets, old signboards above old corrugated-iron and wooden buildings: 'S. Perilly, Fine Handmade Cigarettes. Head Office Glasgow, Scotland' ... dee dee deederik ... 'Fancy Goods. Drapery. Imported Shawls' ... 'Goodchild & Rothschild, The Auction Mart' ... 'Watchmaker' ... 'Hairdresser' ... 'Licensed Diamond Dealer' ... 'Oldest house, 1877 – manufactured in England and brought to Kimberley by ox wagon' ... 'Vooruitzicht' – the name of the farm on which the town was founded. She remembers that the British Colonial Secretary at the time, Lord Kimberley, complained that he could not pronounce the name Vooruitzicht, and so gave orders that the place had to be given a name worthy of the British Empire: Kimberley.

She finds a tap and waits until the water runs cold before she drinks from her hand, and sprinkles some on her face and arms ... The place makes her uneasy;

244

perhaps it's the heat. Perhaps she should go back to her car. But she sees an arrow pointing: 'Big Hole'.

Moments later she comes to a large wire cage which the people are entering . . . she goes in too . . . it's a narrow cage built on a platform projecting out over the edge of the hole. She walks up to the front. She hears herself say: it's not true, it's not true. Before her the most terrible, incredible hole plunges down into the earth: the biggest man-made hole in the world. No picture she has seen of it showed how big and frightening it was! Across the void, in the distance, lies the city centre. She does not want to look down again, but she must. From the top of the hole yellow-brown earth walls slant down till they become sheer curtains of blue rock, plunging into a pool of green water far below. It wants to pull her down. The knuckles of her hands are white as they grasp the wire mesh in front of her.

Dee dee deederik . . .

Don't look down, she says to herself. Round the hole, there are still patches of lonely veld with grass and thorn trees; trees and grass grow on the slanting walls down to where there is no more soil for roots to cling to. It's as if they're trying to hide a little of the wound. Somewhere in the air is a sharp, endless twittering noise . . . it sounds like swallows, but there are no swallows, only hundreds of large moths far below, circling round and round above the water.

Then she realizes that they are not moths – they *are* swallows.

'Are you feeling all right?' the woman standing next to her in the cage asks.

'I'm all right, thank you.' Go away.

'It's incredible to think that this was once a hill, isn't it?'

'Yes.' Go away!

The woman goes away.

She'd forgotten that it was once an ordinary hill in the

veld. Until someone picked up a handful of diamonds on its crown and prospectors came flocking. They dug and dug, and brought up from the earth riches such as had never been found before in the whole world. When the hill was levelled to the ground, they started digging down. Deeper and deeper and deeper. She sees it before her eyes. Later, when the wheelbarrows could no longer get up the slopes, a network of steel cables hauled up the large heavy buckets of earth to the top, and all the time a town was growing up around the hole. 'It's a place for those who want to sell their souls!' a visiting preacher cried out in despair.

The best whores came on ships from over the sea and by ox wagon all the way from the Cape: £1 a time, £5 for the whole night. Gambling-houses, canteens, merchants by the wagonload, concerts, thieves, swindlers. The mining magnates had the shacks of the thousands of black workers fenced in so as to have better control over them; especially in order to curb diamond stealing. To keep them on the mines for longer periods of time, they gave them plenty of strong drink . . .

She feels sick.

Then gradually there were fewer diamonds in the sieves, and no more yellow earth down in the hole. The diggers had come to a hard, blue rock – and panic. Two brothers by the name of Bernato appeared on the scene from London. And another, a preacher's son from a village north of London: Cecil John Rhodes. Together they started buying up claims from the disheartened diggers until almost all of the hole belonged to them. Then came the machinery they had ordered from England, for what the ignorant diggers didn't know was that the hill and the yellow earth beneath the hill were just the cap of a volcanic pipe that had burst out of the earth millions of years ago. The best diamonds were still waiting down in the blue rock for those who had suspected that that was the case.

Dee dee deederik! It was not the bird, it was she herself.

Deeper and deeper went the machines, digging out the earth until water started rising from the bottom as if to say: no more. Not far from there they started digging the next hole . . .

Slowly she starts moving back, away from the wire . . . her hands, her arms, her feet, her whole body is stiff and sore because she had held on so tightly. She must get to her car, she no longer wants to be here. If something had wanted to punish her for thinking she could spit from a bridge and get rid of her anger, she has had her punishment.

Perhaps she suffers from a fear of heights without having realized it . . .

Immediately outside the cage she looks up and sees the board. She did not notice it when she went in. It is like a giant tombstone on which the particulars of the deceased have been recorded: diameter of hole 1:6 km; depth to the water level 165 m; depth of water 230 m; work abandoned August 1914; 22,500,000 tons of earth removed . . . Behind the posts on which the tombstone rests, three cocopans – three large trolleys, stand in a row, filled with little pieces of glass, representing diamonds, so that visitors can see what 2,722 kg of diamonds looks like, because that is the quantity of diamonds that was taken from the hole.

Three wretched cocopans full of diamonds and one monstrous hole in the earth?

First she feels anger. Then helplessness. Then a consuming pity and guilt and compassion, making her crouch down and put out her hand to touch the warm yellow soil, saying she's sorry because she doesn't know what else to say. And from the earth rises a sadness that swells up in her as if she should shed the tears that have been withheld.

She suddenly knows that she made a mistake when she sent the Priest down the river and out to the sea – the

Priest did not go away, he crept into the earth to hide. Only when the earth finally dies will he go away.

'Are you all right, miss?'

'Yes.'

She gets up painfully. She must get away from this place and go to her car. It's half-past twelve already.

The man at the window who sells the tickets is reading.

'Excuse me.'

'Yes?'

'What did they do with the soil that they took out of the hole?'

'The municipality put it at the back here,' he says, indifferent.

'Where?'

'There, where the caravan park is, the blue mounds you see there. They sieved it again first, and found quite a lot more diamonds.'

'Why didn't they put it back in the hole?'

He looks at her, surprised. 'Funny you should ask. Only last week a man came here asking me the same question. Man from England, as if it has anything to do with him, as if I'm responsible for the hole. I told him it would be impossible. You know what he said to me?'

'What?'

'He said, if I had a hole in my leg, would I want it to be healed, or would I display it at a fee for others to see. I told him I'm just doing my job. And now you come here, asking the same daft question.'

'I'm sorry, I just wanted to know.'

Don't think.

The earth is our mother, the sea is our grandmother . . .

Don't think, just get to your car.

For three cocopans.

248

Thirteen

THE OLD RED COMBI is already parked under one of the last pepper trees.

It's five minutes to one.

When she puts on the indicator and starts to pull in, the front doors of the vehicle open and the two of them get out: Angeline and the man in the blue overalls: Piet Sinksa.

She pulls in two trees away from them.

'We were getting worried that we might have missed madam as you went past. This is my brother.'

'How do you do.' The hand he holds out is rough, the hand of a labourer. He's short in build and very dark-skinned; he has a friendly face.

'Angeline didn't tell me madam was so young.'

'Thanks for the compliment, but you're mistaken.' There is a scar starting above one of his eyes and running into his hair like a parting. 'I'm sorry if I've kept you waiting.' Angeline has the same skirt and headscarf on; across the white T-shirt she's wearing is written UNIVERSITY OF CALIFORNIA in a semicircle.

'I don't know what madam has in mind,' Piet says, cautiously. 'Perhaps it would be best to drive out a bit further from the city. It's not a good idea, us standing here.'

'I want to see the diamonds first. Right here.'

'Trees have eyes, madam,' Angeline says, warningly.

'I know. I'll tell them to close their eyes.'

She laughs. 'I said to Piet, madam's not like most of the other white people, madam's got a heart that's warm to us black people, madam won't get us into trouble. Piet, show her the diamonds.'

He doesn't want to. 'You're making a mistake, both of you. We've been standing here too long already.'

'I want to see the diamonds first.'

'Show them quickly, Piet; the road's quiet at the moment,' says Angeline, encouraging him.

Piet is still not happy. 'Then madam must open the car bonnet first so that it looks as if we've stopped to help madam. Then we can be examining the engine.' To Angeline he says, 'Go and loosen them.'

They wait till the bonnet is open. It's obviously a well-practised ritual: Angeline gets into the front of the Combi and fidgets with something on the floor while Piet gets in under the Combi. They work fast; the next moment he crawls out with a plastic bag in his hand, tied with a short cord that had obviously been secured under the Combi. In the bag is a dirty old cloth and in the cloth . . .

'You see, madam,' Piet explains, 'if something goes wrong, we cut it loose at the top as we're driving and let it drop on to the road. That way they won't find anything on us if they search us.'

In the cloth lie three, six, nine, ten diamonds. The largest is the colour of an orange . . . two are green like new leaves . . . three are pink and the others are white and clear like huge drops of water.

'Madam is rather overwhelmed,' says Piet, proudly.

'Are they all *diamonds*?'

He gives a little snort. 'Of course,' he says, beginning to fold the corners of the cloth back over them.

'Wait!' she cries. 'Let me hold them in my hand for a moment, please.'

'Put them in madam's hand,' says Angeline.

'We've got to get away from here!'

'Put them in madam's hand, so that she can have a proper look!'

He hands them over reluctantly.

They are blessed stones filled with ancient light . . . in the most beautiful one, it's a golden light . . . She cannot make out whether they're happy or not. Piet Sinksa does not give her enough time to hold them. He takes them and wraps them in the cloth.

'We must get away from here!' he says.

'Madam can go on ahead, and we'll follow you,' says Angeline.

'I don't want them.' She hears herself saying it. She sees astonishment come into their eyes as they look at her in disbelief. 'I'm sorry. If I could afford it, I would buy them and make little holes for them in the ground and put them back where they belong: in the earth.'

'What?' Piet asks, flustered. 'We have to sweat to get them out, and madam wants to go and put them back in again?'

'I don't want them. I don't want to buy diamonds any more. I'm sorry for the trouble I've caused you.' She closes the bonnet.

'Just wait a minute!' Angeline says, stepping in front of her. 'I don't think I understand. Are you saying you're not going to *buy*?'

'That's right.'

'May I ask why not?' she says with contempt.

'Simply because I don't want diamonds any more. I'll manage on my own. I'm sorry if this doesn't make sense to you, it does not even make sense to me at the moment.'

'It's not a matter of making sense, madam,' Piet chips in from behind Angeline. 'I just don't understand. I've kept the best ones for madam, I sent away the other *baas* who was offering ready money. I told him I had given my word to someone else. Now it seems that there's something wrong with the diamonds and they're not wanted any more.'

251

'I didn't say there was anything wrong with the diamonds!'

'Forget it!' says Angeline, abruptly. 'Madam doesn't want them.' She's cross. It's as if she's telling Piet: don't bother with her, to hell with her. 'It seems to me she doesn't know what she wants.'

She turns round and walks away to the Combi. Piet stays behind as if to have a last try. 'Madam,' he says, 'it's not my funeral – it's madam's. If madam lets these diamonds go, you're never going to get another opportunity to buy from Piet Sinksa.'

'I know. Tomorrow, when I regret this, I'll think of you because I've waited a long time for this day. And please, do me a favour, be good to those diamonds while they're with you. Put them in your pocket or somewhere – diamonds don't sparkle in dirty cloths.'

The next moment Angeline shouts from the Combi, 'Leave the white-arsed Boer alone; she's wasting our time!'

Immediately she feels the old spittle on her face. She turns round and looks the woman straight in the eyes. She wants to say something to her, she wants to spit at her with the hardest words she knows, but she cannot get the words across to her – she's standing too far away.

All she can do is to get into her car and drive off. Southwards. Home. When she looks in the rear mirror, she sees the red Combi driving in the direction of the city.

Long after she's crossed the river, long after she has passed Hopetown, her mind starts to clear and the tension in her body begins to ease.

Somewhere, something has gone wrong. It's inside her, but she doesn't know what it is. She only knows that she had waited a long time for Piet Sinksa and when he finally came she turned away because she had been overcome by three cocopans filled with bits of glass. Because she had crouched down and imagined herself feeling the heartbeat of a dead old Priest beneath the ground!

*

252

She will go and work for the rest of the money. She will not cause the hole to be made bigger in order to provide her with a short cut. She'll manage by herself.

Not because of Koos Malherbe's law, but because she herself has decided to do so.

If perhaps an angel had pushed her to the edge of that hole in order to tell her something, he had succeeded. Africa is cripple, Africa's feet are hurting. She can only promise that she will tread as softly as she can while she is still here. She will never again say she's going away because Africa does not want white children – she takes those words back. Its his white children that helped to dig the holes and are still helping to dig them.

She will say she is going away because she is ashamed of having thought that she could stand up against a mighty empire and extort a lesser sentence for this little nation between the West and the East. She'll say she thought that if one kept on clinging to injustice, one would get to justice in the end.

Now it seems as if she has got nowhere.

She will admit that deep in her heart she had hoped that Africa would shed one tear over her.

Now she knows that the earth can feel pain. Stones too. The Bible says stones can hear. If stones can hear, they can feel too; and if stones can feel, they can feel pain – and stones are but petrified earth, millions of years old . . .

Britstown. She won't be home before dark.

They say that if you want to know what millions and millions are – if you want to know how old the earth is – you must think of it as being forty-six years old. No one knows anything about the first ten years of its life and not much about the next thirty. When it was about forty-five years old the shrubs and the woods and the grass and the flowers started growing, and there was food and air for the animals and the birds that were about to appear. When everything was prepared and the table was laid and running over with abundance, modern man arrived – and that was about four hours ago.

Four hours ago.

Three cocopans filled with diamonds.

And man began increasing and destroying and killing and making holes. Those that have must fight to keep what they have; those that want, must fight to get it. And she, Araminta Rossouw, is only on the earth for a fraction of a second and she did not buy the diamonds!

It's too late. She can't turn back.

Victoria West.

She must get petrol. 'ANC PLAN TO INTENSIFY CAM-PAIGN OF MURDER, SABOTAGE, ARSON.' The words are displayed in a red metal frame in front of the filling-station café, big black letters on white paper. They do not disturb her any more.

About thirty kilometres south of Beaufort West, she stops to stretch her legs and rest a while. She always wanted to know what it feels like to stand on a wide open, semi-desert plain where one can see a long way and no one can sneak up on you unawares . . .

First there's an almost deadly silence . . . watching her . . . eerie . . . then a movement . . . the call of a bird, an insect. The sky is blue, the breeze is cool . . . all around the plains are empty: the bushmen are gone, the Koikoi are gone, the wagons and the oxen are gone . . . she is alone on the veld spinning silently through infinite space. She's inside it. It's alive. She's alive. It's the same aliveness. It's Now.

A little grey bird sits on a twig, chirruping away. The sound that comes from his throat is yellow . . . In the distance a moorcock takes wing with a screech – a purple sound . . . She stoops down to let her fingers stroke a little shrub – it's green . . . A grasshopper with a fat red body . . . big brown ants . . . small white flowers. When the rains come, a carpet of wild flowers will cover the plains from the tiny little seeds the earth has hidden and kept alive . . .

What is life?

Who is she, living between the West and the East, where it is South . . . where the summer lives, where the full moon lives? Her life comes from the earth which is her home, her mother. She's a child of Africa's feet, where the mountains and the wild, barren places are mercifully still whole. Most of them. Did the Priest come here to hide his peace on the outstretched, desolate plains around her? Is that what she feels closing in around her, giving her solace . . .

In the distance a car is approaching.

She must go.

When she turns round, he is sitting on a post on the other side of the road, looking straight at her: a big brown eagle.

Fourteen

WHERE KOOS MALHERBE APPEARS from, she doesn't know. When she stops, his car pulls in behind her.

He carries her suitcase up the stairs.

She puts the bag with the money on the bookshelf and opens the curtains. The mountain is not asleep, it has waited up for her.

And Koos Malherbe stands with his hands in his pockets, staring at her as if he wants to find the answers to the questions on his face in hers.

'I am not in trouble, if that's what you want to know.'

'I tried to get hold of you yesterday, but you had already booked out of the hotel.' Cold.

'What did you want to get hold of me for?'

'I wanted to know if you had come to your senses.' As if she is a disobedient child standing before him.

'I've never been out of my senses and I'm too tired to get angry with you.'

'The fact that you are back tells me it wasn't a trap.'

'It wasn't.' I'll save the rest. 'Sit down.'

'I don't want to sit down. I also assume that you didn't find the Priest you were looking for.'

'I did. But he's very cold and dead. It will take many big fires to bring him back to life again.'

'I take it that you've had your spit?'

'The wind blew it back in my face.'

256

'Did it make you feel better?'

'Lighter. Only half of me has come back. And by the way, your "nothing for nothing" does not hold water. The didric cuckoo pushes the eggs of other birds out of their nests and lays his own in their place.'

'Have you ever heard a didric sing a happy song?'

'Do you have an answer to everything?'

'No. Especially not when it comes to you. I take it you'll be going to Cape Town shortly?'

It's a little red warning light.

'What?'

'To sell the diamonds.'

'What makes you think I'd go to Cape Town?'

'Because your buyer is in Cape Town.'

'How did you get that into your head?'

'I know.'

'How do you know?'

'You told me.'

'Am I under cross-examination? Am I in some kind of trouble I don't know of?'

'If it wasn't a trap, you're evidently not in trouble. Unless your bridge starts toppling in on you.'

'I think you're playing a game with me. Why?'

'Because something does not fit. You.'

'Then let me make it easy for you, because I'm tired, Mr Malherbe. You see, I didn't want to be a member of the most hated people on earth. When I found out that I had no choice, because that's what I am, I decided to fight what I am. But little by little, I came to realize that we're not as bad as they say. So I got even angrier. When I came to the conclusion that there is in fact no place for us here, in this country, I decided to go and look for somewhere else to live. I *did* have a choice after all. But now I know something I didn't know last night: Africa never wanted us to leave. We are the children of its feet. It did want us, but truth and lies and right and wrong got terribly mixed up. It can't take care of us any longer, it's tired of its children. *All* its children. And I did not buy the diamonds.'

'What?'

I thought I'd get you off your pedestal with that. 'I decided to cross the river on my own. South Africa owes us nothing. We've helped to devour it.'

'You didn't buy the diamonds?'

Touch me just once. Hold me a little, please. 'No. Though I held them in my hand, they were very beautiful and it wasn't a trap.'

'Why didn't you?'

'My sister once stole a pack of sweets and the shopkeeper gave her a talking to. She told her an old Jewish legend: that for every good deed, you get a good angel, and for every bad deed, a bad one. If you've acquired enough good angels, they'll plead for you when you're really in trouble. Long afterwards, I found out that the woman had only told half of the legend. Peoples, nations, are awarded good or bad angels for their deeds too. I feel sad because my people, in spite of everything, have not gathered enough good angels to plead for them now. We are in trouble.'

'We are.'

'How did you know I would have gone to Cape Town?'

'You had an appointment there once before that you didn't keep.'

'How do you know that?'

'Let's just say that one attorney talks to another. When you did not turn up, your buyer assumed that you had been caught, and that they would put pressure on you to reveal his name.'

'Was it he that paid my fine?'

'He was a day too late. It had already been paid.'

'Who by?'

'Perhaps by a good angel.'

'Did you pay it?'

'No.'

I thought so. 'Have you ever considered leaving the country?'

'Yes.'

'Would you?'

'When I no longer had a choice. Yes.' He looks at his watch. 'You must get some sleep. I'm glad you're back safely. That's all I wanted to know.'

As if he were saying: the court is adjourned now. Case dismissed.

Everyone at Carr & Holtzman had also been worried that she might have got into trouble, for one after the other their faces brighten when she walks into the office the following morning.

'You make me feel like a lost sheep!'

'Well, just about the whole town was looking for you,' says Christel. 'Mr Blom wants you to phone him. A Mr Williamson came in and asked to see you. He wants to buy a plot or a house with large grounds. The Shirleys recommended you to him. Then there was a friend of the gentleman you sold the beach house to at Herolds Bay; he said he'd come back.'

'Don't let Elvin hear all this. He'll threaten to appoint an extra agent this very day.'

At five o'clock that afternoon, she sells a house to Mr Williamson from Johannesburg.

And Wynand Blom has a second appointment for the Friday morning; she has to make a final offer on his behalf for business premises in the industrial area. It's a difficult transaction, in a world of steel and scrap-iron and oily cement floors and noise, and neither the seller or the buyer are prepared to budge a cent. The one wants his price or it's no sale, the other says he can keep it then, but he still wants the place all the same.

She spends the whole of Friday morning negotiating between the two. Elvin gives advice, Bernard makes

259

suggestions. Somewhere during the day, Lizzie informs her that someone has sent her flowers; they're in the kitchen, dripping water.

At half-past four the two hard-headed businessmen agree to meet each other halfway and a very happy Wynand Blom buys the concern. When he has signed the contracts, and she is showing him out, she sees a woman standing at the desk with Christel – actually, it is her beautiful shoes she notices: soft green high-heeled sandals.

When she comes back in, the woman is still there. The rest of her outfit is as smart as the shoes: green striped two-piece suit with puffed sleeves; thin gold bracelets; large gold earrings; hair short and very chic . . .

The woman turns round and says, 'Hallo, Araminta.'

It's Angeline Sinksa.

For one blinding moment, overcome by shock and fury, she has only one desire: to spit in her face.

But she can't. She has no spit, her mouth is as dry as dust from fright.

It was a trap and she hadn't realized it!

'We haven't really met; I'm Lieutenant Grace Ngobeni.'

She would like to ask her what she wants, but she can't get a word out.

'I was working in George this morning, so I thought I'd come and say hallo. Maybe we can talk?' Well-spoken. Amiable.

'I have nothing to say to you.' The words sound as if they're sticking together. Where's Lizzie? What happened to Christel? How much can they hear of what's being said?

'I can understand your reluctance, but I would very much like to talk to you. It's important to me.'

She has to get her away from wherever Lizzie and Christel are. 'Come in to my office,' she says, curtly. In her heart she adds: Don't think for a moment you'll get anything out of me with a new approach. 'Sit down.'

'Thank you.'

Don't let her see that you're trembling. 'What did you say your name was?'

'Grace Ngobeni.' She sits down as her name says: gracefully. And with self-confidence. 'Please let me put you at ease, I'm here as Grace Ngobeni, not as part of my job.'

'I have nothing to say to you.'

'There is something I would like to ask you, because if I don't, it will bother me for the rest of my life.'

'I have absolutely nothing that I want to say to *you*.'

'No one, either guilty or innocent, has ever looked at me with so much hatred as you did when I called Lieutenant Sixaxeni back to the Combi. You're still doing it. I'm sorry about the crude words I used. I had to. Two of your old acquaintances were lying at the back of the Combi under a blanket: Major Kruger and Lieutenant Botha.'

You can take just so much terror, and no more. Then you react. 'I don't think I like black people.'

'Don't feel bad about it. I know many black people I don't like myself. And just as many whites. What bothers me is that a person like you can look at me with so much hatred. A good person.'

'Do you mean you – or me?' she asks acidly.

'Let's stop beating about the bush, Araminta! You're no ordinary woman and neither am I. If *we* start hating each other, there's no hope for either of us. Nor for the rest of us.' Quick, intelligent.

'If you think that you and I can make any difference . . .'

'I don't only think it, I believe it. Wait until you've seen the world as I see it. It would be as dark as hell out there, my friend, had it not been for the ten of us who carry the other ninety.'

'What do you mean?' There is an irresistible challenge in Grace Ngobeni's eyes.

'I see them, I count them. The good people. Ten in every hundred. A hundred thousand in every million.

Walk down the street, count them yourself. I do it regularly, it keeps me going, it makes me fight. Then suddenly and unexpectantly I pick one up on a pavement in Kimberley one Sunday afternoon, and I wonder what she is doing there and why she is so very angry?'

'I'm white. I'm a member of the most hated people on earth. If you think I'm saying this out of self-pity, you're quite wrong. It no longer matters much.'

'There was a time when the Boer women were the strength of this land. Because it did matter to them.'

'What is it you want from me?'

'Through all the years that I've been doing this work, I've never seen any of my quarry handle diamonds the way you did. Afterwards, I asked one of my colleagues what the word for "compassion" is in your language. He said, *ontferming* – "to care for". There was something of that between you and those diamonds. It hit me so hard, I was jealous of it. But when I called Lieutenant Sixaxeni away, you swung round, hating me.'

'Why did you call him away? Why did you seem to lose interest in pushing me to buy? Was it one of your tricks?'

'My mother will be ninety next month. When she was a little girl in Lesotho, the women of the kraal used to go and burrow for clay in the foothills of the mountains. One day my mother joined them. Late in the afternoon, when they got back, the women went and showed the headman the strange little stones they had found in the clay that day. When the headman saw the stones, he sent them back to the hills immediately, to go and put them back where they had found them. They were diamonds. Then you stood there saying that if you could afford it, you would buy the diamonds and put them back in the earth.'

'I meant it.'

'The reason why I didn't push you, was because I didn't want to see Major Kruger and Lieutenant Botha get their hands on you.'

Mountain?

It's the cool spray of mist – the touch of a bird's wing, lightly brushing her face and sweeping away the old spittle. There is no deceit in the woman's eyes and she is waiting for you to take her hand . . .

'Had you pushed me in the right way, I might still have bought.'

'I was afraid of that.'

'I don't know what to say. I'm sorry that I said I didn't like black people . . .' She gets no further. Lizzie, nosy Lizzie, comes in with a bouquet of flowers so big she can hardly get through the door.

'Sorry to interrupt, Araminta – I'm just bringing in your flowers.'

'Is it your birthday?' Grace asks when they're alone again.

'No.' There is an envelope with the flowers, not the usual florist's card. 'Appreciative clients sometimes send me flowers.'

'That's nice.'

'It is.' And these are the most beautiful flowers anyone has ever sent her – fairies could play in them. 'I didn't mean it when I said I don't like black people. We are all in trouble, we've built too many bridges across each other's truths. The most beautiful diamonds on earth are black. Often, when they're cut, they're pure and white inside – oh dear, that does not sound the way I wanted it to.'

'I know what you mean,' she says, smiling.

'I got such a fright when you turned round and I saw who you were; I still can't think properly. I don't know what to say to you, I want to give you these flowers . . .'

'You owe me nothing. You're a good person. Good people don't owe one another anything – we *are* one another.'

'You are the good person, not me . . . What did you mean when you said ten people must carry the other ninety?'

'It's an old legend: ten strong ones carry ninety weak

263

ones. If the ten strong ones lie down, the ninety rise up and destroy everything: the tens, and the legends as well. The ten are lying down, Araminta, the ninety have started the stampede.'

'Only one tenth of all the diamonds that are mined are suitable for gems. But all diamonds are made of holy material, from the highest to the lowest.'

'Why didn't you buy the diamonds?'

'I wanted a short cut out of this country and I thought the diamonds would provide it. Then I saw the terrible hole that had been made in the earth. As if someone had been maimed to satisfy man's greed for a moment. I can't explain to you how it felt; I only know that I didn't want to buy the diamonds after that. I couldn't.'

'Do you really want to leave the country?'

'Yes. I've thought for a long time that Africa does not want white children, only black children. That's why it doesn't bother about us. Now I know that even if I go away, I will always be a child of Africa. And Africa cares for us too – we are all its children. But we do not care for Africa.'

'Africa is not bothered whether his children are black or white, Araminta, but Africa desperately needs its good children! Don't tell me this is an idealistic dream. The drought breaks when we dream that the rain is coming; it will not break while we believe in the drought.'

'Dreams cost money. There is not enough money; the people will not understand. In any case, the more I think about it, the more I'm coming to believe that we're actually building one enormous bridge across the whole world and it is leading nowhere. No one will have anywhere to live. We just keep on digging holes.'

'The tens will make the miracle happen!'

'I'm sorry, I don't believe in miracles any more.'

'That's a pity. I am here, because I had hoped you might.' She gets up. 'I must leave for the airport, I have to catch a plane to Johannesburg.'

'I wish I had something to say to you.'

'Say you'll break down the bridge you've built over me.'
'I say it.'

When she comes back after walking with Grace Ngobeni
to her car the faint scent of flowers hangs in the air.

It's quiet. Christel and Lizzie have gone home. Somewhere she can hear one of the others opening and closing
drawers.

It was not Piet Sinksa after all. It was a trap and she
hadn't known it! It is as if she had stood on the edge of an
abyss and someone had pulled her away – the shock hits
you afterwards and freezes the very blood in your veins!

She takes the envelope from the flowers and opens it.

'Did you hear?' Bernard asks at the door. 'Nick Wehland
was caught for buying diamonds this morning. Apparently
by a woman detective from Kimberley. Araminta?'

'Go away. I don't want to know.'

'What's this enormous bouquet?'

'Go away. It's mine.'

She reads the words over and over until she believes
they're true: 'Marry me. Koos Malherbe.'